PULL
FOCUS

PULL FOCUS

A NOVEL

HELEN WALSH

Published by ECW Press
665 Gerrard Street East
Toronto, Ontario, Canada M4M 1Y2
416-694-3348 / info@ecwpress.com

Editor for the Press: Susan Renouf
Cover design: Caroline Suzuki

LIBRARY AND ARCHIVES CANADA CATALOGUING IN
PUBLICATION

Title: Pull focus : a novel / Helen Walsh.

Names: Walsh, Helen, (Writer and producer),
author.

Identifiers: Canadiana (print) 20210176237 |
Canadiana (ebook) 2021017627X

ISBN 978-1-77041-579-9 (softcover)
ISBN 978-1-77305-791-0 (ePub)
ISBN 978-1-77305-792-7 (PDF)
ISBN 978-1-77305-793-4 (Kindle)

Classification: LCC PS8645.A4725 P85 2021 | DDC
C813/.6—dc23

We acknowledge the support of the Canada Council for the Arts. Nous remercions le Conseil des arts du Canada de son sout-
ien. This book is funded in part by the Government of Canada. Ce livre est financé en partie par le gouvernement du Canada.
We acknowledge the support of the Ontario Arts Council (OAC), an agency of the Government of Ontario, which last
year funded 1,965 individual artists and 1,152 organizations in 197 communities across Ontario for a total of $51.9 million.
We also acknowledge the support of the Government of Ontario through the Ontario Book Publishing Tax Credit, and
through Ontario Creates.

PRINTED AND BOUND IN CANADA

PRINTING: MARQUIS   5 4 3 2 1

For my mother, Jessica,
and for Michael, with love.

CHAPTER ONE

DAY 1: *What Ever Happened to Baby Jane?*

T minus four hours. I glanced nervously at the wall clock behind Jacob, as words slithered out between his thin lips, one coiled phrase after another.

He'd cast himself in the character of Dark Messiah, that much was evident in the words he used, the condescending politeness, the pained expression when someone disagreed. Mere civilians might cringe mid-apocalypse, but he'd stay on the horse, semi-automatic rifle in one hand, the burden of seeing the world for its shit-bucket self curled up in the scarred palm of the other. The baddies would quake, the babies would live, and if there was collateral damage of the slow-moving who couldn't get out of the way, whoever said life was fair was a loser anyway.

Jacob Ray owned a successful crisis management firm, BFA, that made problems go away for people rich enough to buy salvation. He'd been recruited as board director of the Worldwide Toronto Film Festival the previous year because his client base brimmed with political leaders and sponsorship-rich corporations. Many of WTFF's multi-year funding commitments were due to expire in the near term; cultivating powerful decision-makers of the kind who owed Jacob a favor, the reasoning went, would have significant upside for the festival.

I'd had little functional connection with him until six months earlier, when Paul DelGrotto, WTFF's former CEO, was suspended amid allegations of sexual wrongdoing and the board chair abruptly resigned. Suddenly, I pole-vaulted from artistic director to acting CEO, and Jacob became my board chair. The organization was in crisis, and the board didn't have to look further than one of its own directors for a seasoned pro in the reputational wars.

"Everyone knows Samantha is fomenting civil war among the staff," I said. "I ask her to stop verbally attacking the veracity of the women involved. The next day she files a HR complaint against me. Doesn't it seem likely that those two things are connected?"

"No need to be defensive, Jane," Jacob said softly, forcing me to lean in to hear him.

"Samantha was Paul's assistant for twenty years. She resents his firing —"

"He's on administrative leave. We won't be hasty in our judgments."

"He sent photoshopped images of his penis to female staff," I said, in exasperation. "From his own email account. There's not a lot of room for ambiguity."

After Lina Garcia, WTFF's head of marketing and public relations, had gone to the human resources department with her complaint, the board originally chose to believe DelGrotto's story of a consensual affair gone wrong, a disgruntled employee looking for revenge. They suspended Lina with pay and a gag order. Two days later, the photos of Paul's genitalia appeared on TMZ, and four more women stepped forward with their own complaints.

Jacob's eyes narrowed. "We don't know for sure that it's his body part." He paused to stare at me pointedly. "Or who leaked the photos to the media. Regardless, Paul's now at home pending investigation, and you've landed yourself in the top job. Temporarily, at least."

The Dark Messiah is not above implicit threats.

It was the opening day of the festival, and a long line of people waited for me to troubleshoot the various firestorms. Jacob's insistence on meeting in my office, despite the time crunch, was the latest in a series of power plays that began immediately upon his appointment as chair.

"I'll talk to HR about transferring Samantha to another executive, at least until the end of the festival. I can make do with an intern as my EA for the next ten days," I said slowly, not wanting to appear eager for an outcome I'd give my John Cassavetes collection to make happen.

"That would be a demotion, and demotion without cause is grounds for a constructive dismissal case. You should know the intricacies of employment law, if you're going to manage an organization this size," Jacob said, making a deliberate motion of looking down at his manicured hands, so as to avoid bearing witness to my management faux pas. "A hundred million in assets; we're a target."

Neutral face, Jane, I told myself, as I swallowed the "fuck you" lump of bile in my throat. "Well, you felt the need to bring this conversation up today," I said finally. "Is there a particular short-term solution you're driving toward?"

3

"It's not up to me to tell you how to do your job. I'm just alerting you to the situation, and letting you know that the board is watching," he said, rising to his feet. "And to offer any assistance to you, of course," he added, reaching out to shake my hand. His flesh was as cold as I imagined it would be, although also sweaty, which was an unwelcome surprise.

As soon as Jacob left, I dialed my partner Bob's cell, then his direct office line, surprised when both went straight to voicemail. "Hi, it's me. Please call back. Darth Vader made an appearance. I could use that strategic mind of yours. Otherwise, no later than six forty tonight, black tie."

* * *

Our COO's booming Scottish accent rounded the corner of my office before Burt himself did. "We need to cancel tomorrow's screening of *State*. An emergency injunction has been issued after someone filed a complaint that it's hate speech. No great surprise who will be behind that one," he growled, refusing to look back at Victoria, our VP of development, who hustled in behind him.

She barely made it to his shoulder, but was twice as tough. Victoria used boxing lessons as a relaxation tool. "Finally, someone's shown some leadership."

"Hate speech," I said, incredulous. "How?"

"Detestation and vilification that will expose a target group to abuse or delegitimization thus rendering them lawless, unworthy, or unacceptable in the eyes of the audience," Burt said, reading from his phone.

I shook my head. "The Chinese government is going to be delegitimized by a film screening in Toronto?"

"Sounds about right," Victoria said. "That settles the matter."

This argument had eaten its own tail for months. "I honored the pledge you and Paul made to exclude *State* from the special showcase," I said. "But you know I never agreed to ban the film altogether."

"You understand, right, that it takes fifty million dollars a year to run this fucker?"

Victoria was gearing up for a fight. I admired her tenacity to do whatever necessary to get her job done; at the same time, I objected to some of her tactics. But she and Burt were diametrically opposed to each other's position on this issue, and a blowout would serve no one well. "You and your team do an amazing job fundraising the yearly budget."

"Cut the shit, Jane. You want the art-house directors like Yin Lee to love you, great. Have as many non-fat green tea lattes with them as you want. Hell, program *State* every day for a year after the festival closes for all I care. I agree, the film's a punch in the gut. Chinese corruption sucks the motherlode. Yin Lee will win an Oscar. But the Chinese government gave us ten million for this showcase, and they don't want a film highly critical of them to screen while they're in town. It took us five years to make this sponsorship happen and if you fuck with it, I'll fucking hang you."

"How much wood would a wood fuck fuck, if a wood fuck could fuck wood?" Burt's scorching tone bounced off Victoria's hide, without making a dent.

I signaled for a time-out just as Samantha scurried in. "I didn't realize there was a meeting in here. What'd I miss?" she said, notebook at the ready.

Samantha's simmering hostility seemed even more apparent now I knew she'd made a HR complaint against me. Was she a conduit of information back to Jacob? "Have you connected with Devlin Ross's people today?" I said, diverting the conversation.

"Did she arrive? Have you gone over the donor stewardship sequence for tonight?"

"I need two more spots," Victoria said, switching complaints without missing a beat. "I can cut them down to thirty seconds each, forty-five tops, but Devlin has got to give some face time with key targets of mine."

We'd negotiated precise deal terms with Devlin Ross, the lead actress of *Shifting Dragon*, this year's opening night film. She'd consented to one circuit of the VIP room at the after-party, sprinkling a little magic dust on the five biggest sponsors, but no single sponsor would receive more than three minutes of conversation. There would be no redistribution of unused minutes to other potential donors if one target was too starstruck to use their entire allotted time, a highly possible outcome given how mesmerizing she was.

"There's no way Devlin's people will agree to a last-minute change in terms," I said. "If the three targets are critical, then I'll lean on a friendly agent or manager tomorrow to get us an opportunity with another A-lister. Samantha, would you please go make sure Devlin has everything she needs?"

Samantha reluctantly left, while Burt began to pace his inner Braveheart up and down the short length of my office. "I'm working with the lawyers. We need to get that injunction lifted if we have any hope of screening before the festival ends."

Veins bulged in Victoria's neck. "We're not going to screen it. The whole purpose of programming *Shifting Dragon* for opening night is to make the Chinese government happy. And now that *State*'s been banned, they're even happier. Ten million dollars happy. Happy, happy showcase. Happy, happy opening night. You get the picture? Their entire delegation disappears in less than a week. I don't want to hear anything about *State* until they're gone. Not a peep."

6

Burt had just informed us of the injunction; how could Victoria have already discussed it with the Chinese partners unless she or someone close to her was the source of the original complaint?

From his expression, Burt figured this out too. "Are you fucking kidding me?" he yelled. "You really did throw us — me — under the bus for a funder?"

Victoria remained silent, but her clenched fists spoke defiance.

"Let's hope your sponsors don't read reviews," Burt said, suddenly quiet, a dangerous sign. "The critics aren't stupid enough to miss what a piece of utter shite *Shifting Dragon* is."

A modern thriller starring one of China's biggest stars, Andy Tse, and two Western actors who play CIA agents in need of rescue after being kidnapped by Boko Haram in Nigeria, *Shifting Dragon* sought to telegraph a more muscular Chinese identity as international peace-brokers. It was billed as the crown jewel in a thirty-film showcase underwritten by the Chinese government and negotiated by Paul DelGrotto and Victoria. No films by Taiwanese directors or that dealt with Tiananmen Square could be programmed for the showcase.

Burt and I, like most of our colleagues, were dismayed by the precedent set in giving a sponsor veto over content. To avoid the criticism, Paul and Victoria had slipped into stealth mode. It was only after Paul's suspension that the commitments he'd made surfaced, ones I was now required to honor.

I listened with one ear as Victoria and Burt raged at each other about censorship, the large domestic Chinese community that deserved programming, and the geopolitical history of Asia while I quickly scrolled through my messages. Still nothing from Bob. His usual response rate was five minutes; more than an hour, unprecedented. I looked up only when Victoria uttered a sentence she had to know would be the powder keg. "We need to be sensitive to our partner's political realities."

"That's it," I said, just as the snot began to combust out of Burt's nose. "Burt, I know you'll stay on top of the injunction. But it's two hours to showtime. Let's focus on tonight."

Burt stormed out. Victoria vibrated with triumph as she moved past Samantha who had reappeared at the door, still clutching her notebook and pen.

"Everything under control, Jane?"

* * *

A retaliatory pinch at my waist; Tassio, the dresser, was not best pleased. "Put the phone down. You're ruining the line."

"I think we're good."

"We're not." His fingers reached under the dress to adjust the spandex underclothing I'd been warned against calling a girdle in public — their brand people hated that — pulling the nylon edges away from the curves of my buttocks, so that it became a de facto thong.

I dialed Bob and again it went straight to voicemail. Tassio yanked the phone away, tossing it over the top of the privacy screen to Samantha, who slipped it into her purse. She disappeared only to reemerge seconds later accompanied by a tuxedo-clad, gray-haired man who was seventy if he was a day.

"This is Gerald. He's one of our volunteers this year. He'd be honored to be your escort for this evening."

"Pardon?"

"Gerald can move when Bob shows up, but we're fifteen minutes away — we can't hold any longer," Samantha said, reading my mind.

"I'm four inches taller than him." I was dismayed to hear a slight whine infect my tone.

Burt pulled up alongside Samantha. "The fat man's in position. Producers are getting itchy to start in case he hoofs it," he said.

#fatmanrising — a hashtag started by a festival staffer to track famed distributor Larry Roth's movements without identifying him directly — had gone viral. Within an hour, it had become the litmus test for whether someone was a festival insider. Unsquelchable. I had turned it over to Lina and the marketing department to discretely exploit.

"It's trending on Twitter," Samantha said. "It'll be number one by the end of the night."

I swatted away the dresser's fingers as he reached into my bra to arrange my breasts. "What I look like isn't important."

"Tell that to Dolce and Gabbana," he hissed. "The dress is going to be unsellable because of the sweat stains, the least we can do is give them decent photos."

"I've read the clothing notes in case anyone from the media asks," Avatar Bob piped up, helpfully tapping his jacket pocket. "Someone was kind enough to loan me their spectacles."

Stepping from behind the screen, I linked arms with Avatar Bob. "Okay, then. I guess we do this."

As we neared the stage, the venue manager appeared to guide my companion to his seat and I walked to the microphone amid the glare of five hundred cameras. Sweat pooled in my armpits and at the nape of my neck; my fingers left marks on the edges of the chic black podium from gripping it too hard. I'd introduced many films over the years, so the mechanics of what I was about to do was familiar, but the import of standing there as acting CEO rendered me momentarily speechless.

Shortly before finishing NYU's graduate film school, I abandoned my dream of being a filmmaker in New York to care for my mother during a prolonged battle with cancer. That fate blocked my first choice was hardly a surprise. Good fortune was reserved for people born into families with cleaner karmas than mine.

But a love of film was in my bloodstream and could not be denied. Four years later, I landed a part-time gig as a WTFF programmer, then moved to fulltime, promoted to senior programmer after a few years, and eventually appointed artistic director once it became clear to Paul I'd work like a Trojan but let him take the credit. Give a foolish, weak man with a Mussolini self-image enough rope and he'll hang himself, or so my hope in retributive justice went. I calculated the odds at 20 to 1 — on an optimistic day.

In the meantime, I kept my head down and ears open. I watched every film that crossed anyone's desk and I slowly perfected my craft. I built a global network among the indie filmmakers who would have been my peers. I had one mantra: Prepare. Prepare. Prepare.

Never, though, did I think I'd get the top job this quickly, or in circumstances that were half opportunity, half poisoned chalice. Turn it down and the board might hire a CEO who'd remain a couple of decades or more, bringing in his own people to take the senior positions like mine. Accept the interim appointment and risk being made the scapegoat for a festival half-baked by Paul, produced during chaos, and mired in scandal-related negative press.

"You've got this, Jane," Bob had said. "And I've got your back."

Except he didn't. The two-headed snake of Jacob's insidiousness and Bob's unexplained absence lay curled in my thoughts as I stood at the microphone. But still, an electric current of excitement fizzed in my bloodstream as I leaned forward to speak.

"Good evening. I'm Jane Browning. As the festival's acting CEO, it's my very great pleasure to welcome you to the opening night of the Worldwide Toronto Film Festival."

Applause broke out around the room, and I waited for it to take its course, willing my voice to steady. "We're delighted you've joined us for tonight's film, *Shifting Dragon*, which kicks off our special spotlight on the vibrancy and complexity of contemporary Chinese cinema. And we hope to see you often over the coming ten days, for films from every corner of our planet, stories that challenge the status quo, from filmmakers who shed new light on what it means to be human, to be a citizen, in this troubled century. Please join me in giving a very warm Toronto welcome to the hundreds of amazingly talented directors, writers, producers, and actors whose work we're honored to present this year."

A guttural sound from the balcony competed with the applause. All heads, including mine, swiveled to witness Devlin Ross stumble her way over a seated Huntley Bartlett, supporting actor in *Shifting Dragon*, who hadn't thought fast enough to get up. She milked his lack of chivalry for every ounce of attention she could get, prolonging and exaggerating her teeter. Her costar, Andy Tse, stood and extended his hand to assist, causing rows of young women to swoon in delicious delight.

Twitter had been vicious about Huntley's performance after a rough cut of the film leaked. Hoping to extinguish the negative momentum, the film's production company ordered Huntley to skip the festival, offering an escalating non-appearance bonus, but his agent had hung tough, labeling it an infringement on Huntley's first amendment rights. Huntley would go where Huntley wanted to go, and neither God nor goddamned Beijing was going to interfere.

Taking pity on Huntley, I began to thank the long list of sponsors, forcing attention back to the stage. Finally, I headed back to my seat but paused in consternation at the end of the aisle. Avatar Bob had melted away as imperceptibly as the real one, replaced by a woman I didn't know. Small, curvaceous, with carefully sculpted blond hair, she seemed exuberant, if that's not too strange a description for someone who was not uttering a word.

A life force so strong, she seemed to be in full motion when not even moving an inch. It was impossible to take my eyes off her, and I didn't even try.

She whispered in my ear the second I sat down. "The tsunami is coming. It's urgent that we speak about Bob."

CHAPTER
TWO

"Johnnie's disappeared. We're trying to trace his movements," Bob had said.

"What?" I muttered, as I typed furiously into my iPhone. Late August, only two weeks out from the festival, and my electronic devices were one long siren call of organizational and media emergencies twenty hours each day. I wasn't paying Bob, or our dinner conversation, the attention I should have.

"Jane, the waiter is trying to put the food on the table."

I looked up and, sure enough, the waiter stood there with my black cod and Bob's lamb shank.

"Sorry." I finished the message and slipped the phone back into my pants pocket. "What were you saying?"

"One day Johnnie was in the office and the next, gone without a word. Alex is trying to find out where he is."

"Is that a problem?" Johnnie was Bob's half brother, and business partner, and my former husband, an unholy trinity of attributes that made me reluctant to let his name pass my lips, never mind contemplate his whereabouts. It'd been a short and violent marriage, the details of which I'd successfully suppressed, at least during waking hours. Bob saw Johnnie at the office of the family firm, but not outside it, and the three of us almost never rubbed up against each other, for fear of sparking a fire.

Bob dug into his dinner without reply. The phone vibrated continuously in my pocket, and I clutched my utensils tightly to stop from answering. "Who's Alex?" I asked, wanting to make amends for my comment that inadvertently sounded flippant.

"Don't worry about it. I shouldn't have brought it up. You just concentrate on the festival, and I'll take care of everything else."

The phone refused to stop. I made the excuse of a washroom visit to check my messages without it being obvious. By the time I got back to the table, Bob had moved on to another topic. If I'd paid more attention then, would our lives still have unraveled so spectacularly? Or was the Trojan horse of Johnnie's disappearance always going to carry the seeds of destruction?

* * *

Samantha's eyes drilled into me as I dialed Bob's phone for the umpteenth time from the back seat of the SUV, one of a long line of cars waiting to approach the venue for the opening night party. "Will Bob be here?" she asked.

"How did that woman get past security to strong-arm her way into the chair beside me?"

A moment's pause. "What are you talking about?"

"The blond in the leopard skin dress? English accent?"

"I have no idea what you're talking about."

"One minute Avatar Bob was in his seat. The next minute, he's gone, replaced by the wolf in leopard skin," I said, waiving my hands in frustration.

A pause. "I'm afraid I'm not really following. Wolf?"

"Movie reference." It wasn't, but Samantha was unlikely to challenge me on it. Even I didn't know what I meant; my survival instinct was kicking in, and it wasn't pretty.

"Did she tell you her name or what she wanted?" Samantha asked.

"I was pulled away too quickly," I said, my fists clasped tightly in my lap, wary of exposing vulnerability to her. "Don't worry about it. I was caught off guard, that's all."

"If there's some kind of threat, I need to report it to security. Protocol. She could be one of the nutters."

"Leave it to me. I'll do it."

Finally, the SUV reached the front of the museum. Our driver opened the door and into the party fray I slid, soon separated from Samantha by the crowd. The clatter of a thousand people bounced off the museum's stone walls, an engorged octopus of strangers each pulsating with a need it was my duty to divine and fulfill.

I steeled myself and plunged in, an introvert camouflaged in a bon vivant attitude. I kissed cheeks and shook hands as I made my way through the room, focus narrowed to one conversation at a time as if my life depended on it. See no evil, hear no evil, evil must not exist.

It was too early for the movie talent to appear, so the photographers languished on the sides, waiting for someone they recognized as a VIP to show up. One snapshot of an A-lister, drink in hand, would secure the booze sponsors for the following year's festival. The festival leaned on talent managers, who in turn pressured the actors and directors to put in appearances. The marketing department bribed social media influencers with free tickets and swag in exchange for scattering the celebrity photographs everywhere. It was an illusionist's game, but one in which everyone was happily complicit.

A hand clamped down hard on my shoulder. Startled, I turned, fists coming up involuntarily. Jacob's eyes took in my overreaction before he slowly released his grip. The blond leopard had thoroughly rattled me.

"Jane, meet Darren McGregor," he said.

I turned my gaze to the Instagram legend beside Jacob. A whole-living guru with tawny skin and flowing blond hair streaked expertly with silver as if to say, yes, he was accepting his age gracefully. Darren McGregor had been born some sixty-odd years earlier in the Bahamas, where his English grandfather was governor and his father an alcoholic who squandered both money and reputation. Sent off to boarding school in the U.K., young Darren ultimately had to forfeit his place at university when the family cup ran dry. Without the school-tie connections to grease his way into the financial center of London, Darren headed to Toronto to remake the family fortune, reclaiming his "Britishness" once he'd become rich enough to buy his way into the establishment.

Out of the blue, Darren's people had telephoned the festival to announce he'd be attending to support his son, an associate producer on a British film in our Next Wave program. Might the festival be kind enough to arrange tickets? Invite him to the best parties?

Victoria and the fundraising department swung into action. Darren's net worth, giving patterns, real estate transactions, listed assets, friends and family — no detail too big or too small was left unexamined as they pulled together a cultivation strategy, including interviews with former employees and business partners to extrapolate data beyond what was publicly available. In three weeks, Victoria's detailed profile rivaled the work of MI6.

"It's lovely to meet you, Darren," I said. He bypassed my outstretched hand to kiss my cheek, making me uncomfortable in his assumption.

Born into wealth, self-doubt extinguished in utero, Victoria ziplined the thin edge of utilitarian flirtation with no worry of consequence, slipping "we" and "us" into conversations with potential donors, creating a suggestion of more to come but not crossing the line. It was a skill I almost admired, but one I found impossible.

I stepped backward, arranging a friendly smile on my face. "Can it really be true that you've never been to the festival? Even when you lived on this side of the ocean?"

Darren nodded. "I was always so busy, you understand, with mundane things like business," he said. "It was only once I was courageous enough to chase passion, not profit, that I had time for the things that really matter."

"I admire your very generous support of our artistic counterparts in London," I said.

Darren's Cheshire smile widened. He ran a hand through hair whose layers cascaded in exactly the right waterfall. His yearly hairdressing budget would fund a staff position. "You've been checking up on me."

"I'm sure you knew we'd do exactly that when your office called with the good news," I said, betting Darren favored an insider sense of frankness. "Festivals like ours need champions like you. I've only just been appointed acting CEO, but I'm determined to throw open the pearly gates to filmmakers who struggle to get their films made and distributed. The indies who operate on a shoestring. Artists of color struggling past the invisible quota system that views one success as the leveling of structural inequity. Do you know that male directors still outnumber women, five to one? The word inclusion is in everyone's press releases these days, but too often that commitment is only an inch deep. Our audiences want the thrill of being talent spotters. Otherwise, they'd pay half the ticket price and go to the movies."

Darren zoomed in like a bird of prey with a tasty canary in his sights. In my haste to focus away from potential dangers in the room, I'd revealed too much.

"I love your passion, Jane. I'm dying to get together and hear more."

I placed my hand on Jacob's arm to draw him back into the conversation, breaking the intimacy with Darren.

"I'm sure that Victoria and Jacob have sorted out your tickets and party invitations," I said, leaving my hand in place with a perverse enjoyment given Jacob's recoil. "But if there are any films or events you want to add to your itinerary, please let someone know, and we'll make sure you're taken care of."

"I'd love the opportunity to see a film with you, Jane," Darren purred. "Learn through the eyes of an expert. It would be a rare honor."

"I'm sure we can make that happen," Jacob said. "I'll have a word with Jane's assistant."

I bet he would. "Duty calls," I said, pointing toward a waving Samantha at the front door. "I believe the talent has arrived. Until the next time, Darren."

I wove through the crowd toward the evening's lead sponsor, Charles Brindamount, who stood talking to Scott, my next-door neighbor.

"Jane, darling, we're so very proud of you," Scott cried, dabbing at his brow sweat with a cocktail napkin, leaving a trail of chicken remnants scattered across his forehead.

The very day the board appointed me acting CEO, Victoria called Bob to ask his company, Smythe Financial, for a significant festival sponsorship. I chafed at the obviousness of the quid pro quo, even while understanding this was how the game was played at this level. In addition to agreeing to the donation, Bob handed over his personal Rolodex to Victoria to exploit.

Like many of our acquaintances, Scott swooned under her approach, excited and nervous to be invited inside an organization he'd only ever seen covered in the media.

Four figure donations meant expedited ticket access, queue jumping, opening and closing parties. Five figures: more exclusive parties, special lounges, and other perks. North of that and everything was negotiable. Forty percent of the yearly budget came from individuals or from corporations, all of whom gave because they felt an experiential connection to the festival. A connection that needed constant reinforcement.

"Darling," I said, drawing it out slightly until he blushed, and I felt bad for poking fun at him. Like most people, I, too, swayed under the secret spice of celebrity, despite my ongoing exposure to it. Why should he be immune?

"You're so kind to come," I continued, more gently. "I bet you've got a great selection of films already, but if you need anything, just call me. Right now, though, I'm afraid I need to steal Charles away to meet the leading lady."

Scott beamed, and I was forced to cull his expectations with a look that made it clear he wasn't included. Tonight was business, and access apportioned according to supporter levels.

"By the way, I just ran into Alexandra. She's looking for you," Scott said.

"Alexandra?"

"English accent. Blond. Do you know who I mean? I met her a few days ago on your front steps. With Bob."

I stared, trying to register Scott's comments. Finally, Charles's discreet coughing cut through the fog. He pointed at Samantha, who'd turned into a windmill trying to get my attention. I bid Scott goodbye and began to drag Charles through the crowd, as my mind churned.

Finally, we reached the front entrance. A cacophony of cameras went off like gunshots as Devlin Ross swept in to kiss me on both cheeks, then slid an arm around Charles's neck for the money shot. Her breasts were too voluptuous for her thin frame, but who cared, they were gorgeous, barely concealed as they were behind the black lace of the dress. Charles stood up taller as they nestled into his chest at just the right angle. She was a pro, I had to give her that. Samantha handed her a drink from our vodka sponsor, the photo was taken, and Devlin handed it back untouched. We were just over a minute.

"Charles and his bank generously fund our Global Connections program. Ten young writer/directors, from Vietnam to Zimbabwe to right here in North America, enter a structured mentoring relationship with a leading industry professional, attend the festival with full industry passes, and have their films screened as well. It's an unparalleled opportunity."

"Remarkable," Devlin purred, simultaneously stepping in closer to Charles and laying her hand on his arm, while she pumped my foot like a piano peddle with sole of her five-inch Louboutins.

"You're such a citizen of the world yourself, Devlin. I thought you'd appreciate knowing about the bank's philanthropic leadership in this area," I said. Charles was a strong advocate for the arts within a bank that preferred football to films, and a significant donor personally as well. He was getting his full three minutes, even at the risk of my walking with a limp.

"Your performance was so moving," Charles blurted out. "You're an extraordinary actor."

The simple sincerity penetrated Devlin's armor. She kissed him on the cheek, even without the camera bulb. "Thank you."

Her publicist's hand now pressing into my back, we bid Charles goodbye and moved on to the next target. Devlin was skilled at disarming the sponsors and the three minutes were shaved down by thirty seconds each subsequent round. We sped our way through the head of the arts funding agency, the chairman of an investment firm, and the president of a private foundation at a pace that was dizzying.

Suddenly, an arm slinked its way through mine and spun me around. The blond leopard's face was even more heavily made up than I remembered, the bronzed tone of the foundation garish against the oversized hoop earrings. "You can't avoid me, Jane," she said, her little incisor teeth marked with her dark red lipstick.

"Thank you so much for supporting the film world's most important gathering," Devlin purred. "But I must run and catch my plane now. Jane's contracted to see me out."

Devlin pulled me away, deeper into the bowels of the museum where containers of embalmed remains surrounded us. I paused in front of what I suspected was a liver, its coloring moving from white to brown to dark, blood-encrusted red as it circled up around itself. An inexplicable fear seized me. First Johnnie missing, then Bob? The blond leopard and a coming tsunami of which I knew nothing? A light touch on my lower back brought me back to consciousness.

"At their best, the English are charming and funny," Devlin said, withdrawing the hand to light a cigarette. "The rest of them go into the battlefield to shoot the wounded. Stay away from that woman. Her karma's black as ice."

Samantha arrived in a rush. "You can't smoke inside," she said, waving her hand to dissipate the smoke. "It's against the rules."

"Sue me," Devlin said, offering me the cigarette, which I took, much to Samantha's chagrin. She held out her hand for it, but I avoided her reach.

"The fire alarm will go off and ruin the event," she protested.

"Then you'd get to go home," Devlin smirked, taking the cigarette out of my fingers with a sigh as I began to cough on the first inhale. "Can you get us out of this crypt?"

She puffed away as Samantha guided us to the staff entrance where a small entourage waited. One assistant took Devlin's cigarette butt, while another swept her hair into a ponytail and covered it up with a baseball cap. Sunglasses and an oversized leather jacket, and she was unrecognizable in thirty seconds. She leaned in to kiss me fully on the lips.

"You need more people."

And, without another glance, they were gone, suction-cupping the oxygen out of the room with them. I flopped against the security desk, as Samantha took my iPhone from her purse and waved it in my direction. "I listened to the messages. Several crises but all related to work." No Bob, she meant.

"Did I ask you to check my messages?" I asked, voice sharper than I meant it to be.

She paused before answering. "I thought I was being helpful."

"I appreciate that," I said, putting out my hand. "May I have my phone back please?"

"You have nowhere to put it."

I pushed myself away from the desk and grabbed my phone, looking longingly at the exit. Several times during the evening, I had turned around, expecting to see Bob in conversation with someone, patiently giving me space to take care of my obligations while he played rearguard action with a board member or one of the festival's business or government funders.

Then I'd remembered. Bob was missing, and in his place, a threatening interloper.

The lessons of my unstable childhood were in my DNA: don't talk, don't feel, and, above all, don't trust. A crater the size of Texas constricted my breathing as much as the spandex. Living with Bob, I'd let my guard down, only now realizing how fully.

"There are just too many stakeholders still here," Samantha said, ever watchful. "We don't have a choice."

On my sixteenth birthday, I had stood in front of the TV to block my mother's beloved soap operas, watched late at night after her shift as a cleaner in a real estate office was over, and told her that there were always options in life, even if many of them were unpalatable.

But had I actually been justified to sit in judgment of my mother all those years ago? A woman too beaten down by the rulebook being thrown to the wind. By the good book slammed on the desk. By the nibbling ducks of self-doubt. By the bullying nature of testosterone squared. Is it any wonder she lacked the power to confront ugly truth?

The blond leopard wasn't getting within ten feet of me until I had a clearer picture of the jeopardy Bob and I faced. Nor was anyone else. I pulled my dress up and slipped the phone underneath the tight fit of the spandex, to the astonishment of the security guard and the displeasure of Samantha. Adjusting my package about as discretely as a hockey player rearranges his, I smoothed the dress down, before walking back into the fray without a backward glance.

CHAPTER THREE

DAY 2: *Eyes Wide Shut*

When I was eight, the widower Pastor Glass and his two school-age children moved onto our dead-end street in the small industrial city where my parents struggled to make ends meet, their early visions of adventurous travels and unbound choices ground down by the dreariness of daily life in the lower one percent.

Suddenly, the word of God was everywhere in our house, and we who couldn't identify Job from Judas found ourselves baptized into the church, listening to Pastor Glass deliver his Sunday sermons from a plain wooden pulpit in an unadorned A-frame neighborhood church.

The pastor's prematurely gray hair framed an unlined face, beautiful in composition but sallow in complexion, except when flushed by the exertion of administering to his flock.

I would sit upright with indignation on the hard, wooden pews, boxed in by my parents on one side and my little sister on the other. My father absorbed with fervor Pastor Glass's lessons that pardon came not by acts of contrition but by absolute faith. My mother was silent. For her sake, I learned to swallow my frustration, until it built a tiered cake of resentment that fed my flight when I turned eighteen. To the overbearing authority of Pastor Glass, and the world, I turned an unbreakable face, and shuttered eyes.

As time went on, my father basically went to live in the Glass household. He returned once or twice a week to make an appearance for the sake of normalcy, and certainly on Sundays for the barbecue that was a staple of our suburban cul-de-sac from April through September.

A group of women would linger around the picnic table, including my mother and Margie O'Flynn from next door, an Irish émigré continually on the angle for any gossip to be hoovered up, as assiduously as she vacuumed the dirt in her carpet night and day.

The men would congregate away from the storm that brewed at the barbecue where Pastor Glass flipped burgers for the sake of communion with the regular people. The alcohol consumed there was a running blight he was determined to conquer. Conquer with love, of course, although it was sometimes difficult to distinguish Pastor Glass's love from his burning indignation.

He'd turn those burgers with a force that increased every time he heard the unmistakable noise of a Labatt's Blue bottle cap. Wham, the barbecue's metal lid would go down as he fixed the trespasser with his glare. More often than not, it was Joe who refused to relinquish his beer, despite God made manifest with a giant spatula in his hand. Whoop, the lid would go back up again, spatula banging and scraping the charred flesh of the animal off the grill as surely as Pastor Glass would scrape the blackened stain from Joe's soul, if he had his way.

My father, his faithful assistant, stood ready to receive the offering onto the Chinet plates.

As I approached twelve, the age when Lutheran children began preparatory classes for their confirmation as adult members of the church, the pressure became intense for me to fall into the conga line of faith. I finally agreed to be confirmed in exchange for a video camera paid for by Pastor Glass, which I pointed at the world around me, desperate to decode the secrets that shaped our lives.

During the barbecues, I let the camcorder run on a tripod inside the open door of the garage, week after week, year after year. Everyone knew but they soon forgot. Like me, it sat confounded at the lack of inhibition around me. As if they felt no shame. That is, except for the Browning and Glass families. The seven of us knew, without a scintilla of doubt, that keeping things close to our chest was the very definition of survival.

Later, I cut together a horror-comedy film from the footage for my application to the Tisch School at NYU for my master's degree in film. I called it *Truly, Madly, Creepily*.

I was only ever captured on tape once, in the grade eight production of *Guys and Dolls*. My mother insisted that my sister film the performance, positioning her in the front row with the clunky, heavy camcorder. The attention it brought from the rows around her was torture for my sister, a prepubescent girl already desperate to disappear into herself.

Years later, I transferred that footage from VHS to digital, and from time to time, I'd watch it. Jane, at thirteen, already taller than everyone else, whose red curls bounced halfway down her back, whose periods started early and hard, whose shoulders hunched to camouflage already full breasts. She looked impossibly young, that Jane, with her long legs, and awkward dance steps, and smooth skin. But not the eyes. I'd pause the frame and zoom in, my own unblinking eyes staring right back at me. A gaze that already had taken accurate measure of the world around it. Thirteen, and fully cognizant of the shit people do. Thirteen, and determined to survive.

★ ★ ★

"Ms. Browning? My name is Dilip Patel. I need to talk with you urgently about Smythe Financial."

Only nine a.m. and the shoe had dropped. "Please come in," I said, ushering him quickly into my office and closing the door. "How can I help you?"

"You're the same Jane Browning who's a board director and officer of Smythe Financial, correct?"

I nodded, slowly. "It's a family firm run by my partner, Bob Walker-Smythe. I'm sorry, who are you?"

He withdrew a card from his pocket and handed it to me. "Dilip Patel, senior forensic accountant, Office of the Whistleblower, Ontario Securities Commission."

The bottom fell out of my stomach. "Office of the Whistle-blower?"

Patel nodded. "It's urgent we reach your partner. Do you know his whereabouts?"

"His EA would know his daily schedule better than me."

"She's being less than transparent."

That made two of us. "I'm sorry to hear that," I said. "Like most of the senior staff here, I stay at our partner hotel for the week previous to the festival and then during the eleven-day run. We work around the clock; everything else gets squeezed out of existence."

"When did you last have contact with Bob Walker-Smythe?"

"Yesterday or the day before," I prevaricated. "It was the launch yesterday. Utter madhouse around here, and I collapsed into bed when I finally left the opening night reception around two in the morning."

"He didn't attend?"

I shook my head and kept quiet, hands clasped tightly behind my back.

He stared at me intently. "We've left messages for all four of Smythe's senior executives without a return call, nor has the official notification we sent Smythe Financial been acknowledged."

Jesus. "What kind of notification?"

"Formal notice of irregularities in the firm's minimum capital requirement."

I picked up my phone and dialed the receptionist. "Please bring a pot of tea," I said, playing for time to quell the nausea before I turned back to him. "What kind of irregularities?"

"I need to review specifics with the firm's management, not its board."

"But you came to me."

"As a courtesy, because of your unique relationship to the company's management," he said. "But make no mistake, Ms. Browning, this is a serious legal situation. And, as a board director and corporate officer, you're liable. I need to hear from one of the c-suite executives by end of day Monday, or the enforcement team will roll out."

A knock sounded ever more ominous for its coming at the exact end of Patel's sentence. I opened the door to retrieve the tea from the receptionist, placing it on the small table in my office. "Do you want a cup?" I asked.

He shook his head. "Please understand that if you're the one left holding the bag, then you're the one we'll be coming after. You could face criminal charges."

"I'll do everything I can to reach Bob, or one of the other executives," I said, slowing pouring a cup of tea and turning to face him. "But I don't take kindly to your tone, Mr. Patel. You show up at my office unannounced, refuse to give me details about your claims, and then threaten me?"

"Not threats, Ms. Browning. A warning. To make sure you're fully in the loop."

Before the loop is around your neck. "I'll help in whatever way I can. You must also understand I have my own responsibilities here that cannot wait."

He put out his hand to shake mine. "Goodbye, Ms. Browning. I need to hear from you by Monday."

As soon as the door closed behind him, I dialed Bob's cell, then his direct line; both went straight to voicemail. "The securities commission has just been here. What on earth is going on?"

* * *

The trees held their breath in the evening's stillness, darkness a sound blanket that muffled intent, ill or otherwise. Walking up the front path had triggered the motion detector lights, illuminating the front yard and the garbage and recycling bins at one side of the house. Beyond that was sheer black.

I collected the mail from the box and went inside. There were several envelopes and the usual brochures from real estate agents proclaiming their successful neighborhood house sales. Was it a week's worth of mail? Or a day's? Hard to tell. I'd talked to Bob first thing in the morning and last thing each night, picturing him lying in our bed, craving his touch as I lay alone in my hotel room. But had he been here? Telephone calls could be made from anywhere.

Closing the door behind me, I walked swiftly through the first floor, pulling down the window blinds and locking the stairs to the basement. It felt ridiculous, but so did Bob's disappearance.

The first year I'd moved into this house, his house, we invited my sister to come for Christmas. Determined to produce a fulsome dinner — turkey, sausage stuffing, a ham, and endless vegetables — Bob set about buying the food on Christmas Eve, armed with a list and an equanimity that I was incapable of in crowded stores. He'd been flush with determined excitement as he came through the front door with bag after bag of food, bottles of champagne and wine. We lit the fire and made love on the settee between tasks.

Tracy showed up the next day for an awkward half hour, clutching her latest liquid diet concoction in an oversized plastic cup, her metabolism destroyed from a war she'd waged against herself. Bob coaxed me out of my funk after her departure with a runny patter of funny anecdotes, and glass after glass of bubbly. We cooked everything, excess be damned, and ate ourselves solid until we could do nothing that evening but tuck ourselves up in bed, wind howling against the glass of the skylight, protected against the outside forces by what seemed like our unbreakable connection.

Pulling myself away from the memories, I headed upstairs. The master bed looked crisply made, top sheet turned over the edge of the French provincial duvet cover. I pulled back the sheets; nothing looked disturbed. The laundry basket and bathroom garbage can were empty.

The long cupboard struggled to contain its usual jumble of different sized roller and garment bags, but did the doors close a little more easily? Running a hand along the suits in the closet, I slipped it in and out of pockets, unsure what I was looking for.

The security guard in the lobby of Bob's office building had been startled by my sudden appearance an hour before, trying to talk my way into his offices without the benefit of a security fob, a set of keys, or a credible storyline.

I moved on to the bedroom dresser, the bedside table, underneath the sink. My search gained intensity, as one by one all the places where things could be hidden within the intimacy of a shared space unveiled themselves. Seven years of a relationship without any strife had lulled me into trusting the space between willful blindness and shared optimism. A rookie's error.

Downstairs in the home office, I turned on Bob's desktop computer and opened his email program. Almost without meaning to, I'd internalized his passwords over the years, as I stood at his back waiting to be shown an email or a YouTube clip he thought would make me laugh. The inbox was stripped down to only a few emails, the sent file and trash completely empty. My inbox bulged with thousands of emails seeking reply; could anyone's be this preternaturally empty?

I clicked on the icon for Smythe Financial; a request for a password came up. After the third wrong attempt, an ominous yellow triangle warned me that I'd been locked out and the activity reported to the system administrator.

Increasingly agitated, I pulled out the desk drawers, putting them on the floor. Methodically, I went through the contents. Getting down on my knees, I examined the bottom of the desk but found nothing unusual.

Finally, there was nothing left to search. I slipped the credit card, bank statements, and several thumb drives into my purse and sat back on my haunches. But my body would no longer be silenced. I sprang up and ran for the washroom, vomit hitting the toilet bowl water and bouncing back up at my face from the force of the expulsion.

Lying on the bathroom floor, I willed my heart back into a normal rhythm. The sound of the front door banging sent it into a frenzy again. I rushed up, hitting my head on the pedestal sink, and ran to the doorway. A dark-colored sedan was parked across the road, idling. Terror made it impossible to swallow; someone had been inside the house the whole time, watching me. I pulled my cell phone from my pocket and angled it to take a picture of the car just as it pulled away.

I wedged the door open with the umbrella stand, not sure if the greater danger was outside or in. Was I alone in the house or not? Every horror film I'd ever seen flashed through my mind, their ominous sound tracks throbbing in my veins. Things didn't end well for women on their own in the dark — either in the movies or in real life.

I grabbed a shoe from the front closet and threw it into the yard to retrigger the motion lights and then ran full speed back to Bob's desk to grab my purse. I stepped out into the night, locking the door behind me, and I rushed to the side of the road with streetlights.

All day, festival obligations and emergencies had foiled my attempt to come investigate. I'd carved out this hour, informing an overly curious Samantha that I had a private appointment. My iPhone alarm beeped ten p.m., and I vacillated between ordering an Uber right away or squeezing a few minutes out for what I wanted to do next, knowing it might be my only chance. I glanced up and down the street for black sedans as I began to walk.

Typing in the address I'd copied from Bob's contact list, I let the iPhone GPS guide the way. I followed it, watching the journey as a director might: a long establishing shot of a city neighborhood, circuitous jungle of one-way streets, dead ends, and glass towers, as a woman walks alone. A black sedan follows her from a discreet distance. She pauses in front of a house, smaller than the last one but no less attractive; its red door and black shutters against the white vinyl siding suggest a bit of whimsy. Bodies are visible but indistinguishable behind the curtains. The camera pans to the woman, across the sidewalk, as she stands silently. Watching. Being watched.

The insistent buzz of incoming texts pulled me back from the imaginary shot, to the reality of the night air. Shivering, I looked around at the bushes and shrubs where people might hide. I began to run down the street, raising my hand to flag down the first cab I saw.

★ ★ ★

The *Vanity Fair* party was so overcrowded the jaws of life couldn't haven't pried open the room. I clung to the corner near the emergency exit, drinking too much.

The exit behind me opened suddenly, and I was pushed to the side by the entrance of several men who looked like they should be in a mixed martial arts cage. Varying skin colors but the same muscle-bound bodies and tattoos. In the midst of the posse was Meaghan Randall, star of a mega-successful horror franchise, recently outed on Twitter for sleeping with the very young actor who played her son in the series.

She stood, body tense, eyes down, demanding attention while affecting an air of resigned duress. Her bodyguards surveyed the room, which yielded not a square inch. The atmosphere had tensed up with the aggressive show of muscle. Meaghan's publicist, Franny, edged around the drama to glue herself to my side. "Where's the VIP room?" she shouted.

"The entire crowd is VIP," I shouted back.

Amanda, *Vanity Fair*'s event producer, picked her way over. "What the fuck is this?" she said, when she finally arrived, panting at the effort of trudging through molasses. "They're slaughtering the vibe."

Franny frowned. "We need a VIP room for Meaghan. What do you have?"

"Sweet fuck all," Amanda replied. "Everybody in here is A-list."

Other actors waved a hand at Meaghan, who was intent on not acknowledging anyone, although I doubted she missed a single salute. The phalanx of bodyguards started to move as one. "Where do they think they're going?" Amanda said, her attempt at crowd control thwarted when the lead bodyguard picked her up as if she was a leaf and placed her to the side.

"I'm betting the stairs. The Borg seems to have figured out there's a second floor."

"Is that a racial slur?" Franny asked. By this time, the three of us were squashed together in the vortex the security detail had created. "Because if it is, I'll have this festival up before the NAACP before you can say 'I quit,'" she said, waving her finger at us.

"Look," I said, words coming in spurts as I fought to get enough oxygen to speak. "Your party, Amanda. You want to evict Meaghan, you or Chantelle own that."

Chantelle Healy, *Vanity Fair*'s influential west coast editor, acclaimed celebrity whisperer, and host for the night's party, held court upstairs. She was mercurial at the best of times, and even someone as thick-skinned as Amanda would quake at having to interrupt her with this.

Franny started to protest, but my hand covered her mouth before she could squeak out a sound. I was going to need a vat of hand sanitizer, who knew what asses those lips had kissed this week.

"Meaghan is B-list in a room full of As. Ain't the room to pull this kind of shit," Amanda said, still angry but clearly weighing her options.

34

"My client has done you the favor of appearing at your festival —"

"Just cut the shit," I barked. "It's after midnight." Franny didn't know what to make of that non-sequitur and frankly neither did I, but by that time our little group was being carried up the flight of stairs. Meaghan finally deigned to lift her head and make eye contact with the room, dramatic in her sorrowful demeanor.

"We'll clear one of the rooms for a VIP lounge," Amanda said to Franny. "But you pull this kind of stunt again with me, and you'll be party planning at Florida seniors' complexes and shopping at Marshalls before you can figure out how to spell regret."

Franny went momentarily quiet. We'd reached the second floor, and the Borg paused to focus their collective brain on next steps. Amanda and I wormed our way to the front, passing Meaghan as we did, who did not look at us. With the extra space, I began to breathe a little easier.

"You wait with them," Amanda muttered darkly, disappearing around a half-closed door. Almost immediately, disgruntled party-goers emerged in various state of undress, staring at Meaghan as they headed for the stairs. Amanda reappeared to give the all-clear signal and, as the entourage headed in, I turned to go. Franny grabbed my arm.

"Give me a sec to figure out who you need to send up. The CAA guy, too, there at the bar, the good-looking Jewish one. He's connected, bring whoever he's with. Any producers in the room, too, and you'd better round up the best-looking actresses, I guess. Make them on the young side. No phones. We can't risk unauthorized photos. One of our guys will collect them at the door and return them. Give them the heads-up on that."

I shook my arm free. "I'm not in the business of procurement."

Amanda snorted. "I'm not going to be within swinging distance of a Hollywood agent being told he needs to give up his phone."

"Jane, come on, you know how this game is played," Franny whined. "It's your job."

"No, it's not."

Franny turned desperately to Samantha, who had finally made her way upstairs. "I need your help rounding up people for Meaghan to hang with."

"Come on, Samantha," I said, as I started to descend.

Franny complained bitterly as Samantha and I picked our way to the floor below. She'd get her way in the end, not matter how pissed off Amanda was. Parties turned on a dime, or in this case, on a pout. Millions were on the line for all the brands — Vanity Fair, Hugo Boss, the booze sponsor, and the festival itself. The key to a successful party wasn't difficult — keep it well lubricated, keep it sexy, and jam it full of celebrities. Vanity Fair's reign as Vibe Houdini was constantly challenged by pretenders to the throne, and a divisive diva in its midst came with a potentially expensive downstream effect.

I'd made my way to the bar when the voice came from behind me.

"Jane, is that you?"

The hairs on my neck bristled at the unfamiliar, silken tone and unrecognizable accent. All night, I'd had the feeling of eyes following me. Of fate come knocking. I'd tried to shake it off as residual fear from the intruder in the house but visions of black sedans, blond leopards, and tsunamis danced in my head. For a moment I longed to be anyone else, but I turned to find a woman I didn't recognize, cheekbones higher than her Manolo Blahniks, long hair blacker than carbon.

"It's a pleasure to see you again," I said, shaking her hand even as my retrieval function drew a complete blank. It was hard to imagine I'd met a woman this remarkable and forgot her. Surely, undercover RCMP didn't wear heels that cost a grand?

"Is Bob with you?" She looked around. "I just arrived and have not seen him yet."

My heart beat a retreat back through the cavity of my chest, sinking deep to rest in a dark place. "No," I said. "Bob was unable to attend this evening. Was he expecting to see you here?"

"Well, you know, our business interests have been dovetailing somewhat."

What kind of business could Bob possibly have with a woman like this? "I've been very preoccupied with the festival the past several months."

"Yes, of course," she said, putting her hand on my arm. "What a fantastic accomplishment. I attended the opening night film and, of course, the party. You really know how to work a crowd."

"I'm sorry not to have seen you," I said slowly. "You should have said hello."

"I couldn't get at you," she said. "You were never alone. And besides, I knew we'd eventually meet."

Across the room, Jacob and a small entourage emerged from the elevator. He'd been quiet all day, which should have been a relief but wasn't. The festival's lawyers had successfully fought the injunction against *State*, getting it lifted just before the courts closed for the weekend. The film could now go forward, if I gave the greenlight. Our eyes met, and I struggled to keep the consternation I felt out of my face. He paused to stare at me, sonar trained to pick up any vulnerability.

"Perhaps you and Bob will give me the pleasure of a drink this week?" the woman said, drawing my attention back.

I looked back at her without reply, body increasingly wired.

"Of course, if you are too swamped with professional matters, Bob and I could have a drink ourselves. And Johnnie, too, if he's in town?"

I smiled thinly. Johnnie? "Let's play it by ear," I said, twitching. "I never know from one moment to the next what will happen."

"A démain," she said, leaning forward to kiss me three times, alternating cheeks, her musky perfume staining my senses. "I'll look forward to getting together very soon," she murmured, as she moved away.

The crowd swallowed her almost immediately, and Jacob was still staring at me. I shivered, pulling my jacket closer around me. The room was suddenly still, as if noise had been suspended and I no longer had ears to hear with but rather gills to experience the vibrations of the room, feeling words as I heard them, tasting colors instead of seeing them.

I was across the floor and down the stairs before my conscious mind registered that the noise rushing to fill the void was the pounding of my heart, telegraphing my flight.

CHAPTER FOUR

"I came to understand those women," Clare said, leaning in so no one could overhear. "The ones who drown their children in the bathtub or hold a pillow over their heads. We're supposed to hate them but . . . I feel pity. You watch this son whom you've nurtured inside your own body, and slowly he's turned against you. Poisoned with lies his father drip-feeds him through the vein of his great authority. You worry, every hour of the day and the night, that he's turning into the same manipulative monster. You know that, just like his father, he'll get more powerful as he gets older and you'll bear the responsibility for whoever he ends up hurting."

Her voice was a long, low stream that bore no interruption. "You know as long as he's alive, his father will control both you and him, your life and his destined to be a misery from which there is no escape. Death is not revenge. It's the only choice left to you, a preventative measure, in a game whose rules were rigged before it began."

With this, Bob's mother sat back, lit a cigarette, and watched for my reaction. I signaled the waiter. The Perrier wasn't going to cut it.

That day, seven years earlier, was the first time I'd met Bob, and the only time I met Clare. Bob and Johnnie's father, Robert, had died suddenly in a single engine plane crash en route to a mining business he owned. Bob returned home from the U.K., and Clare from New Zealand; they'd both fled twenty-five years earlier. Wearing hot pink, Clare demanded to sit in the front row at the funeral, "to make sure the bastard is actually dead."

I sat on the other side of the aisle trapped between a weeping Johnnie, whom I had left three years earlier, and his mother Hazel, whose pregnancy at twenty-two promoted her from nanny to wife number two. Neither Hazel nor Clare shed a tear.

I'd have been more attentive to Clare's story if I knew she herself would be dead of an aneurysm within the week. But, like Michael Corleone, I just wanted to escape this family and kept getting dragged back in.

Johnnie stalked me for months after I moved out. He was adamantly opposed to a divorce, emotionally devastated at my leaving. Eventually, I was forced to accept Robert's deal: he'd guarantee Johnnie's distance and honor the basic support payments of the draconian prenuptial agreement I'd signed. In exchange, I'd stay silent about my broken arm and collarbone, and punt the issue of divorce down the field. I carefully folded the urge for real freedom into a little compartment in my mind, along with suppressed echoes of my mother's powerlessness, telling myself I could deal with it later, after the passage of time had leached off the inflammation.

"You've heard what an unremittent asshole he was to me?" Clare asked that day at the wake.

I had nodded, ordering a double gin and tonic when one of the waitstaff approached.

I watched her watching me from behind the cigarette and wished like hell that I hadn't agreed to sit with her. Hazel was passed out inside, Johnnie huddled with his uncles at the make-shift bar drinking scotch after scotch, plotting a coup, which later failed, against the iron-clad trust that had handed control of the family firm to Bob, the eldest son.

Bob stood by himself fifty feet away on the patio grass. I was fascinated by his sculpted, patrician face. It appeared stoic and dig-nified, but if you looked carefully — and I found myself completely unable to look away — his dark green eyes were pools of emotion.

While Johnnie and I were still together, Hazel would often show up, drunk, at the condo where we lived. She was like a dog with the desiccated bone of the family Smythe caught in her jaw. One day, she dumped a box of weathered kodaks over the kitchen table. In them, she aged from a sweet, open-faced twenty-year-old to an increasingly harder-looking woman approaching thirty, a tumbler of spirits always in her hand, the smile too forced as the fantasy of happy ever after curdled. Johnnie, with his loopy smile and need for attention, was usually dead center. Hazel picked up one final photo and looked at it a long time, before she thrust it at me and went to the fridge for her second bottle of Chablis.

"If it wasn't Shangri-la beforehand, it was certainly shit after," she said.

Balloons and decorations on manicured grounds establish it as an outdoor birthday party. Food and drink and people are littered everywhere. Off to one side stands an eighteen-year-old Bob, caught on celluloid as Hazel lands an intense kiss on his lips, one hand on either side of his face. Johnnie looks on from a distance. Within weeks of the "incident," Bob left for business school in Europe; a distraught Clare gave up saving the soul of her only child from becoming his father's doppelganger and fled to join her sister in New Zealand. Johnnie was left alone with a mother in whose affections he was secondary.

Clare waited for a response, withdrawing further into her self-protective mantle as I silently sipped my drink and let a movie reel of an alternative life play in my head. At the time, I thought she wanted a fellow outsider to listen to her bitter tale, and I chafed at the compulsion I'd felt to attend the funeral for Johnnie's sake. What I failed to recognize, at least until it became impossible not to, is how the kind of intense anger that burned inside Clare justified its own set of rules. Or just how much it would come to mirror my own.

★ ★ ★

They descended on me as soon as I stepped through the revolving door into the hotel lobby. Samantha sprung off the low Italian sofa, followed more slowly by a shambling bear of a man lugging a television camera in one hand. A dark-haired woman in her thirties, phone glued to ear, stopped pacing the moment her eyes locked on mine. I recognized that intense, devouring focus immediately: Cynical Yet Intrepid Reporter. I beelined for the bank of elevators, but CYIR would have stepped over the decapitated head of a child to make sure she got there first.

"We need official festival comment on the Alexei Panov arrest immediately. We're live on Ukrainian breakfast television in twelve minutes."

"It's two a.m. Jane would be pleased to make a statement in the morning," I said, poking the elevator button with brute force.

"You are Jane Browning, yes?" she asked, frowning, as Samantha jockeyed to get past her.

"Ventriloquist trick," I said, as the elevator arrived.

I stopped a foot over the threshold to make it difficult for the Ukrainians to follow, but the camera guy was surprisingly fast, using his considerable height and weight as a human wedge in the door. His face was suddenly so close I could see the dirty white spittle on the side of his mouth. My fist, thumb to the outside — too easy to break it otherwise — went for the bridge of his noise. Conscious thought kicked in the split second before contact, and I was able to pull back enough before cartilage followed the blood now running down his nostrils. Years earlier, my self-defense teacher had motivated me through months of early morning lessons by telling me that, with enough practice, the instinct to protect one's self becomes subrational.

The camera guy backed up in shock, Samantha slipped in, and I jammed the close button. "So sorry for that," I murmured as the door closed, simultaneously worried I was losing control and proud of my self-defense mechanism. "Statement tomorrow."

Samantha stared at me, gobsmacked. "How did you know how to do that?" she whispered.

The doors opened on the sixth floor. "Television."

"Why are we getting out here? You're on seven," she said, recovering her voice, as she followed me into the hall.

"Misdirection." I headed for the stairs. "What's going on with Alexei Panov?"

"It's been two hours since you disappeared. You can't just go off the radar screen."

"I'm sorry," I said, impatiently. The news crew was now ten minutes to live, and there was zero chance they'd give up. "Panov?"

43

I listened to her recital with morbid curiosity as we climbed a floor. Alexei Panov, oil oligarch turned director, had been charged earlier in the evening with sexually assaulting a hotel maid. Infamous for becoming a billionaire in the 1990s sell-off of Russian state energy assets to members of the Kremlin's inner circle, he'd thrust himself onto the film scene a decade earlier with a series of violent, gangster movies that glorified male machismo. Panov's new movie was a slick, empty spectacle that doubled as a thinly veiled love letter to President Putin. I failed to understand why Paul DelGrotto had programmed it — Eastern Europe and Russia were his geographic specialty — unless the Russian government was financing a showcase the following year, or the allure of sexting had befuddled both his heads.

The Russian bear wasn't growling so loudly now. Samantha and I ogled the photo of Panov, hair unkempt, his suit jacket thrown over his hands to disguise the handcuffs that adorned his wrists. A quiet swoosh of a door interrupted our schadenfreude as we rounded the last hallway bend before my suite. A head peered around my door.

"What the hell." The door closed just as we got there, and I banged on it with one hand while spearing the fob out of my purse with the other. Huntley Bartlett's thin body lay curled up in a fetal position on the edge of the couch by the time we entered.

"Get your shoes off the furniture," I said, slapping his legs lightly until he sat up long enough to rearrange himself against the arm of the sofa with an exaggerated whimper. "What are you doing in my room? And why the dramatic tableau?"

"Everyone is tweeting the most horrible photos from the screening. Why can't your press department make it all go away?"

"Most people consider it polite to get up when a woman is trying to get by," I said.

Hartley's spite made him sit up taller, despite himself. "You think Devlin's the weaker sex," he complained. "She put out a cigarette on the arm of a makeup artist who complained about her chain-smoking on set. Devlin is an alpha bitch."

"A bit harsh but he makes a good point," Samantha muttered.

"Go back to your own room and get some sleep," I said. "Our social media director will meet with your manager in the morning."

"But those media scum are all camped outside my bedroom door. And I can't bear the crowds in the hospitality suite. I just can't, Jane. There's nowhere to lie down in there."

"That's because you're meant to drink and eat and otherwise avail yourself of all things free in the hospitality suite. In your bedroom — you know the room with the big bed in it — that's where you sleep."

"I'll just stay here on your couch tonight, okay? I'd be as good as a little lamb, you won't even notice I'm here." He lay himself back out to provide his point, smiling up at me weakly.

"You're already yesterday's news," I snapped, walking toward the bedroom, too tired to massage the message. "The media found someone else to shove in the barrel."

I closed the connecting door and collapsed on the king-sized bed. Lifting a leg as high as possible, I stared at the runs in my nylons. If Bob were here, he'd have them off in a flash. Or maybe he wouldn't bother. Maybe he'd just tear the seam all the way to the top and push my panties aside. Bob kept his hereditary anger zipped up inside, out of my sight, almost always gracious but I knew it was there, lurking, waiting. I glimpsed it occasionally in the cut of his eyes before he turned away to compose himself, or in the cold abruptness of a tone that brooked no compromise. Its potentiality trembled under the cover of our sheets almost nightly, gripping my arms as he shuddered into me with the intensity of his orgasm and then gathered me up softly in his arms in the aftermath.

Samantha walked in, unknowingly followed by Huntley. I dropped my leg to the bed and sat up. "You. Out. Now." I spat the words at him until he withdrew, but without closing the door. "He's a liability," I said to Samantha.

"Our liability for another day and a half."

The door opened wider, and Huntley and the news crew squished into the room. "You're trespassing," I said, with as much dignity as I could, as I scrambled off the bed. "Samantha, call hotel security."

"Mr. Bartlett let us in. The two of you are lovers?"

"Don't be ludicrous," I said. "Huntley, tell them what's going on."

A momentary silence. "Jane and I are only very good friends," he murmured, completely unconvincingly.

"Don't be ridiculous. We're not friends." Even exhausted, a part of my brain began to calculate the percentages in my various options.

"The police are no comment," the reporter said. "Everyone attached to Panov's film have gone AWOL. The half of Ukraine who watches us wants something negative on the Russian. You will give a statement on Panov, yes, or I will report on the rumors of your affair with Huntley. And we will report your nose punch to the authorities. It is, as they say, up to you."

Film festival director rests marginally north of civil servants in being newsworthy, but a female festival director alone in a hotel room with an actor trending on Twitter was just salacious enough to fill some dead air until a better angle came along.

"You understand that I have no actual information, right? I've been off radar since this broke."

"Doesn't matter. Our producer's family lives in eastern Ukraine. Nothing is more important to him than slamming the Russians."

"Give me two and wait in the other room," I said.

"I could use some good media," Huntley said. "I'll just stand beside Jane, and she can do the talking, and I'll be the strong, supportive friend."

Mind the gap. The woman's voice from the Tube echoed inside me. There's reality, and then there's celebrity. "That won't work, Huntley," I said, as gently as possible. "The point is to avoid people thinking we're having an affair. I'm not single, remember?"

"I met Panov once," Huntley said, ignoring me to focus on the reporter. He wasn't so thick he didn't understand the need to double down to get on television. "Wanted to have a three-way with his wife. Or maybe she was his mistress, I can't remember. I could comment."

No one but me was going to barter in my own hotel room in the middle of the night. "Huntley, if you go on television, you're doing it alone, and the loyalty you've enjoyed so far from the festival is kaput."

"We're down to two and a half minutes," the reporter said, taking out her lipstick and compact. "We're going into the other room to set up. We tape whoever appears."

Huntley started to protest, but Samantha seized his arm. "Come on," she said. "I'll escort you safely back to your room. We'll fix the other little thing in the morning."

I locked myself in the bathroom after everyone left. My face was pale and bloated from tiredness; the idea of going on television looking as dispirited as I felt was alarming. I did as much as humanly possible with red lipstick and mascara, before slipping on a jacket and walking into the living room.

The reporter positioned me in front of the camera, and the interview was over almost before it began. The cameraman wearily moved the camera from his shoulder, touching his nose gingerly while glowering at me. "Thank you," the reporter said, as they left.

"Ready," I texted. A quiet knock two minutes later, a look through the peephole, and I opened the door again, this time to a man I'd lobbed an SOS to earlier after fleeing the *Vanity Fair* party.

Suit jacket off, a tight black T-shirt tucked into slim black pants showed off a torso that was taut and strong. His olive skin was unlined, and his alertness was both compelling and a rebuke against the wear and tear of the past few days.

"Come in," I said, putting out my hand. "I'm Jane. We spoke on the phone."

"David Levy." He walked into the suite, violence implicit in the very economy and precision of his movements. A man who could do what was necessary, in the fewest steps possible. "I was in the lobby when you arrived but thought it better to wait until the camera crew had left."

"I didn't see you," I said, frowning to replay the scene in my head.

"That's kind of the point."

I moved to the couch and sat down, nodding for him to follow. "We need to go over things fairly quickly. I'm getting picked up in five hours and need some sleep before my peripheral vision completely disappears."

"Shoot."

"When I asked the festival's head of security for a recommendation for some help, I didn't expect her to suggest an ex-spy."

"She always recommends me. My aunt wouldn't speak to her otherwise," David said. It took me a minute to pick up on his deadpan. "Shoshanna is my first cousin. Tell me what you need."

I leaned back against the cushions, weariness evaporating the tension that had been holding me upright. "This is in confidence, correct?"

"Absolutely."

"I haven't spoken to my partner, Bob, since six a.m. Wednesday morning. I stay here at the hotel during the run of the festival because my workday is eighteen hours long, and it's just easier. Normally we speak or text throughout the day, but he went silent yesterday and failed to show up for the opening night. He knew how important it was to me; Bob never fails to do what he promises."

"Is it unusual for him to drop out of communication?"

"Yeah. He's obsessively connected."

"So, either he can't be in touch, or he's choosing not to for some reason."

"Yes."

"You haven't called the police. You think it's the latter?"

I nodded slowly, then shook my head. "I don't know."

"Fill me in from the beginning."

"A woman, English accent, showed up at the opening screening, saying she needed to talk to me about Bob, that a tsunami was about to descend but no concrete details."

"What else?"

"A few hours ago, a second woman corners me at the *Vanity Fair* party. Far more sinister, some kind of Eastern European accent but with somewhere else mixed in. Claims she has business interests in common with Bob, and she also mentioned Johnnie." I paused for a minute, deciding how much of the truth I needed to reveal. "Johnnie is my former husband. He's also Bob's brother. Bob said something last month about Johnnie going AWOL, but in the midst of all the festival drama, I forgot about it."

David took it in. "Did either woman give a name?"

"No. But I figured out tonight that the blond leopard works at Smythe. Her name is Alexandra Hanlon. She's the new head of compliance."

"Blond leopard?"

"Sorry," I said. "The first woman. The one with the English accent. Smythe is the family investment firm that Bob runs. I briefly met her about six months ago at a board meeting, but she was all buttoned-up suit and glasses then, not the glam look from last night, so I didn't recognize her out of context. I also don't remember the accent, but she was new at the company and the CFO presented the compliance report, instead of her."

"Smythe Financial. Mid-sized, second-generation family firm. Approximately a hundred and twenty staff, fifteen billion in assets on the portfolio management side of the business. Solid reputation as value investors. The other business division is investment banking, mergers and acquisitions, taking companies public, sometimes taking them private. That division is run by Johnnie Smythe."

I raised my eyebrows.

"It was more efficient to google them than my horoscope while I waited," David said, a flick of humor in the eyes, if no actual smile.

"About sums them up. I don't have much to do with the running of the firm."

"You're listed as one of the three directors," David said. "Along with Bob Walker-Smythe and John Smythe."

"That has more to do with family tensions than my brilliance at bonds and equities."

David looked at me for a moment without replying.

"What else do you need to know?" I asked, picking at the threads in the cushion.

"How did Bob's mother get away with hyphenating her child's name, but the latter one didn't?"

"Not the question I was expecting," I said. "How is it relevant?"

"I'm trying to figure out what makes you all targets."

I looked at him for a long moment before replying. "Bob chose to hyphenate it as an adult, to honor his mother at a time when she wasn't speaking to him. In his quiet way, I suspect he also wanted to establish independence from a brother and father whose values were so different from his own."

"For a family with interesting dynamics, there's less about you all on the internet than one would expect. I only had a half hour to search, but in any interviews I found, mostly you or Bob, the focus is resolutely, almost pathologically, on the professional. I couldn't find one that mentioned where you're from or what your family background is. You don't seem to attend society galas, or at least if you do, because you must with your job, you don't get photographed, which has to be deliberate. Your looks would stand out in any crowd. The plane crash that killed your father-in-law was covered in the business section, but for a family of considerable wealth, and for someone who now heads up the most important cultural organization in this country, you fly under the radar more than can be an accident. Are there reasons you fear publicity?"

"Wealthy in this town means at least a hundred million or more. Bob's not in that league," I protested.

David remained silent. Misdirection wasn't going to work. "But yes, okay," I said. "Their father was obsessively private. He'd say, 'Let the clients be in the news, their money manager shouldn't be.' Robert built up a communications team whose job it was to sanitize our public image. Any inkling of a story, or any bad behavior, was to be reported immediately. It became a habit we continued even after he died."

"And the delicate romantic history?"

"Even more reason to duck attention," I snapped, defensive as always about a marital situation that belonged on *The Jerry Springer Show*.

David paused. I twitched at the directness of his gaze. "What aren't you telling me?"

I took a deep breath. "I need to make sure this is completely inside the vault."

"If being tortured as a soldier didn't turn me into a blabbermouth, I doubt anything to do with this case will."

I looked at him ruefully. "I'm sorry, I don't mean to question your judgment. It's just . . . a securities regulator came to see me today. He said there are financial irregularities with the firm. That all senior executives are missing. And that I have until Monday to wave my magic wand and make them reappear or I'm up shit's creek."

David's inscrutable expression took it all in. "What is it specifically that you need from me?"

"I need to know Bob's okay. And I need to protect myself."

"I think your first priority should be a lawyer."

"When I went to the house earlier to investigate, someone had gotten there before me. Fled while I was in the washroom. May or may not have followed me in a car."

"I correct myself. You need a bodyguard *and* a lawyer."

"I can't afford for my board or staff to find out what's going on in my personal life," I said. "This organization's in crisis, and everyone is looking to deflect blame. Situations like these don't bring out the best in people." I paused. "If you come to light, it'll be easier to explain that you're a bodyguard than an investigator."

"Why?"

"Women in the public eye get threats. And the festival is even more high profile than usual, given the controversy surrounding my predecessor."

"Have you been getting threats?"

"Sure. The normal ones. Mostly anonymous emails, sometimes telephone calls. They want to stab you with their favorite knife and watch the specially carved handle go in and out. See you die in the most violent way possible and laugh doing it." My voice was beginning to fade with tiredness, and I sank back further on the couch. "Cunt, shithead, idiot, twat, asshole, bitch — the combinations of words the trolls string together in a sentence can be extraordinary. As far as I can tell, there are a lot of really angry men out there. But nothing out of the normal."

"You understand, none of that should be normal?"

I sighed from exhaustion. "Spoken with the insulation of your gender."

David was silent. I closed my eyes for a minute. I must have dozed off, because my toe being gently shaken brought me to with a start.

"Jane, go to bed. I have my briefing. I'm going to bunk down here on the couch until it's time for you to leave. Give me fifteen minutes notice in the morning."

"I don't think anyone's going to break into my hotel room."

David gave me a little push toward the bedroom. "Someone broke into your house. Anyhow, it's part of the retainer," he said, closing the door once I'd walked through.

I dropped all my clothes on the floor and crawled into bed. Ghosts from the past crawled in beside me, scratching along my skin, talons yellowish and overgrown, laughter cold and brittle.

CHAPTER
FIVE

DAY 3: *The Gathering Storm*

"I don't like to see people hanged on television, either. But Saddam Hussein wasn't a nice man," Bob said the second time we met, six months after his father's funeral. It was the Human Rights Watch gala dinner, and I was battling imposter syndrome in a room full of rich and powerful people. It was the first time I'd acted as the festival's ambassador at the invite of a corporate sponsor. DelGrotto hadn't wanted to attend, and eventually the invite got passed down to me.

"The West liked him well enough when they were propping him up."

"For sure. We turn a blind eye to dictators when it suits us —"

I scoffed. "The CIA rig elections to get the candidates they want, and then execute them when they no longer serve their purposes."

"Saddam was sentenced and executed by Iraqis —"

"You can't be naive enough to think the Americans don't pull the strings?" I said, pointing an insistent finger. "Follow the power, expose the bullshit."

Bob paused for a moment, eyes mischievous. "Might I be allowed to finish a sentence?"

I blushed at the realization that I was drunk. I'd survived the endless reception where I knew no one by having one too many glasses of wine and trying to insert myself into conversations with strangers. When the dinner bell finally rang, I arrived last at the assigned table where most of the occupants were still standing, looking around for contacts. But two men were absorbed in conversation at the far side and with a shock, I realized one of them was Bob.

It took him a few minutes to notice me. Meanwhile I watched him, as intensely as a child watches an animal in the zoo. Bob's wavy dark hair was a tad on the long side given his corporate job; it hinted at an inner rebel but was counterbalanced by the distinguished silver starting to streak itself through. He was quite tall, one of the tallest in the room, with a slim build and well-tailored suit. His hands were in motion, telling what I assumed was a good story, given his companion's laughter and Bob's animated engagement. I wished for him to look at me with the same kind of mirth.

And, finally, he did. He spoke briefly to the man beside him, who picked up his wine glass to move to a seat across the table. Bob waved, a wave that turned into an outstretched hand when I made my way over.

"This is a surprise."

"Indeed. A pleasure to meet you again, Jane."

We sat, and soon were wrapped up in a cocoon of conversation that refused all interruption.

The quiet strength of his self-possession excited me. His hand ran through his hair, pushing it back as he leaned in and the conversation became intense. I watched those fingers and imagined them inside me with that same combination of determination and patience. Repeatedly, I went to the washroom to cool my thoughts by running my wrists under the cold water, only to get caught up in exactly the same way upon my return to the table. It was crazy-making. The wine flowed, and I drank, and the attraction intensified as surely as the tides of the moon.

To my surprise, he understood an oblique reference I made to Sylvia Plath and we began to speak at length about American poetry. I was so completely captured I put my fork into my dinner without looking at it, only giving a yelp as the piece of lobster came into view.

"Is there a problem?" Bob said quietly, leaning toward me.

"You may need to stab me in my thigh," I smiled, as I tried to make eye contact with one of the waitstaff.

"Is your allergy anaphylactic?" Bob's eyes were serious, his voice was calm and deep. "Do you carry an EpiPen?"

"Yes, and yes," I said. "But it's okay, I'm sure they'll bring me something else to eat."

"Hand me your EpiPen, will you?"

I reached into my purse and handed it to him. "I'm perfectly fine. I've managed my allergy for a long time."

"I'm sure that's true," Bob said, placing the EpiPen carefully beside his plate. It remained there for the rest of the evening, even after he'd gotten a waiter to come over and remove not just my lobster but his as well. Just to be on the safe side, he'd said, and we both tucked into the unappealing ratatouille.

Weeks earlier I'd tried to initiate divorce proceedings from Johnnie for a second time, wrongly thinking he'd be too pre-occupied with the family business to put up further roadblocks to our inevitable dissolution. A damning of jurors deliberated in my head in the warm intimacy of Bob's car as he drove me home. Bob was legally my brother-in-law, although that felt like a technicality, given he'd been a Smythe in absentia for decades. It was an accident of birth that connected us more than any-thing else. He was so different, and so removed, from the family dynamic that I was caught up in that he was more a stranger to it than I was.

Or so I told myself.

We both understood the inevitability of what was happening. The sexual tension was exquisite, and almost as soon as we were inside my place, he was inside of me, not a word spoken since we'd stepped into the car. "I've been thinking about that since almost the moment I sat down beside you," I finally whispered, as Bob quietly undressed me and tucked us both into bed. "Me, too," he said.

★ ★ ★

Samantha and I sat again in the back of a SUV, this time en route to a luncheon for the Chinese showcase, as she read Twitterverse bon mots detailing the arrival of Alexei Panov's wife, Sophia Bennini, from London to post bail. The Italian former model, two decades younger, was infamous for naked wild-child photos circa age twenty, alongside salacious quotes like "One must only choose between a man or a woman? One at time?"

Samantha had spent the morning sorting out Huntley Bartlett's problems, while I threw myself into meetings with an energy that belied my lack of sleep. That morning I'd handed over the house keys and Bob's desk contents to David, promising to stay surrounded by others until we could reconnect after his day spent investigating.

"How much longer until we get there?" I asked, after working our way north through the city for close to an hour.

"Almost there, Ms. Browning," the driver said. "They said it'd take a half hour from downtown, I don't think they anticipated how bad the traffic would be."

"It's not your fault Victoria planned a donor recognition event in the middle of the day, in the middle of the festival, in the middle of the suburbs."

"Why shouldn't it be held in Markham?" Samantha said. "A lot of Toronto's global Chinese live up here."

"Global Chinese?" I asked. "That's an odd expression to use."

"I've heard our Chinese guests use it several times, Jane. Global Chinese. Overseas Chinese. Ethnic Chinese. I think they would know best the appropriate phrases to use."

I bit my tongue at her prickliness. We were all a little on edge about this politically sensitive luncheon. An online petition against the *State* injunction continued to grow, drawing even more attention to the issue when worries about losing face were paramount for our sponsors. We couldn't put out a statement that the injunction had been successfully fought without saying if we'd be screening the film.

Additionally, the morning's media frenzy had picked apart the Panov rape arrest, and muckraked through the Paul DelGrotto sex scandal once again. Jacob and the board, several of whom were scheduled to attend this event, would not be happy.

The showcase had been a fraught exercise from the beginning. The Toronto Chinese community was a mix of people from Hong Kong who immigrated to Canada in the decade before the 1997 transfer of sovereignty and a later influx of Mainland Chinese who reportedly saw Canada as a more stable economic bet than China for their new wealth and a safer political bet than the United States.

News of the showcase was met with a mixture of pride and wariness, given the community's bifurcated sentiment toward the Chinese Communist Party. Chinese-Canadian artists, many second generation, were often highly critical of anything that smacked of censorship. The continuing crackdown by Beijing on pro-democracy protests in Hong Kong sharpened the tension.

Ten minutes later, we careened into the parking lot of a massive restaurant whose red and gold dim sum sign towered twenty feet tall. A festival intern hurriedly escorted us upstairs to the private dining room. Exquisitely embroidered red silk fell from ceiling to floor across the windows, and heavy gold chandeliers lit the room in a Neverland hue. Two hundred people sat at round tables with one long one facing the rest, as if a head table at a wedding. A single seat sat empty at one end of it.

Victoria rushed over and put a hand under my elbow. "I said no seats for staff," she whispered urgently, jerking her head at Samantha. "I can't believe how late you are. You missed the opening remarks."

I smiled in what I hoped was a friendly fashion at the table as Victoria frog-marched me to it. "Perhaps you might have ordered me an Uber helicopter given the distance we had to travel," I sniped back.

I wanted to slip quietly into the seat at the end, but the entire table had risen and gesticulated that I was to sit closer to the center. The woman occupying my intended seat apologized profusely as she moved to the end, only to come back repeatedly for her water glass, and her cardigan, and her half-eaten plate as a bevy of waiters clucked, scolding her for trying to carry them herself. It took repeated attempts to explain to the head waiter that indeed, despite what Victoria had said, I really couldn't eat any kind of shellfish at all, which was basically every course on the set menu. "Can you just shoot up with an EpiPen and deal?" she hissed, as I finally sat in my seat.

I turned my back on her to speak with Norman Chiu, the director of *Shifting Dragon*. "Glad you were able to stay in town for this."

"A little United Front work to reinforce the agenda of the ancestral land is the least I can do to repay the debt for my film." Norman took a drink of his beer. "And they have my passport, of course."

I had no idea if he was being ironic, or what my response should be, so I turned to introduce myself to the man seated on the other side. Yaya Hui, the Chinese cultural officer, sat three seats down. When rumors about *State* being programmed into the general lineup started to surface, Yaya relentlessly campaigned to keep it out, telephoning, emailing, and showing up unexpectedly, day after monotonous day.

Anxious to avoid her gaze, I expressed profound interest in the seafood wholesale business that my seatmate owned. At a hundred million in revenue per year, it was hardly a modest undertaking, and his detailed explanation about marginal costs took us through four courses. He was just getting into the challenge of weight discrepancies on frozen shrimp, when a tall, well-dressed man approached the podium set up on one side.

"Hello, my name is Raymond Cheng. On behalf of everyone in our community, as well as the board of the Toronto Chinese Business Council, thank you for attending this celebration of modern Chinese cinema. We're privileged to have with us Norman Chiu, director of *Shifting Dragon*, programmed in the prestigious opening slot for this year's Worldwide Toronto Film Festival, and our very honored guests who have traveled all the way from China to join us. Canada and China share core interests and values, and we welcome the opportunity this showcase provides to extend the boundaries of unity."

He paused for the obligatory clapping. The purse on the ground beside my chair danced with the vibration of a call coming in. I twitched to pick it up, as Cheng went on interminably. Finally, he introduced Norman, who spoke briefly, followed by Matthew Li, a writer/director at the leading edge of the Chinese documentary movement.

Then it was my turn. I underscored how beneficial the showcase was, enabling us to educate and entertain our audiences, many of whom were encountering Chinese cinema, in depth, for the first time. I meant the words I said, but I chafed at the words I couldn't say. The films in the showcase were mostly excellent, but they represented a narrow slice, excluding Taiwanese directors and most of the so-called Sixth Generation of Chinese filmmakers, whose anti-romantic view of contemporary urban life and negative take on China's capitalist leanings had produced some very provocative films.

Yaya approached the stage as I beat a hasty retreat to my chair. She raised a small hand and Raymond Cheng nodded for her to come to the microphone.

"Hello, my name is Yaya Hui, and I'm with the cultural affairs office of the Consulate General of the People's Republic of China in Toronto. I'd like to thank Jane Browning, and everyone at the Worldwide Toronto Film Festival, for their sincere cooperation in programming films that properly represent China's long and impressive history. Many films are made every year, some of higher quality than others, and I am delighted that we have only the highest quality for the audiences. It is important to promote Chinese directors who are trustworthy and talented at the festival. I encourage you to see all the films, many times."

Message sent and received. I picked up my purse, hoping the end was nigh. I'd protected a two-hour window in my schedule to see an Africanfuturist film based on Nigerian folklore by Lagos-based director Hawa Mwangi. It was a rare pleasure to watch a film during the festival itself, to be reminded of the power and beauty of film at a time when the machinations necessary to do my job seemed utilitarian and even cynical.

Raymond Cheng took the microphone again. "Before we close, we have one final speaker. Please join me in welcoming Darren McGregor to the stage."

My chair shook as the sands shifted underneath me. I'd noticed Darren beside Jacob during my remarks, and assumed his presence was a smart cultivation play by the board. But why was he addressing this crowd? And why hadn't I been told of the change in plans?

Darren glided to the podium, his beautifully cut linen suit a nod to the importance of the occasion, but his jettisoning of a tie in line with the rugged individualism of his brand.

"Hello, 你好, 你好, thank you for your patience in allowing me to speak for just a few moments. As Mr. Cheng said, my name is Darren McGregor, and I'm attending this luncheon as a guest of the board of the Worldwide Toronto Film Festival."

I glanced sideways at Norman Chiu as Darren paused for the obligatory clapping. "First in Mandarin, then in Cantonese," he murmured. "The man knows his politics."

"Some of you may know me as an erstwhile Canadian," Darren continued. "I immigrated to this country when I was a young man, and spent much of my life here, before moving to London a decade ago. But I've never forgotten the welcome Canada gave me, a far more egalitarian acceptance than I ever received in

Britain. The strong Canadian economy gave me opportunity to chase my dreams, to build a business and a good life, to provide for my children. I imagine many of you in the audience have followed a path not dissimilar to my own."

Darren had a natural way of connecting with audiences, I had to give him that. People nodded, paying closer attention now.

"I believe passionately that art is the very foundation of life. It is the prism through which we examine ourselves. It reflects back to us our best hopes and our worst excesses, showing us both how we fail as human beings and how we might strive to do better. I've been fortunate over the past decade to become a substantial supporter of visual art, sculpture, dance, and literature. But arguably the most important art form of the past century has been film."

Darren paused, everyone seemed to move an inch forward in their chairs in anticipation, me included.

"Inspired by the tremendous leadership of the Chinese government in supporting this exemplary showcase, I'm ready to take the leap. Today, sitting here during lunch, it became clear to me there's no time like the present to make a commitment." He paused for a deep breath and a wide smile before continuing. "I'm delighted to announce that it'll be my privilege and honor to donate twenty million dollars over four years to the Worldwide Toronto Film Festival."

The clapping began in earnest. Victoria and the attending board members jumped to their feet, prompting my head table to do so as well. After a minute, Darren put up a hand to quiet the cacophony. "I appreciate the opportunity to support this great organization that illuminates the world's humanity back to us. I wish you all a terrific rest of the festival."

By now, the whole crowd had risen, many of them surreptitiously glancing at phones and taking tiny steps in the direction of the exit as Darren McGregor made his way back to the table and Raymond Cheng closed out remarks. The suddenness of the announcement, and the size of the give, stunned me. Had Victoria and her team known about this in advance? What was Jacob up to? I bid Norman a quick goodbye before scurrying over to where Victoria had commandeered every photographer to take pictures of Darren with Jacob, as well as the filmmakers and dignitaries.

"What a remarkable gift," I said, as Darren pulled me in for a picture, his colonizing arm tightly around my waist. "I'm sure the others have already thanked you extensively but let me add my voice to the chorus of appreciation for your generosity."

"You inspire me, Jane. I want to give you the freedom to take programming to the next level. Working together we can achieve great things."

"Absolutely." I stepped back from his embrace. "I'm afraid I need to leave shortly to get to my next commitment, but I'll ask my assistant to sort out a time for us all to get together. The programming team will be so delighted to meet you."

"Cancel whatever you have next," Darren purred. "Let's go have a coffee, just the two of us, blue sky the possibilities."

"You're an enthusiast," I said, punching him lightly on the arm in what I hoped felt like friendly comradery. "No doubt the key to your success. I'm really sorry, but they keep my schedule so tight that sudden changes during the run of the festival are impossible. But Samantha will make a window appear very soon, I promise."

Darren stiffened. A man unused to being told no.

"I'd like a word before you go, Jane," Jacob said, from behind me. Had he been lingering nearby, listening, and I hadn't sensed it?

"How's Johnnie keeping these days?" Darren said, as I turned to walk away with Jacob. I froze in my tracks, head swiveling toward him like a marionette.

"Pardon?"

The look in Darren's eyes chilled me. "Johnnie."

"I wasn't aware you two knew each other," I said, Jacob standing shotgun beside me.

"Quite well, actually," Darren said, my discomfort his quid pro quo for having turned down the command performance. "Smythe Financial handled the sale of my holding company, a little over a decade ago now. Took months of protracted dealings and negotiations, so I got to know Johnnie, and Robert, too, of course. Bob hadn't yet returned to the fold."

"Johnnie was pretty junior then," I said, hyper-conscious of my private life splayed out in front of the attentive Jacob. "He wouldn't have been the lead on a sale that huge. I'm surprised you had the opportunity to become close."

"Robert ran things, of course. Very creative on structuring the business vehicles necessary to handle such a complex deal. But Johnnie is his father's son, smart as a whip and just as innovative. We shared an appreciation of similar things, including winning. And, it goes without saying, beautiful women."

A shiver ran down my spine as I thought about the fraud investigation and Dilip Patel, while filing away the sexist comment for later revulsion. What did Darren mean by innovative? "What a small world," I said, infusing my voice with every ounce of steel I could muster. "The deal must have made you a wealthy man, given your remarkable gift to the festival. Another thing for us to discuss when we have that coffee."

"Indeed." Darren stepped back, point made.

Jacob and I walked a few paces away. "When did the decision get made for Darren to speak?" I asked. "Seems an odd choice to make such a major donor announcement here."

"We need to immediately turn the tide on all the negative publicity," Jacob said. "Do it here and the media photos include the Chinese dignitaries as well. Gives them a win against this ridiculous petition."

He'd ignored my question about timing, but pursuing it would make me look petty. "The cultivation of Darren has been a great success," I said, aiming to mend fences. "A remarkable coup for the festival."

The Dark Messiah leaned in, his breath pungent with crustaceans and garlic. "I trust you got the message in Yaya Hui's speech?"

"I heard what she said."

"Then the rumor you're still considering screening the film must not be true."

I paused for a split second. "You know it's been cleared of the hate speech allegations."

"This is your first time operating at such a senior level, but why are you the only person who didn't see the injunction as a blessing in disguise? Our government gets blamed for censorship in the film seizure, we spare our Chinese partners a black eye, the tickets holders get a refund and a voucher for a free screening after the festival closes. It was a win-win-win."

"Not for Yin Lee."

"Who?"

"*State*'s director. She devoted five years of her life to making this film. She's constantly threatened, and family members who don't enjoy the benefit of foreign cameras on them are physically intimated and beaten. If we cave to this censorship, we may as well hang up a 'not wanted' shingle on the festival for every filmmaker who takes a risk against authoritarian regimes."

Jacob stabbed his stubby finger at me. "You should never have invited her in the first place."

I worked to control the emotions that ran from temple to gut and back again, fed by the tiredness and stress of the past few days. Moral arguments would never sway someone like Jacob, whose realpolitik swamped any sense of right and wrong. "I've adhered to the terms of the sponsorship agreement Paul DelGrotto signed."

"A foreign government is unwilling to be judged by the standards of a society not their own. That seems completely unreasonable to you?"

"What about films criticizing the invasion of Iraq? Would you ban those, too?"

"If the Republicans gave us twenty million dollars to help us meet payroll, yes."

"Human rights abuses in Saudi Arabia?"

"The House of Saud has a lot of money."

He sought to deliberately provoke me. "*State's* buzz is strong and growing," I said, voice now steady and firm. "Yin Lee has a long relationship with our festival. Not fighting for her film would undermine the credibility of our organization which, at the end of the day, is our stock in trade."

"If you want to stay in this new position, you need to be conscious of the wider issues beyond the artistic."

"I'm very conscious of the multitude of issues at play," I said. "And fully committed to the long-term financial health of this organization. Our relationship to the international film community is the currency we trade."

Jacob looked at me for a long moment before he spoke. "It's become clear you need help. We must maximize the McGregor announcement, especially in light of the brutal Panov coverage. Our brand is suffering with all these mishaps. My staff and I will assist with media and stakeholder relations going forward."

Trying to kill two birds with one stone. Jacob had been gunning for Lina because of the DelGrotto complaint. Usurping her authority as the VP of marketing and public relations while the same time mine as CEO was a power move indeed. "That's kind of you to offer. But it risks introducing conflicting messaging, not to mention further tension into our operations. Lina and her team are excellent at their jobs," I said. "They've got it under control."

"As board chair, the overall health of this organization is my responsibility," Jacob said. "I'll decide."

Samantha materialized as soon as he left. "What did Jacob have to say?"

"Checking on his party tickets," I said, silently fuming. "Let's go."

The driver opened the front door as we approached the SUV, but I slid in the back, closing my eyes as I leaned back onto the headrest, exhausted. There was no way I'd make the Nigerian film. "Take us to the office, please."

Burt pounced as soon we returned. "I need to talk to you about *State*," he bellowed, Samantha scurrying in before I could close my office door.

"Isn't there any other film that people want to talk about?"

Undeterred, he continued. "In today's whack-a-mole news, an appeal has been filed against *State*'s 14A rating. Will be heard first thing Monday morning."

"Someone's determined," I said, shaking my head. "Do we know who?"

"Not yet. I'd finally found a venue to do a makeup screening. Franklin Square, ten p.m., Monday night."

"I haven't approved a screening. And if the rating gets made more restrictive, there's zero chance we could do an outside event."

Samantha's mouth gaped. Burt turned his back on her and kept talking. "The lawyers feel confident the appeal will be thrown out. We need to be prepared."

"This is a huge gamble you're asking me to make, Burt."

Burt's stubborn Scottish face wasn't budging an inch. "The Poets' League has Franklin Square booked for the evening but their show is scheduled to end by nine. They'll do us a solid and create a later slot for us, including riding on their outdoor permit which is good until midnight. We'll do our sound check early before their gig starts. There's a quid pro quo, of course. We guarantee them fifty reserved spaces right up front, and George, the head poet, gets to hang with you. He's the kind who lives for insider access. Programming in that square needs to be free, though."

Samantha spoke up. "A large-scale, free screening will bring exactly the kind of publicity the board doesn't want."

"We'll send out a notice Monday offering all existing ticket holders a reserved premium space and open up the rest on a first-come, first-served basis," Burt said, talking right over her. "Whip up some publicity about censorship and people will understand the last-minute nature of the screening."

"I want to go on the record that I'm opposed," Samantha said, increasingly agitated.

Burt turned back to her in a flash. "This is way beyond your pay scale, who gives a flying fuck if you're opposed," he hollered, slamming his hand down on the desk, and sending the stapler and paper clips flying. That Burt had anger control problems was known to everyone in the office, in part because of his perfectionism; he personally sweated every detail of the festival instead of trusting his team to share the load. A trait we recognized in each other. But this level of aggression was beyond the pale for him. I needed to take him for a beer and have a quiet word.

Jamila, the receptionist, peeked around the door. "Sorry to interrupt. Panov's manager says she's called you several times today. Didn't want to leave a message. So, she's showed up here. And guess what?" Jamila paused for dramatic intent. "The *wife* is here, too."

Samantha and Burt moved faster than a napalm bomb, knocking each other out of the way to get a better view out the office window. "Please show them in," I asked Jamila. "Bring coffee instead of tea. I want to be alert for this one."

I'd met neither Panov's wife nor his manager. As I watched them make their way across the floor, I was struck by their similarity.

Attractive brunettes, svelte but not too thin, expensive-looking. The wife wore over-the-knee, dark brown leather boots, with slim pants tucked into them and a tailored, short jacket. Her long hair was pulled back into a smooth ponytail, sizeable diamond studs in her ears. One of her famously provocative quotes was about the pleasures of a good spanking every now and then. Whether the riding crop would be in her hand or on her bare bottom was difficult to discern, but I imagined she'd enjoy either scenario.

"I'm sorry I've been difficult to reach today," I said, putting out my hand to shake. "This is Samantha, my executive assistant. And Burt, our COO. Please have a seat."

"I'm Sophia Bennini," she said, shaking my hand briefly and the others not at all. "And this is Georgina Koch, my husband's manager. We will speak with you alone."

Jamila paused on the entrance to the office, a pot of coffee and cups in her hands.

"You may leave the refreshments," Sophia continued, arranging herself on the couch.

I raised my eyebrows in apology. Burt's snort was audible as he and Samantha left. Jamila placed the coffee on the side table and leaned over to whisper in my ear. "A woman, blonde, forties, no appointment barged in, insisting on seeing you, but she refused to give her name. Security escorted her out."

"I'm very sorry about the situation you find yourself in." I said, closing the office door a little more forcefully than required. "It can't be easy."

Sophia looked at me with disdain. "This *situation*, as you call it, is patently absurd. We expect your cooperation to rectify it."

So much for the pleasantries. "What did you have in mind?"

"You agree, of course, that my husband should be at the premiere of his film?"

"We always want the director to attend the gala screening of their film," I answered carefully. "But if they're unable to attend in person, we ask that they appoint someone to introduce the film on their behalf. Generally, that ends up being the producer. We've made overtures to your husband's production company to discuss, given the screening is tomorrow, but so far have not heard back."

"We seek a special ministerial permit to have my husband released from custody for the screening. You must call the justice minister and support this request."

"I see," I said, sitting down in my chair before I spoke again. "This isn't my area of expertise, but I believe those kinds of permits are generally for a mercy reason, like a family funeral, and not a gala movie screening."

Sophia frowned, or at least gave the general semblance of a frown since her forehead was incapable of movement. Not even thirty, she wasn't taking any chances with aging. "My husband labored for four years on this film. It's a masterpiece. Not allowing him to celebrate his triumph with his audience would be a travesty."

I took a moment to drink my coffee before replying. A travesty was having all the billions that stolen state assets can provide and still making a film that was both trite and shite. "I will speak to our legal department, but to be transparent with you, I don't feel confident. It's difficult for me to imagine any politician circumventing due process for a filmmaker."

"You refuse to help?"

"I said I would look into it and help as much as I'm able," I said. "I'd suggest your lawyer is best suited to pursue any temporary release or push for an expedited bail hearing. Being the weekend, it's challenging."

"It's ridiculous that a man of my husband's stature should be held captive on the word of a maid looking to capitalize on our money. Do you know she's planning a civil suit against us already?"

"I'm not sure how that's relevant to this conversation."

"You believe my husband is guilty of rape?"

"I didn't say that."

"You should see the men Alexei is sharing his cell with. Tattoos, missing teeth, drug pushers. You believe my husband should be treated like them? This is perhaps for you an issue of egalitarianism?" The sneer on the last word was slight but unmistakable.

"I believe Mr. Panov is caught up in a legal process that will need to play itself out. But, as I've said, I'll consult with our legal department and see what action would be appropriate for us to take."

"My husband bought sex with a chambermaid. She's trying to shake us down for a bigger fee. Surely, you understand that women lie about these kinds of things?"

I stood up, abruptly. I didn't have a bird's-eye view of the truth but listening to the powerful wife of a corrupt pig like Panov slag our shared gender was more complicity than I could bear. "That's all the time I have for today," I said. "I'll let you know what I find out from our legal department. It's important to have a backup plan on the film intro, so please have the film's producers contact the festival. The masterpiece should be publicly represented by someone who made it."

Georgina Koch stood as well. "Our apologies for showing up unannounced, Jane. Thank you for your time."

"There will be no backup plan," Sophia said, as she rose. "I'll do whatever it takes to get Alexei out of jail by tomorrow's screening. I guarantee you that."

She stalked out, the manager following her. I closed the door and locked it, before dialing Bob's number; it went straight to voicemail. Eighty hours and counting without communication. It took me a minute of focused breathing to calm the nausea. The second number I dialed also went straight to voicemail. Apparently, Johnnie had kept the same cell number, all these years later. And I had remembered every digit, without meaning to.

CHAPTER
SIX

Clare's life ended in seconds, a bulging, weak point in her arterial wall, previously a quiet predator, now Mount Vesuvius, a mountain of blood as angry as Clare herself.

My own mother slipped away as silently as she'd relinquished her resiliency to my father. Gone at 3:08 p.m. on a sunny afternoon, resurrection yet another myth Pastor Glass had peddled.

I'd moved home three years earlier to nurse her through cancer of the esophagus. I'd tasted freedom living in New York as a student, and what a compelling taste it was. No one knew my background, I didn't need to be anyone's fixer, just . . . Jane. Jane, aspiring filmmaker, maybe less earnest than the others, certainly less outgoing than the Americans with their easy camaraderie.

But singular vision, strong aesthetic, tremendous worker, or so my evaluations went.

Foreign students were granted one year to work in the U.S. after graduation. Twelve months to build a track record and make connections fast to qualify for a more permanent work visa and membership in the largest indie filmmaking community in the world. My student debt was also due to come knocking. NYU gave me a serious scholarship, but I'd still owe more than fifty grand by the time the program was through.

With the help of my thesis advisor, I lined up a production assistant gig on Spike Lee's new film to shoot the summer I finished. Toronto Jane would have understood it was too good to be true. But New York Jane had seduced herself into believing in the possibility of happy endings.

The night my mother called, I boarded the bus back to Windsor with a duffle bag and a box of Kleenex, stunned to find myself crying, face turned toward the window and pressed into my sweatshirt to muffle the sobs. Suspected stage three cancer, curable, even if the treatment would not be pleasant.

My sister, Tracy, crawled underground. A week after my return, I went to her on-campus student-housing digs. I'd worked out a treatment plan with the doctors and met with my father to brief him on the situation — by then, Pastor Glass had moved to another church, and my father had rented a basement apartment nearby.

I laid out what I thought was a reasonable compromise: Tracy would live with our mother for the next few months while chemo-radiation started, and I'd go back to New York to graduate, work on the Spike Lee film, and shop the script for my own first feature. I'd be back before Tracy's fall term started and see my mother through the surgery and the post-surgical care.

My sister balked. "You're the strong one," she said, burying her head in her hands. "You know I can't face vomiting, or diarrhea, or hospitals, all that pus and blood and shit. Can't we get a social worker to drive her back and forth to treatments? Or Mrs. O'Flynn? The cancer society must have volunteers."

"So Mrs. O'Flynn can poster the details of Mom's illness around the neighborhood?" I said. "We're her children. We owe her more loyalty than that."

Tracy turned away from me. "No, we don't."

I walked for a long time before finally boarding the bus back, heels rubbed raw and bleeding from ankle boots more attractive than functional. By the time I got home, I'd made my decision. It took me a half hour to cancel my post-graduation plans. I received my MFA in the mail, but my dream of being a filmmaker was functionally dead.

For all his faults, my father never missed any of his meagre monthly support payments. I made up the rest of our income by getting a production assistant job at the local television station. Days were long and routine: work, run, cook dinner for my mother, work, sleep. Repeat. Six months later I made assistant producer, then producer on the nightly news.

Almost three years later, Johnnie swooped in, a Chagall painting superimposed on the boxed realism of my life. Through its private equity fund, Smythe Financial had acquired a majority stake in an industrial manufacturing company, the second-largest employer in the region. I taped a preinterview with Johnnie on his press swing through town, to determine whether to have him on air for the local public affairs show.

Compellingly out of control, no gesture too grand, Johnnie overrode all of my hesitations to have dinner with him that first night, to visit him in Toronto the following weekend, and to marry him six months later. He entirely charmed my mother, frequently sending her flowers or fruit baskets, texting each day to see how she was doing. After three years of worry — and celibacy — I allowed the attention to settle around me like a massage.

All through childhood, I hid a dog-eared photo of my mother under my pillow. In it, she wears a yellow T-shirt, with a sunflower decal in the middle, tucked into a high-waisted pair of jeans. A slight swelling of the belly threatens to pull the T-shirt askew. She is transcendent, smiling coquettishly at the camera, one hand holding back her long curly red hair, the other touching her stomach.

When I was growing up, my mother refused to have any kind of conversation with me about what was going on in our house, in their marriage. There's no point going over all that, she'd say on the odd occasion I broke our family's unwritten code of conduct. *Leave it alone.*

The day Johnnie and I married, I reapplied my makeup three times in the washroom of the county courthouse, unwelcome tears ruining my mask each time. My mother wandered in and out of the ladies, patting me on the back, telling me not to worry, that every bride is nervous on her wedding day. I nodded at her through the tears. She smiled, not with the coquettish lightness of the young pregnant woman in the sunflower top, but with the relief that she could pretend, at least near the end, that she'd been a mother like any, about to shepherd her daughter through a normal ritual of adulthood.

A month later she slipped away in the afternoon, as I sat by her side. I'd made a binding commitment to a man who could provide my mother a sense of security she'd never had, who would willingly provide for her should she get sick again. But, convinced of my well-being, she let go.

* * *

I lay on the office couch, curled into a ball. Hearing Johnnie's voice on his cell phone message had prompted the unwelcome walk down memory lane. Whether it was that, or dealing with Sophia Bennini's arrogance, my stomach was one unhappy camper.

Samantha walked in. "Ready for an update on Huntley Bartlett?" she asked.

I groaned for comic relief, as I sat up. *Keep your friends close, and your enemies closer* was one of Bob's favorite sayings. I needed to sway Samantha into a less Judas frame of mind. "Do tell."

"It seems playing second media fiddle to Panov wasn't sitting well with him."

This time I groaned for real. All day our media director had planted stories intended to divert attention away from Huntley, many of them historical tidbits about Alexei Panov. Panov's lawyers were sticking to the consensual sex line, despite the implausibility that, after a long day of scrubbing toilets and making beds, a cleaner would be so struck by him that she'd drop to her knees out of a sheer desire to put a penis in her mouth.

"In an interview with the *Guardian*, Huntley was asked about his relationship with Devlin Ross," she continued. "He said that, contrary to erroneous reports, the two shared quite a warm relationship. One might even call it intimate."

"In his dreams."

"He went on at length about his admiration for her strong mothering instincts. The pièce de résistance, though, was when he offered to give her real children if she desired."

I doubled over in laughter, leaning sideways on the couch.

"Yes, apparently adopted children are not as real as ones that come from Huntley's sperm," Samantha said. "He did say that he wasn't suggesting a relationship per se, though he couldn't help but notice she was an attractive woman —"

"Glad he's not blind as well as dumb."

"It's just that they would make such wonderful co-parents, and of course he'd be happy to step up for the four adopted children as well."

"The unreal children?"

"That's it," Samantha said. My position on the couch's edge seemed an unfortunate reminder of Huntley on my hotel room sofa; I forced myself to get up and slowly walk around the office. Samantha sat down in a chair, her arms for once not crossed against her chest.

"And the story doesn't end there," Samantha said. "After the interview dropped last night, Devlin emasculated him in a hundred and forty characters or less — Huntley's sperm can get up? #dreaming. It broke the internet. His publicist wasted no time putting out a release claiming Huntley was misquoted. That, on the issue of Devlin's adopted children, Huntley only mused that he'd be willing to serve, hypothetically."

"Because he's such a mensch."

"Unfortunately for Huntley's publicist, though, Huntley had agreed to a recorded interview."

"Ouch."

"The *Guardian* released the audio this morning to back up their claim. And the irresistible tidbit is that it was Huntley himself who sought out the interview. The *Guardian* had already run advance press on the film, including an interview with Devlin. They felt they were doing him a favor to try to divert attention away from the negative advance reviews. And then, of course, that little incident on opening night."

"That's him cooked," I said. "Isn't he scheduled to leave, like, any second now?"

"That's become a little murkier," Samantha said. "Apparently someone from Jacob's firm contacted him about image control. I'd calmed him down, but they just riled him up again. He's prostrate in bed, morose if his Twitter feed scrolls for more than ten minutes without a mention of his name, but equally unhappy if he finds anything negative. He's desperate for praise."

I sighed. High Noon with the Dark Messiah was creeping ever closer. "Okay, keep an eye on Huntley. And keep the BFA staffers away from him, while I figure out how to handle it with Jacob."

If I wasn't mistaken, there was a glint of revenge in Samantha's eye as I mentioned Jacob. Her expression itself was completely smooth, though, as she continued. "Another problem. Fatmanrising's people are asking if we've seen him."

"They lost their guy?"

"Maybe," she said, scrolling through her messages on her iPhone. "Their emails started this morning kind of jocular, how great the *Vanity Fair* party was, could they get some extra tickets for screenings, casual mention that Larry must be sleeping it off somewhere since he wasn't answering his phone. But then they started calling various staff under one pretense or another and asking more directly about Larry. Doesn't seem like they've seen him since the *Vanity Fair* party. They implied that he didn't leave alone."

I put my head down on the table. Men's insatiable desire for female flesh; was there no acceptable limit? I looked back up. "Female and young?"

"They were looking for a data upload, not the other way around."

"Put the word out discreetly amongst our own staff to keep their ears and eyes open. But give his people nothing about what we find out. They knew enough to ask, let them swing."

"His wife's been tweeting the hashtag," Samantha said. "I've started following her. She's actually pretty funny."

"In a smultchy 'look my husband's so famous and we're good sports' kind of way? Or a 'where's the Vagina Vulture' attempt to keep track?"

"Unclear," Samantha said, heading for the door. "Unless you need me for something, I'm going to go check on Huntley. I'll meet you at the theater at six thirty."

"Great, thanks."

She had barely made it out the door before Jamila was through it. It took me a minute to realize there was someone behind her. Yin Lee, director of *State*, so slight that she fit within the outline of Jamila's silhouette.

I invited her to sit at the small conference table in the corner. She perched on the edge of the chair, declining an offer of coffee. We made small talk until Jamila returned with a double espresso for me and left again.

"Please, Jane, what is going on with my film?"

"You know that the injunction claiming it's hate speech has been denied?"

She nodded.

"Whoever's working to stop the screening has tried another route. They've applied to overturn the 14A rating it received and make it more restrictive. We expect that, too, will fail."

"And if you do, a screening will definitely go ahead? This is your promise?"

She'd honed her slightness into an arrow that pierced through pretense. Her film was similarly devastating in its quiet insistence on the truth. "There are many forces that would like that not to happen," I said carefully. "Not just the Chinese government, you understand, but my board and some staff as well. They're probably behind the attempt to delay the screening."

"The Chinese secret service follows me everywhere."

"Here in Toronto?"

"Of course, Jane. Borders mean little." Her directness was a rebuke against a naivete I didn't think I had in me. "They make themselves as conspicuous as possible. I've moved from the hotel to the condo of a friend of a friend. Better security."

"I can arrange personal security for you, Yin. The kind of security that will make sure you're safe. Better than a festival would normally have access to."

"I don't think they'll grab me here; it is intimidation they seek. They've already banned my film in China, said the content is harmful to the dignity, honor, and interests of the People's Republic. But they worry about the film's influence on Chinese people living overseas, white lotuses who still cling to outdated concepts like democracy or freedom of expression. *Twentieth-century values*." Yin used air quotations to underline her point. "They surrounded me at the airport while I waited for my luggage. Said I should not embarrass the other Chinese directors by creating all this fuss around my film. That I was selfish to create trouble for everyone, for one film that was full of lies and mistruths."

"Your film is brilliant."

She bowed her head slightly toward me in response. "Do I have your promise?"

My inability to say yes and have the power to enforce it deeply shamed me. I crushed the little espresso cup I was holding and wished it was Jacob's bobble head. "I can't promise something not fully in my control," I said. "It will get screened in Toronto." I paused for a minute, trying to figure out how best to word the rest. "Even if that proves impossible over the course of the next seven days."

"You're not sure you want to make a stand."

"It would sour the relationship between your government and this festival. And it may get me fired."

It made me feel small to say it. Yin's life had been turned upside down by her government; now mine had added insult to injury by trying to block her film. My own considerations seemed petty in comparison.

"I understand your predicament. But bullies shouldn't win all the time. Then everything we do as filmmakers is a lie. We may as well disappear, like they want us to, because we've failed our function in society."

I looked at her, failure clogging my throat. "I'm trying to do what I can," I said, as she waited for a better response than I could give.

Yin leaned forward to place a hand on my shoulder. "I know." She dropped the hand as she stood to leave. ""An independent filmmaker doesn't have a better ally than you, Jane."

It was the highest compliment, and it only made me feel worse. She opened the office door to leave, and a dozen people stood waiting, all with some kind of emergency that I needed to solve. The festival was an overflowing river, while my life was being reduced to rubble in the background. I answered all their questions, before indicating I needed to use the washroom. Grabbing my purse, I walked toward it but out another door and down the service stairs, as if the devil himself was in pursuit.

* * *

The Toronto Club, Canada's oldest private club, with more influential Canadians — dead, alive, or some fossilized state in between — per square inch than anywhere else in the country. The red brick of its renaissance revival architecture had held strong against Americans, separatists, and cell phones for longer than the country had been a country.

I considered my assault. Bob and Johnnie's Uncle Frank, faced with a wife in serious decline from dementia, often took his evening meals at the club, even on the weekends, and a hundred dollars slipped to his condo's concierge confirmed that this evening was no different. I knew where he was, but how to scale the walls that privilege made thick, was more difficult to discern. My phone rang, and checking the caller ID, I answered.

"Go in and say with a serious and quiet undertone that you have an emergency and you must speak with Frank Smythe. Give your name when they ask, but as soon as the concierge goes up the stairs to the dining room, follow him quietly. Pass him just as he rounds the entrance. No one should want to make a fuss, so if Frank has any sense about him, he'll thank you for coming and escort you to another room to talk."

I looked around to see where David could be, but he was nowhere in sight. "You won't find me," the voice in my phone continued. "But I'm here."

"Thanks."

"Remember to put away your phone. And if you see someone else you know, don't say hello. Breaking the house rules will probably anger the Protestants more than forcing your way in."

I slipped the phone back into my bag and squared my shoulders. Up the stairs I went, smiling in what I hoped was a respectable way into the discreet camera over the door's entrance, and rang the bell.

"It's a family emergency, and I must speak with Uncle Frank now," I said, once the heavy oak door had swung open to admit me. "Frank Smythe, I mean. Apologies for the intrusion."

The balding man of indiscriminate age didn't blink. "Please wait here. I'll be back in a moment."

As his back retreated up the stairs, I waited until his peripheral vision was consumed by the heavy framed paintings of prime ministers that lined the walls and silently slipped up behind him. By the time I reached the top, he was leaning over to whisper in Frank's ear. I crossed the room and enjoyed, more than I probably should have, his look of annoyance, as he straightened up and saw me. But by the time he could do anything about it, I'd leaned in to speak sotto voce to my uncle-in-law.

"Frank, I can't leave until I speak with you about Smythe."

Frank took an inordinate amount of time dabbing his mouth with a napkin, before he finally stood. It's unfortunate our Johnnie has married down, he'd said to Robert, standing only a few feet away from me at the first family New Year's Day levee I'd attended at Eagle's Nest, his pretentiously named house in the expensive enclave of Forest Hills.

"Perhaps the cloak room," the concierge said, moving us discreetly toward the stairs. There were less than thirty people in the room, but what muted conversation there'd been previously evaporated in the face of my intrusion. He waited until the three of us reached the bottom of the stairs before he spoke again. "I'll make sure there are no further interruptions."

The cloak room turned out to be an antechamber of connected rooms; Frank led me to the far end where two chairs were located, although he made no move to sit.

"This is quite extraordinary, Jane," Frank said. He kindly left off the "even for you" evident in his tone.

"What's going on with Smythe Financial?"

"Whatever do you mean?"

"The OSC showed up to warn me there is money missing from the firm. Said all the c-suite execs, including you, are playing hide and seek. I can't reach Bob or Johnnie, so as a board director, I'm seeking a report from the next most senior officer in the company. The chief *financial* officer."

"You're only a board director because you slept with the other two."

The one thing about extreme tiredness was that the fuck-it button was a lot closer than normal. "The mask is slipping,

Frank. You'll need to tighten the screws before you go back upstairs."

Frank searched his repertoire for a poison pill that would annihilate the working-class rodent who'd scurried her way into their Fine Old Ontario Family. The FOOFs didn't move quickly, though; the lifetime of china cups accumulated up their asses made sudden maneuvering difficult, so I spoke again. "I need a briefing before start of business Monday on what the hell the financial risk is. As well as all deals, mergers or acquisitions, current or pending, that Smythe handled over the past ten years. I will not be caught unawares in the financial dealings of an organization for which I have a fiduciary responsibility."

"Where's Waldo?" Frank said, slipping back into his groove again.

"I don't know where Bob is. Only that we must have a serious problem for him and Johnnie to both be unreachable."

"I think your first course of action should be to find the man you live with, *if* you can. Are you quite sure he's disappeared for business reasons?"

Birth order hadn't handed Robert all the bastard genes; there'd been enough left over for his younger brother, too. "You tell me, Frank."

"It's Bob's responsibility to brief the board, and I shall leave him to it," Frank said, smoothing down the tie he wore under his gray cardigan. "I must get back before the veal gets even colder."

Frank lacked enough red blood cells to be a Malicious Villain and was not rich enough to be a Man-of-Wealth Villain. I watched his back retreat and stopped myself from feeling sorry for his lonely dinner waiting upstairs at the club table, where they sat people who had no one to eat with. The Frank I knew would kick his dog if it dared eat scraps that he dropped, not hard enough for anyone to notice, mind you, but deliberate enough that dog and owner knew exactly who was in control. *For whatever a man soweth, that shall he also reap.* Frank could go fuck his solitary self.

David was waiting across the street, when I reemerged from the club. "Anything?" he asked, as I crossed to meet him.

"He knows something, but he's not giving it up."

"So, Bob's disappearance is connected to the business?"

"What the fuck else would it be?"

David was silent as I worked to regain my composure. Life lived with the unhyphenated Smythes was as much in the weeds as my own family, but a million-dollar brush painted over their peculiarities. "I'm sorry. Let's go, okay?"

David looked back over his shoulder as we began to walk. Saturday evening in the financial district, both the foot and pedestrian traffic was lighter than normal, although that would change dramatically in a few blocks as we got to the festival's main hub where large crowds awaited celebrity appearances, the audience jostling with paparazzi looking for a sellable shot. He put his hand out to stop me as the light turned green. "Let's wait for the next one," he said.

I glanced at him quizzically, but my mind was on the conversation with Uncle Frank. David suddenly grabbed my arm and pulled me across the light as it was turning red.

Car horns blared at us; as we reached the curb on the other side, David spun us around to face two men that stood on the other sidewalk, looking for a break in the traffic to dart across themselves. "Jesus," I said. "We're being followed?"

"I clocked them in a car outside the club before you went in. Hard to do surveillance from a vehicle on a street where there's no stopping."

"Surveillance? They're Dilip Patel's people?" I asked as the light changed and the men began to advance.

"More serious than that, I suspect," David said, stepping us both out of the immediate foot traffic.

By now, the two men had reached us. "Ms. Browning?"

I slid another few feet down the rabbit hole. "Yes."

"I'm Inspector Wallace of the RCMP. We'd like to speak with you privately."

"Do you have identification?" David said, voice pleasant and calm.

Inspector Wallace looked down at me. At least six four, his bald head reflected the waning rays of the sun. The second man, no taller than me, a head full of dark hair, and half Wallace's age, was silent.

"Who are you really?" I asked.

Wallace took out his identification. I made a point of examining it closely, although I'd never seen the ID of a federal police officer before and had no idea if it were real or counterfeit. I handed it to David.

"Thank you," I said. "I'm due to introduce a screening in fifteen minutes, so we need to talk briefly and here. How can I help you?"

"That's not the way this works," he said, as he stepped closer.

David grabbed my hand, just as it was turning into an instinctive fist. "Do you have a warrant to compel Jane to go with you?"

The officer looked from David to me. "Does Ms. Browning have something to hide?"

I shook my head. Being followed by the RCMP should have induced fear but dealing with Uncle Frank had shifted my gear stick to angry, and it was stuck there. "Did you honestly just think you'd show up out of nowhere and bully me into getting into a car with you?"

"You're perfectly safe with us," Wallace said.

I shook my head. "Tell that to the thousands of female RCMP officers who've been sexually abused on the job. So, I ask again, what is that you want?"

"Smythe Financial." Wallace sized me up. "And some of the people you've been in contact with recently. It'd been in your own interest to cooperate with us."

"Ms. Browning will consult counsel and be in touch," David said.

Wallace reached into his breast pocket and handed me a business card. "In the interest of your own safety, you should do that very soon."

Both men turned to cross the street again. I began to walk in the other direction, David beside me. "You okay?" he asked.

"We're not in Kansas anymore, Toto," I said, dread settling in as the adrenaline of the unexpected encounter wore off. "Do you think the second guy was police, too?"

"Not RCMP. He would have identified himself."

I nodded. "Something is really fucked with Smythe."

"Possibly," David said. "Could be they're watching you, or someone else you've rubbed up against."

"Like the carbon-haired woman from the *Vanity Fair* party."

"Or Uncle Frank," David said. "They were in situ when you arrived at the club. We just don't have enough information. One thing is clear, though, Jane. It's got to be about something bigger than securities fraud. The RCMP don't generally step in prior to an OSC investigation."

"Maybe I made a mistake in not going with them. Find out what they're after."

"Don't ever speak to them without a lawyer present," David said. "They'll pump you for information, and use scare tactics and intimidation to get what they're after. They'll pressure others by saying 'Ms. Browning is assisting with our enquiries' to imply you're under investigation even if you're not. They'll hold a press conference and say it publicly to ramp up the pressure on you to cooperate. They either charge someone or remain silent; they never publicly say once they clear someone during an investigation."

"Jesus," I said. "Do you think they're who broke into the house the other night and followed me?"

"If they had a search warrant, no need for them to hide. And it'd be illegal for them to break in otherwise. Not to say that doesn't happen, but hard to see why they'd risk that."

I stopped in my tracks. By now, we were only a block away from the festival theaters; I was about to get swallowed whole by the evening rounds of films and parties. I shivered, my blouse suddenly thin against the ill winds that blew.

"Someone else, then, following me?"

David laid his hand on my shoulder. "I got your back. Any progress on a lawyer?"

I shook my head. There just hadn't been time. "I'll do it tomorrow," I said, silent for a moment. I fished the phone out of my purse. David started to move away but I put my hand up to wave away his effort. Searching through my contacts list, I hit dial.

"You rang?" the Scottish accent answered.

"Yin Lee's right. Bullies shouldn't win all the time, especially those in power," I said. This was one concrete action I could take, one small thing I could put right as everything else spiraled around me. "Pull the trigger on the *State* screening."

CHAPTER SEVEN

DAY 4: *Eastern Promises*

Sophia Bennini climbed out of the limo before her husband, one long, leather-clad leg at a time. Bustier tucked under Valentino jacket, red stiletto heels.

She didn't look back at Panov as his thick frame lumbered its way out after her. He hustled to catch up as she stood in front of the phalanx of photographers, simultaneously looking bored while being keenly aware of her best angles. When her husband wound his arm around her thin waist, she didn't move an inch, although she seemed to grow taller and more rigid. Or maybe I was projecting. The pair moved so slowly up the red carpet that the film's cast were forced to take a snail's pace so as to not steal the spotlight.

"Any longer, and the screening will be next week," I grumbled to Samantha as we stood in a little cordoned-off area at the entrance to the theater.

"You're trumped on this one," Samantha replied. "You deny any of these people the spectacle they've come to see, and they'll have your head on a platter."

She had a point. People swarmed like bees, all higgledy-piggledy. Volunteers struggled to herd the crowds into their designated queues: regular ticket holders in one, the rush line for those who didn't yet have tickets, Visa Infinite line for those lucky cardholders with expedited access. Except rebellion was in full stride. The buzz had gone up that Mr. and Mrs. Panov were walking the red carpet — an unprecedented second red carpet for the film, a hastily made accommodation after Panov got sprung from jail a few hours earlier.

"How long before she leaves him, do you think?" Samantha asked.

"Depends on the prenup," I replied. "Might be better to wait until the next wife comes along and he wants a leveraged buyout."

Within minutes, the photos taken would be splashed across the web; within hours, across television screens and in print media around the world. Sophia Bennini was a master of the spin. Hard to say from her expression whether there was triumph in the moment for her or just grim satisfaction. When the couple finally reached us, they swept right by me, deliberately failing to acknowledge my presence. I lingered. The screening couldn't start without me, and they'd look like fools hanging around with nowhere to go. Finally, Samantha nudged me, and in we went.

Mr. and Mrs. stood huddled with Jacob. I turned my head to Samantha. "That's how the ministerial permit got issued?" I asked, working to keep the anger out of my voice.

Samantha looked away. "I've heard a rumor to that effect, but I don't know for sure."

"I can't believe he used our political currency for a man accused of sexual assault."

"I imagine he has his own. Besides, Sophia Bennini is complaining to anyone who will listen that the festival, namely you, aren't supporting the filmmakers we invite."

"That's ridiculous."

"Perhaps Jacob was worried about the fallout."

Perhaps Panov was one of Jacob's clients, and having him photographed without handcuffs was the first step in the whitewash campaign, an all-out attack on the victim to follow. But I kept the thought to myself. Jacob had a reputation for ignoring conflicts of interest, and besides, a Dark Messiah could justify anything during a crisis.

I walked toward the three of them, only to find my path interrupted by the carbon-haired woman from the *Vanity Fair* party. "I'm sorry to startle you, Jane," she said. "Just a quick word before you go in."

I stepped aggressively toward her, catching her off guard. Strike first and strike fast, my self-defense teacher had drilled into me. "I'm at a disadvantage," I said. "I didn't catch your name the other evening."

Undaunted, she ran her hand along my arm and grasped my hand. "Forgive my rudeness. Anna Basmanova. A pleasure to be more formally introduced."

Alexei Panov stared at us intently. I wondered at his sudden interest, when only a few minutes earlier he was determined to snub me.

"What business do you have with Bob?" I asked, as I dug my knuckle into her palm until she released my hand. "You failed to mention that as well."

"Johnnie and I are partners in a new venture. But perhaps you knew that already?"

"I haven't seen or spoken to Johnnie in quite some time."

"And Bob?"

"What about Bob?"

"I understand he's returned from London. Did you tell him it's important that he see me?"

My expression froze. Bob had been in London the whole time? "I've haven't had that opportunity," I said.

"Others will come calling, Jane. It's much healthier if we conduct our business first. Do tell Bob or Johnnie they need to be in touch."

Panov made his way over. "Ms. Basmanova," he said, making a small formal bow to her. "It's a surprise, to put it mildly, to see you here."

"Hello Alexei. You're out of the slammer, as they call it in this part of the world. You must have fixed your little legal problem, yes?" She tutted with exaggeration. "One day you'll learn to deal with the ladies properly, yes?"

Panov barked out a sound — a laugh or a warning, I wasn't sure. "I wouldn't have thought you ran in the same circles with a woman like Anna," Panov said to me. "How do you know each other?"

"From the party circuit," I said, conscious that Jacob watched from a few feet away. "And the two of you? Ms. Basmanova one of the investors in your film?"

Panov barked again. "Anna's interests are simple. Money. Making it and cleaning it."

"A little ironic coming from you," Anna said. She turned her gaze to me. "Alexei exaggerates, of course. He is so dramatic."

Alexei let out a tirade in what I assumed was Russian to Anna. Now I knew what her accent was. She smoothed down her hair, inspected her fingernails, and gazed around the room, presumably bored by whatever Alexei was saying. His voice grew louder.

I watched as her gaze met Jacob's, two vipers sizing each other up. I looked about to see who else might be watching.

Alexei continued to rant, at one point grabbing Anna's arm. In a split second, she had his arm pinned behind his back while making it seem like a caress to the casual viewer. Her training was better than mine; I'd need to remember that.

Randy, the venue manager, stepped in between Alexei and Anna, forcing them to retreat to a respectable distance. "So sorry to interrupt," Randy said smoothly. "The audiences are anxiously awaiting your film, Mr. Panov. I really must take you and Jane backstage. Would you do me the pleasure of accompanying me?"

Anna smiled, fully in control. "My apologies for detaining you, Jane. I'll be in touch again very soon," she said, striding toward the door without a glance at Panov.

"You have no idea what you're getting into with that one," Alexei barked.

"I barely know her," I said, in a tone designed to shut down conversation.

He shrugged. "It's your funeral. I couldn't care less."

Randy nudged us forward until we reached Jacob and Sophia Bennini. "Mr. Ray, someone will show you to your seat in the front row. I'll just take the others backstage for the introductions."

"Thank you," I whispered to Randy, as we walked the short distance to the back wings.

"I'd avoid Octopussy in the future, if I were you, Jane. She looked at me like I was the dead mouse getting dropped into the cage for dinner."

A little push from Randy, and once again I stood in front of a microphone, thanking the audience for coming, the funders for making it possible, and the indispensable volunteers, who always got a round of applause. I cut short the complimentary comments about the film that had been scripted for me.

When Panov took the stage, Sophia at his side although she was not credited on the film, they declined to shake my hand or kiss my cheek when they passed me. He started by introducing his cast, who had gone through the show-and-tell routine the previous night at the real premiere. When all fifteen of the actors were finally assembled, Panov bowed his head, before looking back up at the audience and raising a defiant finger.

"I thank you, dear audience, for your faith in me. I've been treated badly by many in this city but not by you. Long live the true cinephile. Long live art."

Polite applause followed them off, and Randy immediately swept Alexei and Sophia away to their seats. I headed for the lobby, running into Samantha almost immediately.

"I had to learn from Burt that you have okayed the *State* screening," she said, biting off each word in sequence.

I nodded. "There's no perfect decision, but in weighing the various options, I decided to not censor *State* from the festival. I was going to discuss it with you back at the office."

"Have you told the board?"

I took a moment to weigh my reply. "Thank you for your diligence to your job. I plan to do that shortly."

She stormed off a few feet, before turning back. "Fatmanrising has surfaced. He may well be in the company of one of our interns. I thought you might want to know."

"Of course, I want to know. I would have liked to have known as soon as you did."

"I would have told you at our next meeting," she said, face perfectly blank.

"If the intern is one of ours, I want to speak with her as soon as possible," I said, refusing to rise to the bait. "And even if she's not, I still want to."

"Jacob incoming," she said, before leaving for good this time.

I turned and indeed Jacob was approaching, this time with a young acolyte who walked with such exaggerated self-importance he could only be a BFA apprentice. "Hello again," I said.

"Jane, this is Storm, a new member of my staff."

"How nice to meet you, Storm. Your parents are environmentalists?"

Storm looked at Jacob, then back to me. "Pardon, ma'am?"

"Nothing important. How come you're not in watching Alexei Panov's masterpiece?"

"I've assigned Storm to assist you and Samantha," Jacob said smoothly. "He loves movies and is delighted to be of help."

"That's very kind of you, and Storm," I said, keeping my voice in check. "But I have several hundred staff and volunteers. It's a full house already."

"I won't get in the way," Storm said.

"I appreciate your interest in the festival, but it really won't work. It'd be a HR breach for you to be at staff meetings, for example, which happen all day long as we juggle issues. Staff have a right to confidentiality from board directors, and your position with BFA could well make them uncomfortable. It has nothing to do with you personally."

"This is for the best, Jane," Jacob said.

"I don't mean to be obstreperous, Jacob," I said. "It's really not possible."

Our working relationship was sinking fast, but I didn't see any other option. Even without my personal life implosion, everything I had said about inappropriateness was true. But trying to hide what was going on from both Samantha and Storm would be impossible.

"May I have a private word, Jacob?"

"Storm is privy to my business affairs."

That I doubted, but Jacob was signaling control. "Two things.

First, is it true that you applied political pressure to obtain a ministerial permit for Alexei Panov's temporary release?"

"I wouldn't call it political pressure. BFA did some legwork so that one of the festival's directors could attend the world premiere of his film. Panov is influential and connected, and he was threatening legal action against the festival."

"On what grounds?"

"That we had maligned his reputation in not issuing a fulsome defense of him."

"There's no legal requirement for us to do so. In fact, it would have been highly contentious for us to imply that he's innocent, when we have no knowledge of what happened."

"Do you have a law degree?"

"No. But I did consult our legal department. Did you?"

"That would be my decision to make, Jane," he said, too quietly.

I nodded. Indeed, it was. "Is Panov a client, by chance?"

"BFA never reveals its client list, Jane. Nor would I ever allow my volunteer activities to be influenced by my business interests, if that's what you're implying."

Right. "That's good to know," I said, momentarily hesitating about what I was going to say next. But he was going to find out soon enough. "Speaking of decision-making spheres," I said, "we've scheduled the *State* makeup screening for tomorrow night, ten p.m., Franklin Square, pending dismissal of the ratings appeal which our lawyers tell us is all but guaranteed."

There was a full moment of silence, during which Storm looked ready to faint from the crackling tension, and I fidgeted while trying to keep my exterior calm. It was clear that Jacob had every intention of advising the board to dump me. Pin all the festival's problems on the donkey and send her down the plank post-festival. He'd run whatever parallel tracks he needed to behind the scenes to diminish my reputation with our stakeholders, including the other board members, and to concoct cause for dismissal. Nothing personal.

"Then the ramifications are yours to bear," Jacob said, turning to leave, Storm hurrying after him.

I walked out of the building into the sunshine, deflating as the adrenaline of the confrontations with Anna, then Jacob, dissipated. I stopped to buy a chocolate soft-serve ice cream cone from a nearby truck. People lingered around the gourmet food trucks, on benches, on the sidewalks, enjoying the evening's warm air, flipping through the festival program, taking pictures of passing celebrities. I leaned against a low stone wall, eyes closed, slightly camouflaged behind the leaves of a tree. Despite myself, my body began to absorb the calm of the crowd, and I was lulled into a contemplative haze before my eyes snapped open again, scanning my environment for threats. Bob was alive. I was in danger. It was time for answers.

* * *

I slid the dead bolt in place after the room service waiter left; I needed this conversation to be as private as possible. Harrison Wex, a lawyer I'd previously known only by reputation, was now on retainer to me. He tucked into the beef short ribs and mashed potatoes with gusto. David ate at a more modest pace.

"So, let me get this straight," Harrison said, opening his mouth to rearrange his food. "The Ontario Securities Commission appears out of the blue to say there's a problem at the firm. Bob disappears, you don't know if he'd dead or alive. Two strange women stalk you, one of whom has something urgent to say about Bob. The other one is anxious to contact him and/or former husband, who's also your brother-in-law. Turns out the blond is the head of compliance at Bob's firm, which means she's a key player who should be talking to the OSC but instead is dodging them to hound you. And the brunette is a Russian who says she's in bed, professionally speaking, with either Bob or Johnnie and seems to know more about Bob's whereabouts than you. To top it off the RCMP come calling. Am I following along correctly?"

"That's about the gist."

"Seems to me we should be checking accounts in Panama."

"Bob would never do that."

"Yeah, sure," he said, ramming another piece of beef into a mouth that didn't have enough real estate left. He nodded at the massive bunch of white roses on the side table. "Which of the players sent them?"

"Darren McGregor," I said, with a slight grimace. "New festival donor."

"That worm is back in town?" Harrison asked.

"Made a twenty-million-dollar donation yesterday to the festival," I said. "Our publicity department is busy pushing the good news story as a way to turn the corner on all the negative coverage."

"Never fear. McGregor will buy the media coverage if necessary. Or the media company." He looked at David. "What have you dug up on the Russian?"

"Anna Basmanova is an oil speculator, Russian by birth, not clear exactly where she lives. At least part of the time in London but definitely also in Moscow —"

"London," I said. "She said Bob was back from London. Is that connected?"

"We'll get to all that," Harrison growled. "First, we talk about the Russki."

"Anna's obsessively private, so it's difficult to get exact data points. What I'm about to say could best be termed as a subjective narrative based on a mixture of fact, supposition, and informed rumor," David said. "She seems to have partial or full interest in a number of oil and gas projects across Russia and central Asia, including several new ones in Kazakhstan."

This just kept getting stranger. "Kazakhstan?"

"Not as surprising as it might sound," David continued. "The country has significant oil and gas deposits and is, by far, the most stable and largest economy in central Asia."

"They're independent from Russia, yes?"

"Yes and no. They were the last Soviet republic to declare independence, and it'd be folly to assume they could take an anti-Russian stance on anything of meaning."

"Anna Basmanova has business interests in Kazakhstan," I said, pouring myself another coffee in a feeble attempt to kick-start the brain. "Are you going to tell me Smythe Financial does, too? If so, this board director doesn't know it."

"There's private chatter amongst stock promoters that Ms. Basmanova has a subspecialty in bilking Western businessmen on oil lease development projects in the region," David continued. "I've heard of a handful of instances, which probably means there are dozens more. Investors are rarely willing to talk about being duped. These things generally have the same pattern — oil leases are distributed, often with a Russian partner holding minority interest so they can smooth the permit process. Initial drilling reports will show large deposits, with big capital needed to start serious exploration, cash that generally comes from the foreign partner. Invariably, there's one delay after another that requires more cash. These oil leases always have a clause that stipulates any delay in exploration over a certain time period means ownership reverts back to the government, since none of these governments are democratic, Kazakhstan included. Then the government flips them to another crony, and the cycle starts all over again."

"That fits," I said. "Anna said Johnnie was a partner in a new venture. She used the past tense to describe it. Maybe Johnnie got cold feet?"

"We have no way of knowing yet. These joint ventures are normally registered as numbered companies; sometimes the money routes through different jurisdictions," David said. "It can take a long time to untangle, if it's even possible to. But my investigator is trying."

"Johnnie's foolhardy, but he's not stupid," I said. "It's hard to figure how he got taken by a scheme if it's as obvious as you say. And if he did, why is Anna looking for him? If it's a fixed game, wouldn't Johnnie be looking for revenge, not the other way around?"

"Maybe Johnnie's already taken it."

"We're talking tens if not hundreds of millions of dollars for one of these investments," Harrison said. "Would Johnnie have that kind of money on his own?"

I shook my head. "No."

"Would Smythe Financial? The firm is an investment bank, too, yes? Not just money managers?"

I nodded. "We have an investment banking division but in those situations we act as advisors. We make our money through fees for putting together deals or helping companies go public, or private, not on buying or selling things ourselves. In Robert's day, Smythe did have a private equity fund that made direct investments, but Bob scaled that back when he took over. It's a riskier business model. Plus, he never wanted to keep value in the business in the form of big cash reserves beyond regulatory requirements, for risk of being a target for lawsuits or hostile takeovers, including from his own brother and uncle. The bulk of money is paid out quarterly in dividends to the shareholders, and in year-end bonuses to the staff."

"The three of you?" Harrison asked.

"Bob and Johnnie, primarily. Uncle Frank and his children have smaller positions, too. I have no ownership in the company. I lack the necessary DNA."

"Well, something's not right," Harrison said, fingers drumming on the table. "Any information on the brothers Smythe?"

"I guess Bob is an accomplice in his own disappearance," I said flatly, eyeing my untouched food.

"I have someone running traces on Johnnie's and Bob's credit cards to see their movements. It might give us a clue to what's going on," David said. "But since we're not law enforcement, it takes a little time and ingenuity. Might they use any aliases?"

"We're not the kind of people who know anything about aliases."

Harrison started laughing so hard that liquid came up through his nose and he descended into a coughing fit. I turned my head away for the several moments before he could get it under control. "If you're an ordinary family," he finally said, "I'm Attila the Hun."

Like Alice, I kept sliding further down the rabbit hole, but life had proven to be one rabbit hole after another, so ordinary was a difficult concept to judge.

"Ordinary?" I said. "Perhaps you could give me a definition?"

Harrison acknowledged the point by dipping his head in my direction, before turning his attention back to David. "We need to get as much information on Basmanova's business dealings as fast as we can. She warned Jane that others will come calling; I'd be surprised if she meant the authorities. Someone was inside that black sedan, we need to figure out who."

"One more thing," David said. "I don't mean to be alarmist, but this was repeated to everyone my people spoke to. Anna Basmanova is apparently very well connected with Putin. Intimately connected is the suggestion."

I reached for my glass of wine and sat back in silence.

"International film festival indeed," Harrison said.

"She knew Alexei Panov," I said. "Panov implied she was very bad business. As if that wasn't ironic."

David put up his hand to silence us for a moment as he peered into his phone. "Just heard back from my investigator. Bob checked into the Four Seasons here in Toronto. He's registered under the name of Bob Walker."

"Was he alone?" The words were out of my mouth before I could help it.

Harrison looked at me closely. "Is there a reason to think he wouldn't be?"

I didn't answer. David stepped into the breach. "It appears yes, he was."

"Bob in hiding. Interesting," Harrison mused, fingers drumming again. "Who is Bob afraid will come knocking on the door if he goes home? Not Jane, since she's living at a different hotel, although she has keys, so unless he changes the locks — which would be pretty hard to explain — he risks the danger of her walking in on anything untoward. The Russian? That would mean Bob knows something about Johnnie's activities. And presumably Bob hasn't been in touch with the OSC, given he's not eager to be found. It would be helpful to know who he's meeting with, David. Is that possible?"

David looked at me. "You'd need to authorize some more personnel, so we can do a full tail. Could get costly."

"Okay," I said. "I'll figure out a way to pay for it."

"I hate to point out the obvious . . ." Harrison said.

"My finances are independent of Bob's," I said. "Let's move on."

My mother's choices had been short-circuited by not having an independent income. Even if she'd been willing to, walking out on a marriage with two children and a minimum-wage job would have been near impossible. I often wondered, over the years, if I hadn't been born, might my mother have taken flight?

Was the experience of motherhood, in the end, worth her sacrifice of self? It was a question I hadn't faced myself. On my wedding day, I got myself injected with long-lasting birth control, so I wouldn't take the chance of Johnnie finding the little pink pills. I had no desire for another generation to carry forward the sins of either family. Let them die with us.

"Noted," Harrison said. "What about the other brother?"

"Nothing so far on Johnnie. There's no sign of activity at his Rosedale home, or at the Lake Rosseau cottage. Trying to get the financial data."

It was bizarre to hear Bob and Johnnie being spoken of so dispassionately by men I hadn't known forty-eight hours earlier.

"Jane, do you have any idea where Johnnie could be?"

I shook my head. But my mind took its own path.

"I'm out of here," Harrison said, heaving himself out of his chair. David and I followed suit. "Chin up, Jane. We'll figure this out. In the meantime, keep people around and let me know what combatants make an appearance."

I locked the door behind Harrison. "I need to change quickly, then get to the rest of tonight's obligations. What are your plans?" I asked David.

"I'll drop you off, and then try to get some traction on what we've discussed."

"Thanks, David," I said, putting my hand on his arm. "I really appreciate your help. I feel immeasurably better having you in my corner."

He rested his hand on top of mine; a flutter of unexpected warmth invaded my stomach. I took a step backward. "I'll be ready to go in fifteen," I said.

CHAPTER
EIGHT

It was the hashtag that rocked the city.

Some time on either side of eleven, and people were pouring onto the rooftop of the Thompson Hotel where the *Operation Bin Laden* after-party was in full swing. Giant sculptures of prawns in the shape of machine guns competed with rivers of champagne made red with Campari. Party actors wearing burkas and thobes mingled with female guests whose outfits were so minimal they must have required industrial amounts of flesh-colored tape to avoid wardrobe malfunction.

"There's a party downstairs in the private dining room, you need to put in an appearance," Samantha yelled into my ear, cupping her hand around it. I twitched, involuntarily; the gesture was strangely intimate for someone I didn't trust.

"We've already done all the parties on my itinerary," I said.

"Jacob promised them this morning you'd join for dessert."

"Who is it?"

"Darren McGregor. He's hosting funders and talent for *The Lakehouse*. Remember, the film his son worked on?"

Yikes. Darren was one encounter I didn't need at the end of a long day of strife, but there was no way to decline that request. As both he and Jacob knew.

"Okay," I said, walking toward the elevator. "What's the drill for this one?" I pushed the button.

The elevator doors opened, but Samantha put her hand out to stop me from getting on. "The elevator opens right into the room, so let's run through before you go up."

I looked at the cheat sheet full of pictures and bios she handed me. "Who's on the list?"

"Three minutes with the son about his career path and how we can help. Three minutes with the director, praising the auteur quality of the film and the terrific acting by the female lead Ryder Wilson. You've heard early Oscar buzz already; distribution by Focus Features, opens wide in early December. Four minutes with Darren himself, congratulating him on the prodigy, thanking him again for his donation pledge. Ask him about his Fidelis yacht and plans to sail the length of the Caribbean this winter. Then I'll intervene nicely but firmly with an emergency you really must attend to, and we'll be out in exactly ten minutes. Whatever you do, don't get sucker seated. I've had a word with the serving staff and they're supposed to serve champagne and hold on the crème brûlée, so everyone is forced to get up and mingle but you never know about some cowboy waiter."

I nodded. "Anything else?"

"Fourteenth floor," Samantha said, as I got into the elevator. "I'll be up shortly."

The elevator silently spilled me into the sleek dining room, all modern walnut furniture and gold accents. As soon as Darren noticed me, he rose from the head of the long table. I walked toward him but stopped several feet short, forcing him to walk toward me and the others to rise.

"You're very kind to allow me to join you for dessert," I said.

Briefed by Samantha, waiters appeared bearing champagne. I took two glasses, handing one to Darren. "You must be so proud of your son, and his work on this film," I said.

"I think I've birthed a winner. And backed one, of course."

Of course. "There's very good buzz for the film. Your investment in your son's future will show an excellent return on investment."

Darren drank his champagne. Like a lizard, his eyes didn't blink, and they were fixated on me. "I want to get to know you better, Jane. I'm sorry if my comment about Johnnie upset you yesterday."

Being in the dark about the connection between Darren and Smythe Financial carried a considerable downside risk, but Darren wasn't the person to give me an unvarnished truth. I quickly cast back to Samantha's cheat sheet. "I understand you have a Fidelis? Plans to sail the length of the Caribbean?"

"You're a sailor?" Darren drew himself taller.

My mother barely afforded the drive-in movies she took me to in the summer; the Brownings didn't ski or sail. "I love being on the water."

"You're welcome on my boat anytime."

Time to run interference. I waved my hand toward Brendan McGregor. "I'd so love to meet your son."

Brendan transported himself instantly. He carried himself quietly, a lifetime cowed by having a personal brand for a father.

"My team tells me, Brendan, that one day soon we'll be seeing a movie that you helmed here at the festival."

"I've got a distance to go before I reach that dream."

"You're listed as associate producer on a film from one of the most respected independent production companies in Hollywood. That's a pretty good perch to jump from."

"I was an intern a year ago. I just showed up every day and made sure I was the last person to leave the set at night."

"With that kind of attitude, you'll do just fine in this business," I said, smiling. He must have inherited his humility from his mother. I asked him a couple more questions about his career path and gave him my card, offering to help in any way. "I just want to have a quiet word of congratulations with Nicholas about his film before dessert is served," I said. "I'll be right back."

I'd never met Nicholas Bruele before, but knew of him by reputation. A master of technical virtuosity in his craft, a complete mess in his personal life. A man who spoke in interviews about his desire to live happily ever after and yet who saw one relationship after another disintegrate because of his predilection for emotionally needy women.

His artistic vision, though, rarely suffered a misstep, and that's what I told him as we stood quietly talking. I felt the hand on my elbow before I sensed the presence of someone beside me. Failing radar; that was disconcerting. There was no chance of survival without it. "I'm very sorry," Samantha said, pulling me away. "I must have a word with Jane."

We walked a few feet to the left. "Let's stand here for a half minute talking," she said, her sedate tone fitting the decorum in the room. "Then you go to Darren and quietly tell him that there's an emergency that you must attend to. I'll meet you at the elevator."

There was little doubt in my mind that Darren understood the score. He slipped his card into my jacket pocket, a transgression so fast and slight it could have been missed. But I got the signal. "Very few people on this planet have my private mobile. I'll be waiting for your call," he said.

And then we were gone. A ground swell of noise sucker punched me the moment the elevator doors reopened onto the rooftop crowd, which had swelled to at least five hundred people. Large steel lamps shot flames out the top of their eight-foot cylinders into the night sky. A DJ rocked the dance floor from a platform high above the crowd. I hoped he didn't have vertigo. I hoped the event organizers had an adequate insurance rider.

There was no way of being heard so I mimed a drink to Samantha. She nodded, and we started to make our way very slowly toward the bar. It took twenty minutes to get there, and another ten to get the featured cocktail. "Fuck ISIS punch," the sign said. I declined the bacon stick offered as a garnish. The party planner's choices were about as tasteful as the movie.

The rum and bitters packed quite a punch, and the warmth of the alcohol wound its way through me. I'd been drinking more than normal in the past few months — a socially acceptable decompression tool — and my liver's displeasure at the increased alcohol and caffeine intake was making itself known. A shake of my arm interrupted my thoughts and I saw Samantha point to her watch and mouth words at me. I shook my head, uncomprehendingly. She leaned over and yelled in my ear, "We've met our obligation. We can go anytime."

A world of problems waited for me beyond the confines of this rooftop. I shook my head and turned back to the bar. I was having a second before I had to go back in the ring.

I'd barely been handed it from the bartender when arms grabbed me from behind, the compression at my solar plexus depleting the oxygen in my lungs. My breath became shallow; the room faded in and out of sight. I was swung around away from the bar and then dropped, hitting the floor. I scurried out of the way of stampeding feet, until my back was against a hard surface, and I could inch my way up. My head knocked against a railing, the same spot where I'd hit the bathroom sink. I was finally able to pull myself to standing, and then climbed onto the bar to survey the room, sending rows of drinks flying as I did.

Half the crowd still moved to the beat, oblivious that anything more sinister was going on. The rest were just beginning to cotton to the strangers in their midst, dressed all in black, balaclavas covering their faces, guns in hand.

Hands went up to take photos while others scrambled, screaming, for cover. Plates of food were transported into flying saucers when the tall cruiser tables put out by the caterers went horizontal in the crush. The rhythmic whoosh of helicopter blades, at first faint but then growing in volume, competed with sirens.

David appeared suddenly in front of me, corralling three of the black-clad commandos. The crowd, sensing the change in power dynamics, butted forward another five commandos using seized guns which, upon closer inspection, looked to be cheap and flimsy.

This was the moment, as I tried to explain later to the anti-terrorism squad, when I understood that the plot had gone off the rails. The DJ, earphones on and head down, ignored all signals to shut off the music, concentrated as he was on his oeuvre. Snoop Dogg continued to rail against the police as the sirens reached top pitch from the front of the hotel. The sense of crisis gave way to a sinking feeling of parody, and I stood there, just shaking my head, imagining how this cockup would play in the media. Play into Jacob's hands.

Suddenly, the music ceased. The DJ took off his earphones and yelled, "Who the fuck is fucking with my fucking electricity?" The night sky lit up with flashes from cell phone cameras. The paper the following day would track that #invasion had trended to the top ten within the first minute of the most ill-advised publicity stunt of all time. More than a thousand photos were uploaded to Instagram in less than five minutes.

Every entrance to the rooftop opened, and dozens of men in uniform spilled onto the rooftop. It was instantly recognizable that these men in black were not like the others. Even the best trained actors in the world, and that was not who the party planner had hired, couldn't replicate the sheer violence and intimidation by which the police officers moved through the crowd. No remorse shown as people were pushed aside. They spread like a tornado across the crowd, seizing control, until they arrived at the unlikely grouping of eight men in Halloween costumes and David. All were on the ground in a blink of an eye.

I scrambled down from the bar and worked my way toward the knot of control, holding on to passing objects with one hand. It was slow going, and more than once I had to duck the confiscatory arm of an officer. Elsewhere, the police rounded up groups of people and removed them wholesale from the room. As the crowds thinned, I limped closer to the half circle of officers and prisoners.

"Step back, ma'am. I won't ask twice," one of the them said to me.

"I'm Jane Browning. I run the film festival."

"Are you in charge of this event?"

"No. That would be the film's producer. Do you understand the men in black are actors?"

The police officer shook his head violently from side to side. "You can't be serious." David was nearby on the ground; the officer kicked him in the leg. "Are you the asshole responsible for this?"

Given his face had been pushed into the ground, and his hands tied behind his back, it was difficult for David to make himself understood, but with a series of grunts and head shaking he managed to communicate no.

"He works for me," I said. "He had nothing to do with this."

Two police officers pulled him up roughly from the ground, bumping him against any surface they could. He grimaced in obvious pain but said nothing. Other officers dragged the black-clad actors to their feet.

"Are you okay?" I asked him.

"Yes," he said. "Panov and another man were right behind you at the bar, did you see them?"

"What?" I said, as I noticed Franny in the middle of a group that included the producer of *Operation Bin Laden*. A freelance publicist, Franny worked for whoever paid, and I suspected her presence at the party wasn't coincidental.

By this time, Samantha had made it over. "Who is he, Jane?"

The officer detaining David took a step toward me, pulling him along. "He works for you, or he doesn't work for you?"

"He works for me personally, not the festival. His name is David Levy."

"In what capacity?"

I calculated the percentages of my various responses and landed on the abridged truth as my only option. "He's my bodyguard."

Franny stepped forward, batting away the hand of the police officer who tried to stop her. "Jane, you're going to need get out in front of the messaging on this one. I'll start tonight, and we'll sort out the money thing in the morning."

"Don't you think you've done enough damage here tonight, Franny?" I said.

Heads swirled toward her direction. "This wasn't my responsibility. I just executed according to the plan. I don't set strategy."

"What do you need a bodyguard for?" Samantha was working hard to regain form. "Are you receiving threats? Have you alerted security?"

"Yes," I said, my eyes holding David's. "They recommended him to me."

The police began hustling David and the actors toward the elevator. The main officer pointed his finger at me and then at the elevator. "You're coming, too."

"Jane goes nowhere without me," Samantha said.

"Get out of the way, or we'll put you out of the way."

"It's okay, Samantha, thank you," I said. "Please stay here and be in charge of whatever containment is possible."

"At least tell me where you're taking her," she said, not willing to address me directly.

"Fourteen Division." He started pulling me, David, and the actors to the elevator.

"Monique," Samantha yelled toward the back of the crowd, where the producer of the film was backing off as nonchalantly as she could manage. "You're staying with me to deal with the hotel people and then we're going together to the police station."

Monique started to protest but Samantha was finally in control and she wasn't about to give it up. "Throwing the talent under the bus is never a good idea for a producer. You'll bail out the actors as necessary. And you'll face the media scrum. Or I'll be naming and shaming, have no doubt about that."

Fanny's strident voice trying to downplay the event was the last thing I heard as the doors to the elevator closed. "Just breathe deeply. We'll be out of here in twelve seconds." David's brown eyes were inscrutable. "Count backward with me. Twelve, eleven, ten . . ."

I mouthed the words with him, but my mind had wandered elsewhere. Twelve seconds. Life begins and ends in less time. Actions taken and regretted. David got to zero and the doors opened, as if exactly on queue.

CHAPTER
NINE

DAY 5: *Our Brand Is Crisis*

The food Franny rounded up for us at the station was pretty tasty, I had to give her that. But after spending seven hours listening to her name drop every person who'd ever hired her in the film industry, and all the just fabulous things she'd done for them, I was ready to shove the leftovers in her mouth.

It was now Monday morning, one business day after the visit by the securities regulator. The threatening presence of Anna Basmanova and Alexei Panov attacked my central nervous system from the left, while the OSC and the RCMP approached from the right. I stared at the walls of the police station waiting room, trying to think.

A strange assortment of people had filled the room through the wee hours. Sixteen of Monique's production company staked ground in one corner. They'd commandeered whatever small tables they could find to set up a makeshift office. Laptops, iPads, phones, and notebooks were scattered everywhere, alongside bottled water, kale chips, and bags of fruit sourced from the all-night Korean grocery store a few blocks away. Someone even brought in a portable espresso maker and set up a barista bar in the corner. They did a brisk trade, providing alms in the way of free coffee to the families of the street youth, drug dealers, and mentally ill who'd been arrested that evening.

Who said Hollywood didn't give back?

Thoroughly fed up with our traveling show, the police frequently told us to pipe down but their communications team had immediately sussed the challenge in evicting a group of social media influencers, and so they reluctantly let it continue. Samantha did her best to control the situation, but they were ground cover that would not be pruned back for long. The entourage grew as the sun rose and agents, managers, families, and lawyers for the detained actors filtered in.

My tailbone ached from the previous night's encounter with the floor and hours spent slouched in a hard, plastic chair, although I was grateful to not be in a holding cell. I'd done what I could to get out ahead of the story by emailing every politician or influential person Bob or I knew in the city. I sent a note informing the board what had happened and stressed that we had had nothing to do with the organization of the event and it had not taken place on WTFF property. I copied the marketing staff, Victoria, and our corporate lawyers, putting blame squarely where it was due: on the event planners.

But there was no doubt the fallout would further tip the scales of power against me.

The police were vigilant about keeping out reporters, but Franny and Monica's team monitored the online news coverage and read out salient bits, including the fact the hotel was next to the children's hospital, and the helicopter was not the SWAT team descending but rather a six-year-old being airlifted in from a car accident in a remote community. There had been seven hundred people at the party, four hundred beyond fire code, so the hotel faced major fines from the city. Dozens of photographers and journalists camped out on the sidewalk across from the police station, with an equal number estimated at the mayor's office, waiting for the official reaction from the city once council opened up for business.

"I'll have a double espresso, and plenty of sugar."

The sheer authority of Harrison's booming voice parted the room like the red sea, as the lumbering figure made his way to the espresso bar. I slipped my phone back into its hiding place down my shirt and got up. Samantha had already beelined in front of him.

"Can I help you?" she said. "Are you here for the free coffee or —?"

"I'm Harrison Wex," he said, twirling his large hand over and over again to indicate the makeshift barista should get a move on with his coffee.

"Everyone with a television in this city knows who you are," she said. "On the steps of the courthouse, always outraged when one of your clients has been charged with a crime they couldn't possibly have committed."

"She comes with teeth, this one," Harrison said, shaking my hand.

"Harrison is my lawyer, Samantha."

"Since when?" she said.

"He's just stepping in to help with this situation."

She shook her head. "Why do you think you need purchased indignation?"

Harrison drank down his double espresso in one long gulp. "We need to talk in private, Jane."

The police officer who'd stared me down hours earlier appeared at the door. I walked toward him, Samantha following, but Harrison dismissed her with a wave of his hand.

The officer didn't speak until we were in the hall. "Of course, you'd be part of this gong show," he said, cocking his head at Harrison. "Nothing you people do surprises me now."

"Ms. Browning has every right —"

"I don't want to hear it," the police officer said, fixing Harrison with a hard stare. "I accept you weren't legally responsible for last night," he continued, speaking directly to me. "But every one of my officers put their lives on the line to save yours and it turns out you film people were playing dress-up. You get all jacked up about whether my officer stepped on the toes of some ex-Mossad agent in a suit, meanwhile that same officer ran up forty-two flights of stairs in full gear worried that a bomb was about to explode."

Harrison raised his eyebrows at the ex-Mossad comment, but I kept my expression firmly in check. "We fully appreciate the difficulties your officers face," I said.

"I doubt it," he said. "On one hand, a strong deterrent is necessary. Any kind of emergency tonight in the city and people would have died. The calls to 911 claimed this was a terrorist attack; we had no choice but to go code three. Every regular and special forces officer that could be pulled to the scene was. The rest of the city had skeletal coverage. Nothing happened, so we look like overreacting assholes in all that video footage. But had someone died tonight, you'd be answering tough questions in the media and city hall. If it were up to me, you still would."

I nodded. He was right, of course, and I didn't have an adequate answer.

"The chief is meeting with the mayor right now. We're unhappy with the monolith the festival is turning into, and we'll be making our sentiments known."

I'd love to be a fly on that wall. With any luck, the mayor would attack the festival, motivating the chief to defend it, given the intense dislike between the two. The irony must have crossed all our minds, as we were silent for a moment.

"For the record, I want to say that while our organization has no fiduciary or legal responsibility for a private party we did not plan or produce, we deeply regret the mayhem the party organizers caused for the city and for your officers," I said. "It was bullshit and I'm sorry they got caught up in it."

The officer nodded, curtly. "On the other hand, this has turned into a PR debacle for us. Lawyers like this one grind down the court system wasting millions of dollars."

"Not —" Harrison didn't get to the second word, before the officer put up a hand to stop him.

"Everyone is free to go in this matter. The actors and the hired muscle are being processed out now. Clear the circus in the waiting room immediately. And I mean now. Morning rush hour is already slowed to a halt with the media trucks parked out there. No gabfest between you and the journalists when you leave, understand? Take it elsewhere or we'll remove you."

I extended my hand, but the officer kept his by his side. "Thank you," I said, making to exit as quickly as I could, Harrison following. I'd only taken a few steps when my name was called.

"You might think about calling us, not a bodyguard, if you think you're in danger," the officer said. "It comes with paying your taxes. Alongside the water and the sewage."

"Thanks," I said. "I'll remember that."

"One more thing. Got a call from a buddy in the RCMP after the news footage; tipped me off that you're a person of interest to them."

Harrison snorted. "First, they ambush Jane on the street, now they try to jam her through you. If she's such a danger, why not show up here to question her?"

"Who said they didn't?" The police officer inclined his head at Harrison. "The captain's not a fan of jurisdictional bun fights in his station, especially when there's no formal request in play. Said you'd be out on the sidewalk between eight and eight thirty this morning, then it wasn't our problem."

I swallowed hard. "Why are you giving me the heads up?"

The police officer looked at me for several beats before answering. "Take care of yourself, Ms. Browning," he said, then walked away.

* * *

I turned up the volume on the television in the corner of my office. The noon newscast was full of dire tidbits. A new virus being tracked in Asia. Worsening job numbers sending tremors through the world markets, wiping billions from pension fund holdings. Yet another cop killing of a Black man in America. Humankind intent on a constant collision course with itself.

I clicked over to E! to check on coverage about the festival and instead found a video that Devlin had released on Instagram earlier in the day. In it, she cavorted with her children in a mock *Sound of Music* setting, juxtaposed against shots of Huntley, from the ungracious moment at the screening to falling on his motorcycle to paparazzi shots of him looking drunk and disorderly. Samantha would need hours to calm him down again.

"He's a buffoon," Harrison barked from the couch, where he sat hunched over his phone, furiously typing away ever since we'd returned from the police station. I'd done what I could to make myself presentable from the emergency stash of clothes and toiletries I kept in my office closet, but was looking forward to a long, hot shower at my hotel later.

"That's a bit harsh," I murmured, thinking back to Huntley's comments about Devlin. There was a deliberate cruelty to her bullying of him that didn't sit well with me.

Harrison harrumphed and went back to his work. Finally, the knock we were awaiting came. I clicked off the TV. "Come in."

Jamila entered with Dilip Patel, as Harrison rose from the couch.

"Hello again, Mr. Patel," I said. "Jamila, please make sure no one disturbs us. I won't be too long."

She nodded and closed the door behind her.

Harrison put out his hand to shake Patel's. "Harrison Wex. Jane's general counsel. She asked me to join the meeting."

"Dilip Patel."

I waved a hand at my small office conference table. "Thank you for agreeing to meet here," I said. "Why don't we sit?"

"As I said to Ms. Browning, Smythe Financial is in violation of its legal obligations necessary for continued operation," Dilip said, as he took his chair. He was clearly not one for small talk. "It's Monday morning. As I don't see any corporate officers here in the room, I can only assume Ms. Browning was unsuccessful in reaching someone?"

"Jane spoke in person with Frank Smythe, the firm's CFO, and expects to connect today or tomorrow with Bob Walker-Smythe as well. She's working assiduously to meet your demands, despite the intense pressure she faces with her own professional obligations," Harrison said smoothly, as he leaned back in the chair. I tried not to stare at him. My pit bull lawyer had morphed into someone so pleasant, I was tempted to give him a little pat between the ears.

"Good. You should know it's our intention to attend at the office tomorrow," Dilip said flatly.

Harrison's smile faded a smidge. "What does 'attend' mean?" I asked, looking from one to the other.

"Starting at nine a.m. tomorrow morning, our compliance investigators will be in the offices of Smythe Financial going through all relevant files."

"Do you need my authorization to do that?"

"No," Dilip said. "We can come in at any time and look at anything."

"Wouldn't it be more advisable to wait until Jane ascertains that the CEO will be present and able to assist in your inquiries?" Harrison asked.

"If you prefer, we can move for an immediate injunction to cease operations of Smythe Financial pending investigation."

"That's ridiculous," I said. Harrison shot me a warning look.

"We gave formal notice of irregularities in the firm's minimum capital requirement more than a week ago and those charges remain unanswered."

"What kind of irregularities?" Harrison asked.

"They were detailed in the letter that was hand-delivered to Smythe Financial. And signed for, I might add."

Harrison put his hands flat on the table. "You're hamstringing Jane's ability to assist by withholding vital information. A judicial case can be made to consider that inadequate legal notification."

Dilip turned his gaze to me. "As corporate secretary, I'm sure you're aware that the firm must file a monthly legal report indicating how much capital liquidity it has?"

"The working capital, yes? How much cash we have on hand for things like payroll or regulatory expenses?"

"Or fines."

"But nothing to do with the money in client accounts?"

"No." Dilip paused to look at me. "Is there a reason to think there'd be a problem there, too?"

"Of course not."

"As you know, Smythe Financial has fifteen billion of assets under management, and over a hundred staff. A minimum of fifty million in liquidity in the working capital account is the legal requirement. And, normally, that's what Smythe's regulatory filings show. Until last month."

"And?" I asked, keeping my voice neutral.

"It dropped to five million without any explanation."

My mouth gaped open. "The firm lost ninety percent of its liquidity in one month?"

Harrison lifted his hand slightly off the table as a warning.

"Either the money evaporated in a short amount of time — suggesting some kind of cataclysmic happening of which, as a corporate director, you should be aware — or the filings have been incorrect in previous months," Dilip said. "Either way, Smythe Financial doesn't have enough cash on hand to legally continue operating."

He looked up at me, letting the silence stretch, expecting me to speak. But I'd spent a childhood learning to read the visual clues; a wrong foot, a misstatement, would put me further in danger.

"If the descent wasn't that uniquely precipitous — for example, if the decline has been more gradual and the filings were thus inaccurate over previous months — then we need to know. Falsifying statements is fraud."

"That's a very serious implication you're making," Harrison said. "Some might even call it reckless. There's no evidence of fraud. And an injunction would panic clients. You know, as well as I do, the minute clients can't access their accounts for even five minutes, the firm's toast."

"That's the firm's responsibility, not ours."

"Smythe's client base on the portfolio management side aren't the super-rich," I said. "Mostly we're talking about people's retirement savings. I would think your first priority as a government agency should be the welfare of the taxpayers who are our clients, not freezing the firm's bank accounts in order to pay OSC fines that so far are nonexistent."

"Jane's understandably upset by all this, especially when she's gone out of her way to cooperate with you," Harrison said, laying his hand on mine to calm me down. "In my opinion, you're being deliberately confrontational in an attempt to intimidate her. It's also counterproductive, since jeopardizing the firm means jeopardizing the firm's ability to pay whatever fines you might ultimately levy. We would vigorously fight any injunction or move to seize assets."

"And speaking of intimidation," I said, still too hot under the collar, "I didn't appreciate being hassled on the street by the two officers on Saturday night."

"Pardon?" Dilip leaned forward in his chair.

I didn't need Harrison's hand flattening my arm to understand I'd just made a tactical error.

"Let's pivot back to the immediate issue," Harrison said. "Since our time this morning is tight. In the fifty-year history of the firm, has Smythe Financial ever faced disciplinary action?"

"Not to my knowledge," Dilip said.

"Surely, their unblemished track record should buy them a fair-handed process and assessment."

"That's our approach with every investigation," Dilip said, standing. Harrison and I scrambled to follow suit. "We'll be at Smythe tomorrow morning. I suggest Ms. Browning be there by nine a.m., or ensure the corporate officers are. The decision will be made about an injunction pending discovery."

"Understood," Harrison said.

"For future reference," I said, grasping an imaginary stiletto in my hand, "Frank Smythe can almost always be found at the Toronto Club, if you don't reach him at the office. He eats there every night of the week, generally around seven p.m."

Dilip put out a hand to shake mine. "Thank you for making yourself available, Ms. Browning."

"One final question," I said. "The regulatory filings are signed by Bob and Johnnie?"

"And/or Alexandra Hanlon, chief compliance officer," Dilip said. "Any two out of three."

I'd stood outside the black-shuttered house, having retrieved Alexandra Hanlon's address from Bob's computer and pieced together the identity of the blond leopard. Alex, whom our next-door neighbor Scott reported meeting on our step. Alex, whom Bob had mentioned during that dinner in August, was trying to trace Johnnie's movements. Alexandra, the new compliance officer, through whose hands forty-five million dollars had disappeared.

"Bob and Johnnie have a shared legal responsibility?"

"Yes," Dilip said.

"And Ms. Hanlon?"

Dilip looked at me for an extra beat. "That would depend on a number of factors, including her contractual duties."

"Thank you," I said. "I'll need to rearrange a series of my own contractual obligations, but I'll see you tomorrow at Smythe."

Dilip left, closing the door behind him.

Harrison gathered together the paperwork he'd spread out all over the couch, shoving them into a too-small briefcase. "We've bought twenty-two hours to smoke out Bob. We'll drag him from his hotel room tomorrow morning if necessary."

I winced. "I'll call and leave him a message about the OSC."

Harrison shook his head. "Not yet. Let's see what his actions today tell us. In the meantime, instruct David to put the pedal to the metal on his investigation. Dilip Patel knew nothing about the RCMP hounding you."

"I noticed that, too," I said, mind spinning.

"Something else is swirling, and unless you believe in the existence of pretty unicorns, you're in more shit than we realize. Keep David digging and in the meantime go nowhere alone, take no calls from phone numbers you don't recognize, and for God's sake, if the president of Russia calls about an investment, hang up the bloody phone."

* * *

As soon as I stepped into my hotel suite, I knew something was amiss. The telltale signs were slight. Darren's white roses were on the wrong table, makeup I'd left strewn on the table in a hurry to get ready the previous day had been tidied, my laptop sat open. But they screamed volumes. I'd instructed the hotel I only wanted the room serviced every third day to change the towels and clean the washroom, otherwise I'd make the bed myself and maintain as much privacy as possible. This wasn't day three.

I texted David. A WTFF volunteer had dropped me off for a quick shower before a five p.m. emergency board meeting, which Jacob had convened with only three hours' notice. The driver was due to pick me back up in thirty minutes. I held my breath as I stood near the front door, trying to sense if anyone lay in wait beyond the shut glass doors that led to the bedroom and bathroom.

I dug into my purse for my keys and threaded them through the knuckles of my right hand, jagged points out. Softly, I put my purse on the floor, using it to wedge open the door. Danger may well lie in the soft plushness of the corridor, too, but getting trapped inside the hotel room alone with a predator was an even worse bet. At the very least David, or the driver, or someone from the hotel would be able to get in the room quickly.

I slid off my scarf. I rolled up my sleeves to expose the hard, long bone in the forearm that could be pressed against someone's neck as you went for the bridge of the nose, or the eyes, or the artery in the neck, with the other hand.

I moved forward, flinging open the glass doors and stepping back. No movement. Most of the bedroom was visible from this angle, although not the corners or the washroom that lay beyond. Dumping Darren's roses and the water onto the carpet, I grasped the heavy glass vase in my other hand. I looked over my shoulder into the hallway. Nothing.

Blessed are the meek: for they shall inherit the earth. Wrong again, Pastor Glass. I strode into the bedroom, roaring into the void, flinging open the closets, charging into the bathroom. God, it felt good to let anger momentarily course through my veins.

Whoever had been there was gone. To be doubly sure, I got down on my knees and checked under the bed; it seemed too low for a grown adult to fit under, but every thriller I'd ever seen taught me about the dangers of leaving that space unexamined.

I'd just gotten to my feet when David came through the door. He took one look at the keys in one hand, vase in the other, hair wild across my face. "Glad I'm not the bad guy," he said, small smile across his face.

I put the vase on the table and slid the keys from between my fingers. "One too many Charlize Theron movies, I suspect," I said, bending over to pick up the white roses. I put them in the garbage pail instead of back into the vase. "Someone was here but now they're gone."

"Any visual?"

"No. But I'm not wrong about it."

"I don't expect you are," David said. "I'll need to talk to hotel security to see if I can get access to any CCTV footage from the hallways and review their key protocol. In the meantime, what are your plans?"

"The driver's picking me up in fifteen minutes," I said, looking at my watch. "I need to shower and change. Then I have another round with Jacob, followed by the *State* screening. I'll be surrounded by people, but it's a giant free event so anybody could be in the crowd."

"I'll wait here until you're ready. Can the driver take you from the Jacob meeting to the screening and I'll meet you there?"

I nodded, heading for the bedroom. "I've got to go slip on a suit of armor."

"You're a warrior, Jane. Make no mistake about that."

CHAPTER
TEN

"Please, Jane, explain to the board your side of things."

The Dark Messiah leaned forward, an expression of strained patience on his face, his right hand slowly making a circle to be inclusive of the ten board members who'd managed, on short notice, to be around the table. They avoided eye contact by looking down, or away, or vaguely in Jacob's direction.

Once I'd received Jacob's notification about the meeting, I phoned the five directors with whom I was the friendliest in an attempt to gauge the pulse of the board. None took my calls. Finally, Carole, a filmmaker, texted me back. "I hope things will work out for you. Any communication from you needs to go through Jacob, as board chair."

"Are we on different sides?" I asked.

Jacob leaned back in his chair and folded his hands in his lap, with a sigh. "We'd like to have this difficult conversation in as nice a way as possible."

Don't show the cards until you have to. Bob-isms floated to the surface, even in his absence. "Of course. If you would elaborate on what specifically you want to discuss, or better yet, ask me specific questions, then I'll know how best to address your concerns."

"Talk to us about your decision to screen *State*."

"It was in the official program from the beginning," I said, without hesitation. "The program you saw almost two months ago before it was made public. When the injunction was filed against the film, we were forced to cancel the first screening. Once the film cleared, though, we scheduled a makeup one for ticket holders. The rumor mill is relentless, and the petition against its ban was in the hundreds of thousands. How could we risk alienating our audience base once there was no legal impediment? And given the appeal against the more restrictive classification was roundly denied, then showing it outside at a late hour was completely defensible."

I looked around the table, staring in particular at the board directors who were artists themselves. The silence grew more uncomfortable. "You directly ignored my request to wait until after the festival to screen it," Jacob said, hands now flat on the table.

"The final decision on programming is my responsibility, according to my contract. To interfere with that is to interfere with my ability to do my job."

"You don't have to lecture me on governance," Jacob snapped.

Henry, the lawyer on the board, put away the phone he'd been looking at under the table to follow the conversation more closely.

"Your report structure changed once you got promoted to acting CEO," Jacob said. "In that role, your direct report was to the board, and specifically to me as executive chair."

"Not according to HR. They say the only contract in place is the original one I signed as artistic director. I was temporarily appointed acting director in addition to that, not in substitution."

"Your duties as an employee are to take direction from me."

"I'm not trying to be difficult here, Jacob. But I think we need to be clear on the facts." *The best defense is a strong offence.* I took a deep breath for the filibuster about to come. "The best thing for this festival would be for you and me to work together to tackle any issues proactively. But in the past two weeks, you've withheld information and been deliberately obstructionist," I said, putting up my hand to ward him off as he began to intervene. "You conspire to get my staff to spy on me and report back. That kind of divide and conquer strategy contributes to a toxic work environment, which puts this organization, and its directors, at legal risk. You've done everything possible to destabilize and undermine me, and generally interfere with my ability to do my job."

Jacob pressed his hands together in front of them. "Do your job?" he said, articulating each word precisely as if he was biting off its end. "Our Chinese partners are threatening to sue the festival for breach of sponsorship contract because of your obsession with *State*."

"There's zero chance they'd win that," Henry said. "It's posturing."

Jacob flicked his hand in the air at Henry. "The board invested years in securing this sponsorship opportunity," Jacob said. "If the Chinese government start bad-mouthing the festival, how many others will fork over a seven-figure sponsorship deal?"

"Let's remember not everyone on this board was in agreement with the approach we took," Carole said quietly from the other end. "The programming team did what we asked, even after we let a sponsor buy our silence. We shouldn't compound that interference in operational matters by turning into Jane's overlords."

Jacob reached down into his briefcase and tossed some colorful printouts on the table, scattering them around. Even at the other end, I could make out the article that had appeared online a few hours earlier in the *Sun*, with a giant photo as the lead. I looked tired and frazzled and guilty of something, walking hurriedly next to Harrison. The photographer had framed us perfectly, the word "POLICE" on one side of us and "14 Division" on the other.

"Am I the only one worried about what a PR debacle we face?"

I shook my head. "It's a brutal image. I agree. But you know the party had nothing to do with us. I made an appearance after you promised Darren McGregor I'd join his dinner in the same building."

"You spent the night in a jail cell."

"In a police station waiting room. And I was cleaning up someone else's mess. Trying to limit any liability for the festival."

"You should have called me in to handle things."

I took a deep breath. And then dove in with both feet. "I followed our legal team's advice to stay out of Sophia Bennini's quest to get an extraordinary release permit for her husband," I said. "Why did Jacob ignore that and instead interfere in the political process for a man accused of rape? Is that how the board best feels our political influence should be used? Especially at a time when the organization is already facing questions about our willingness to make real change?"

There were audible gasps around the table. "Jacob, is that true?" Henry asked. "We didn't authorize such a potentially divisive action."

Jacob fixed me with a stare. "Sophia Bennini is threatening a defamation suit against the festival. She claims that Jane's lack of public defense of her husband, and the comments you made in the meeting with her and Georgina Koch, paint him as guilty. They are furious with you."

Henry shook his head. "Difficult to imagine she'd win with that argument."

"That's not the point," Jacob said. "We'd still need to defend any lawsuit."

Henry frowned. "We get heavily discounted legal. Any arts organization is going to deal with the threat of libel. We can't cave every time someone raises that flag."

"If it's his word versus her word, then the festival has no right to take a position," Jacob said. "I'd go as far as to argue that we owe the benefit of the doubt to the filmmaker we invited to the festival, not to an anonymous maid who's trying to drag his name through the mud and shake him down for money."

The tension around the table was at fever pitch. Sheila, the board vice chair, put up her hand. "If I may. Let's take a step back here," she said. "The issue of being a party to the judicial process around Alexei Panov is a board discussion, so we'll wait for the in camera. The *State* screening is tonight, so there's nothing to be done about that, but try to manage the fallout with the Chinese delegation, which I'm sure we agree is probably also best done at this level?"

But Jacob had no intention of giving up the counterattack. "The papers claim you have both a bodyguard and the city's most notorious lawyer in your employ. Why?"

"Women in public positions are exposed to all kinds of threats."

"Threats that our own security couldn't handle?" Jacob continued. "If there is a major threat we need to know. There are insurance issues involved."

"Thank you for your worry," I said, managing to keep my face straight. "Our security director recommended David. I didn't think it appropriate to divert organizational resources to deal with my own personal security. So, I hired a little private help this week. It's under control."

"Last night proves nothing is under control."

"I well understand your concern," I said, pinching myself under the table to keep my voice neutral. "Although we've surpassed fundraising and audience targets, it has been an unusually fraught festival, and last night's events with the police were extremely unfortunate."

"Unmitigated disaster is what those of us in the business would call it."

"I've tried my best to contain the fallout from an event we had nothing to do with," I said. "I've reached out to the police with an olive branch I hope they'll take. We're planning a free screening of films for police officers only. Tomorrow night. I'll keep you posted as things firm up."

"Crisis management is what I do, more effectively than anyone else in the country. But you've spurned my offer of free labor to effectively manage these fallouts. You put your ego above the needs of this organization."

Crisis creation, misdirection, and character assassination is what you do, I thought, but held my tongue.

"I planned to bring this up in camera, but it's better to be upfront, since we agreed we'd speak as one voice to Jane but seem to have splintered off in all directions," Jacob said, taking control again. "I table a motion for her immediate dismissal. I'm willing to put my own skin in the game. With the assistance of my staff, and that of the festival, I'll take over her responsibilities for the remainder of the festival. We need to cauterize this liability before it gets even worse."

This wasn't a surprise — I'd tried to steel myself for this eventuality as I prepared for the meeting. But my heart grew heavier as the seconds ticked by and the rest of the board remained mute. Finally, Sheila spoke up. "We have Jacob's motion on the table. Given the immediacy of the festival operations, I suggest we need to discuss it now, rather than let it fester as an open question in every one's mind. Are there any further questions of Jane before we request she leave for the in camera discussion?"

"Jane should be allowed to make a proper statement on her own behalf," Henry said. "We demanded her presence at short notice without explanation of the agenda, and this has been an ad hoc series of complaints, to put it mildly."

"Thanks, Henry," I said, taking a deep breath and launching in. "I've worked flat out for this festival. I take responsibility for the mistakes that have been mine. And for the successes. Jacob's confrontational stance means important issues we should be discussing now — including key media messages, or the relationship with the police and city hall, or even how to raise money from the potential new donors all the controversy has turned up — are getting lost. I think he's right, and the board needs to decide whether to continue with me for the second half of the festival or risk the destabilization of further change at this juncture. As a board, you were slow in response to the Paul DelGrotto situation, and firing me is going to raise your culpability again in the eyes of the media. That's your choice to make, but you need to make it quickly."

Jacob stood. "Wait outside," he said.

I walked into the hall, closing the door behind me. I sat in one of the chairs and closed my eyes, too weary to even look at email, cycling through a lifetime of decisions, mine and others', which had brought me here, faced with dismissal from the job I loved, possible legal charges against me, a partner hiding out in a hotel room, and being hunted for a reason I couldn't identify.

A half hour later, Sheila called me back in. The temperature in the room was at spa level, and the directors looked exhausted.

Jacob was gathering up all the *Sun* article pages that had skidded across the table.

"The status quo will remain for now," he said, without looking at me. "We'll have another board meeting at the end of the festival to take a more considered decision."

"Keep us in the loop as to how we can help, and any major exposures we have," Sheila added. "Especially legal. And know that we're paying very close attention."

I nodded at everyone and quickly left the room. Bob always said if someone is backed into a corner, they come out kicking. Leave someone a graceful exit whenever you could. That was never going to be possible with Jacob, but I'd failed in my attempt to inflict a death blow on him. He was a big game animal, unused to the leash the board had just clipped on him. He had nowhere left to go but for my jugular.

★ ★ ★

Larry Roth stood stock-still in the middle of Franklin Square, as if he owned it. Next to him, a fraction of his height and weight, was Yaya, the Chinese cultural officer, and Jacob.

"We cannot allow this journalistic distortion of Chinese society to go forward," Yaya said, speaking directly to Jacob. "Western forces are always trying to portray our society in a negative light, when really it is the Chinese solution that offers hope for the world."

"Are you fucking kidding me?" All two-fifty of Larry vibrated as he yelled down toward Yaya's face. He moved closer. Unphased, she didn't budge an inch. "Lee's one of yours. What is this 'Western forces' crap?"

There was no way that Larry, as *State*'s distributor, was going to let an audience miss his film. The more buzz the film generated at the festival, the better the box office gross would be when it opened in theaters. That Larry had scooped up *State* but passed rather vocally on *Shifting Dragon* was proving a bitter pill for Yaya to swallow.

"I ask you not to use profanity with me," Yaya said. "I know you desire to destroy Chinese moral models and replace them with American sanctimony and intolerance. But I cannot allow that."

Jacob dominated my immediate line of vision, a jack-in-the-box whose freakish smiling head delighted in my downfall. "This debacle should never have happened," he said, enjoying my discomfort.

"Debacle? Thousands of people at a screening is a fucking wet dream. What's wrong with you?" Larry yelled. "You're going to tell them the Communists wanna take away their movie?"

Every inch of the square pulsed with people. The barriers strained at the effort to separate those on the inside from those wanting to be. The Chinese machine had ramped up its anti-*State* campaign all day. Freelance propagandists charged with guiding public opinion had used a mass of fake Twitter and Facebook accounts to attack the filmmaker, the film, and the festival for programming it. Reviews of the film sprouted up, giving it one star or less. On a parallel track, posters of every film in the official Chinese showcase were blanketed on every street surface, and online outlets ran stories with pictures of happy Chinese people, smiling officials, and cityscapes full of construction cranes showing modern progress.

"Freedom of expression is by definition PEN's issue," yelled Beth Hollett, the executive director of the non-profit organization devoted to protecting writers from persecution, from my other side. She awkwardly clutched the front-page newspaper article about the screening as well as a four-foot picture of a Saudi Arabian journalist currently jailed for pissing off an authoritarian regime with his writings. "I'm only asking you to hold for a half hour while we locate a chair. The festival can't just waltz in and become the spokesperson for freedom of expression. We own it in this city."

"You want me to start my screening a half hour late, and you want carte blanche at the microphone. Am I getting that all straight?" I asked Beth.

"You said no film," Yaya said, staring at Jacob. "Do the honorable thing and cancel this screening; there's still time. If you refuse to respect our friendship, the minimum you must do is allow me to make opening remarks."

Yin Lee, State's director, stood immediately behind me. She wouldn't acknowledge Yaya's presence, but neither did she want to be left out of what was being decided.

"My assistant is nearby with one of his deck chairs." Beth wasn't giving up. "The traffic is a total nightmare, so he's ditched the car. He says five, ten minutes, tops. And I just need three or four minutes for my spiel. He's got donation forms, too. Can we get some room on a merch table?"

I could see Burt ahead of me with some crowd-control officers. I weaved my way between people, pulling Yin along as best as I could. I reached him just as he yelled, "Those cars are stuck there until this is over. But we need to get these people off the street. Get the film started now. The faster the show goes on, the faster we clean up this mess."

People jostled us from all directions. The crowd was quickly morphing into a mob scene, and I was momentarily stunned by the chaos.

Burt pulled me closer and leaned down to my ear. "Don't give those bastards on the board or Victoria any more ammunition. You got this," he said into my ear, concern nestled amongst the gruffness.

He pushed me toward the outdoor stage as he set off in the other direction. Yin reappeared, piercing my paralysis. Her eyes were so large in her face, and so solemn, that it kickstarted my rage at the unfairness of it all. "It floats, babe." Johnnie's trademark saying was out my mouth before I realized it.

I pulled out my phone. "Alex + Russians + OSC breathing down my neck. They attend Smythe tomorrow. I need answers," I texted as I got jostled from all sides, before slipping the iPhone back into my pocket.

Burt was right. The longer we delayed, the more chaotic this would become. The Falun Gong continued their slow, hypnotic movements, signs denouncing the Chinese government's harvesting of organs propped around the parameter. Chisel-featured men with wires down the sides of their neck made circuits around the square. Vendors sold food and bootleg movies, and the crowd continued to build.

"Showtime, Yin," I said. "Just focus on your film. Let me do the rest." We inched forward, Yin clutching the back of my shirt.

Marc-André, the venue manager, waited at the edge of the stage, tapping his fingers on his clipboard, all six-feet-six of his willowy frame telegraphing his unhappiness at the delay.

"Our run of show had us starting ten minutes ago," he said.

I sensed Yaya closing in even before I saw her. At the same time, Poet George had caught sight of me and beelined over from his place in the front row.

"I insist on accompanying you on stage to make comments," Yaya said, as they both reached me at the same time. I shoved Yin ahead of me up the stairs to the stage, while trying to block Yaya from following.

George read the situation and put himself between Yaya and the stairs. "I'm with Jane. No one else," George said.

"Really, I must insist," she said, but George was having none of it, and suddenly a swarm of bodies I assumed were his posse of poets showed up to help. I scrambled up the stairs behind Yin, catching sight of Larry Roth, dead center in the second row, arm around the shoulders of a very young woman I assumed to be the intern. Jesus.

The crowd began to clap as Yin and I stepped forward to the microphone. Car horns sounded everywhere; I chose to hear them as excitement from the captured drivers about to see a free film. Bob Marley came unbidden to me and I stood still for a moment, humming under my breath. Every little thing was not going to be all right but sometimes in life, you just needed to pretend. Otherwise, you'd swallow the whole bottle of Ativan and be done with it.

The Chinese security picked their way through the crowd to where Yaya was fixed in place by the scribes. George had determinedly made his way up the stairs, and now stood stage left, triumphantly part of the action. It was little wonder he kept managing to get himself published. There would be trouble to pay later with my board, the sponsors, the police department — pretty much everyone. I signaled to the sound technician to ratchet up the volume — Yin's gentle voice was going to need all the help it could get — and spoke into the microphone.

"Thank you all for coming. We're delighted to premiere Yin Lee's latest film, as we have for her previous four. Like all the great independent filmmakers, Yin's film seeps truth from every frame, using cinema verité techniques to reveal contemporary social tensions. Corruption happens in every country, within all systems of government, in business, even in the hallowed ground of NGOs and the arts community. People are people — sometimes we're capable of tremendous integrity, kindness, and compassion. Too often, we're diminished by fear or greed. To say that any one government is incapable of dark acts is to strip them of their humanity, and to turn a blind eye to the possibility of a better future. This film refuses to take that road."

My iPhone vibrated in my pocket. My hand twitched but stayed where it was, gripping the mic stand.

"This is not a documentary. It's not a morality film. I selected this film because it's a human story, incredibly well told. Ultimately, the judgment is for you to make. You're among the best and most dedicated film audiences in the world. I ask that you watch this film with an open mind, but first please give a very warm welcome to the writer and director of *State*, Yin Lee."

I squeezed Yin's arm as I stepped back.

"Thank you so much, Jane, for programming *State* at the festival. I am truly honored to be here. I've always been made to feel very much at home here in Toronto." Her soft voice carried like a caress over the microphone. "Jane took a great risk to bring you my film. She is a true friend to world cinema. I hope you like what you see. I tried my best to tell a story that regular Chinese people confront every day. Thank you for coming."

I nodded at Marc-André to roll the film. Beth, the now beat-up cardboard photo, and a man holding a lawn chair jostled with Yaya, the poets, and the Chinese agents at the bottom of the stairs. I darted for the other side of the stage, Yin in tow.

Marc-André had read my intention and waited for us. "You'll get a raise next festival," I said, as Yin and I descended down the back ladder, with his help.

"If you still have a job," he said.

"I need you to assign someone to protect Yin tonight," I said. "And tell my bodyguard where to find me."

Marc-André nodded, gave my shoulder a squeeze, and was off, Yin tucked under his arm, before the latter could finish thanking me. My phone vibrated again. Just as I reached into my pocket to fish it out, a hand touched my back. I turned. Alex stood so close her breath slid across my lips. She was dressed all in black; no wonder she managed to slip back here unseen.

"Hello Jane, I'm glad we finally have the chance to speak," she croaked in a hoarse voice. "It's been impossible to get access at your office or hotel."

I look around, but David was nowhere to be found. I pushed away from the stage aggressively, catching her off guard. "What happened to the missing forty-five million?"

"Excuse me?"

"Smythe Financial? Your job? The Office of the Whistleblower came calling."

Her voice hardened. "Why you?"

"Because you're all avoiding them."

"What did you tell them?"

"That's none of your concern. This is a family business, and you're not family."

Alex pulled out her phone and started texting. "You have the potential to really screw things up."

I snatched her phone; she tried to grab my arm to get it back. My self-defense training kicked in before my thought processes did. I pinned her arm behind her back and forced her to her knees, before either of us recognized what was happening. "What the hell are you doing?" she said.

Good question. I released her immediately and walked several steps away, focusing on my breath in and out until it became less ragged. I could hear the short ads for the festival sponsors finish and the main film start. *State's* opening sequence, where a police officer executes a business executive by shooting round after round into his torso, never failed to startle me. The film had been finished quickly for the festival, and the sound was uneven, much too loud and then much too soft. They were going to need to remix before a commercial release.

The film had competition for decibels, though. Slipping Alex's phone into my pocket beside my own, I turned around to see

Beth, George, Yaya, and a block of Chinese muscle in a suit all coming toward me.

I ran in the other direction toward a group of orange-shirted volunteers standing at the outside perimeter, all of whom were too busy staring into their own phones to talk to each other, or notice me, until I was virtually on top of them.

"Sorry to startle you," I said. "Don't let these people follow me. Call security if you need to."

Placing my bum on the edge of the plastic crowd barrier, I swung my legs over the edge and was off like a shot, weaving my way through one back alley after another until I found myself back down at King Street. I slipped into the first hotel I saw and sat at the back of the darkened bar, ordering a double gin and tonic.

I pulled both phones of out my pocket. My own had several missed calls and four texts, one of which was from Bob. "Do nothing until we talk. I'll call as soon as I'm able." Alex's iPhone, although password protected, showed her unread text messages on the lock screen. One was from Bob. "Come after 11. Room 4602."

CHAPTER
ELEVEN

DAY 6: *Margin Call*

"Let's walk," Harrison said, as soon as I exited the taxi in front of Smythe Financial.

I frowned, confused at his delay tactics. "You know I told Dilip Patel I'd be there at nine. It's quarter to."

Harrison put his arm through mine and pulled.

"I gave my word," I said, tired and grumpy and determined to see this through. "I'm not going back on that."

I'd grabbed my phone time and again during the wee hours of the night, determined to force Bob to tell me the truth. And time and again, I'd slumped back down in front of my laptop endlessly googling all the main players, looking for clues.

"Dilip Patel and his team are already inside, working away like little clams," Harrison said. "There's a Starbucks around the corner, David is meeting us there. Their espresso tastes like shit, but at least it'll be hot."

"But —"

"I don't want to have this conversation twice."

I kept quiet all the way to Starbucks, as Harrison filled the dead air with tales of his workout that morning, and how difficult it was to not fall off the treadmill as he read his email. David sat at a table near the door with three coffees.

"I found Bob at Smythe when I arrived an hour ago," Harrison reported, plunking himself down. "Along with Alexandra Hanlon. Uncle Frank completed the trifecta. All the c-suite execs managed to find their way back just in time, like good little homing pigeons. Except Johnnie. As far as I can tell, he's still a no-show."

"I see," I said, staring into my drink. After the disappearance and reappearance, the worries and the fears, the fact I was about to see Bob was discombobulating, and depressing. There was no putting the genie of our lives back in the bottle. "Did you speak with him?"

"Briefly. He asked to be told as soon as you arrived."

"Why did you hustle me away then?"

"The immediate legal obligation is being met by the firm's staff, as it should be. Beyond that, we can't risk Bob throwing you under the bus if they question you together."

I shook my head.

"This has been a week of things Bob would never do," Harrison said, blowing on his coffee to cool it down. "He seemed too anxious to see you for it to be lovey-dovey stuff, no offense intended."

"Wouldn't the point be to find out why?"

"How flexible is your time today?"

"Well, I'm locked in a death grip with my board chair to see which one of us is fired first. Larry Roth's cavorting with one of our young female interns. I'm being followed by the police for an unknown reason, and powerful Russians are breathing down my neck, so . . ."

Harrison peered at me closely. "What's with the sarcasm? That's not like you."

I wrapped my hands around the coffee. "Sorry. I didn't sleep well."

"Just because Bob says meeting you today is urgent doesn't mean it's urgent for you."

"Let's do it," I said. "We know that Alexandra Hanlon was in touch with Bob at his hotel. And now we know they've reemerged to deal with the OSC. But Johnnie's still AWOL, and all the other threats must be related to him."

"Johnnie is Bob's brother. Let him deal with it," Harrison said.

I shook my head. Bob was constrained by his basic faith in right and wrong; he'd never been able to grasp how Johnnie lay outside of that. I knew it intimately, like his father knew it. With Robert dead, the responsibility of reining him in could only rest with me.

"You really don't want to get in the middle of something you can't control."

"Control is proving an elusive concept."

"Would now be a good time to report what I've learned?" David asked.

"Saved by the bell," Harrison grumbled. "What?"

"I finally tracked down a phone number for Anna Basmanova. We spoke before I came here. She says she'll only meet with Jane, Johnnie, or Bob. I said that wouldn't happen until we knew what she wanted. She hung up but called back. She was brief with the details; I got the sense she was telling me the truth, even if it was a circumscribed truth."

"Which is?"

"Johnnie and an unnamed partner bought a sizeable oil lease in Kazakhstan. Anna Basmanova had a minority stake — I couldn't get her to reveal whether that was from the beginning or not, or even when the beginning was. But, at some point, she moved to assume control. Reading between the lines, I'd guess that Johnnie's partner was also Russian. The partner signed the legal paperwork, possibly because he had no other choice. But Johnnie bolted. She's most anxious to find him and make him sign."

"That has to be the missing Smythe money," Harrison said. "Which makes it Bob's problem."

I shook my head again. "Not that simple," I said, looking at my watch. "Let's go talk to Bob. We can game plan the rest after."

"If you insist. But play your cards close," Harrison said, staring at me for an extra beat. "As close as Bob has played his."

* * *

The same green eyes, the same wavy black hair, yet I found myself looking at him as if through a viewfinder. This man with whom I'd shared the minutiae of life over the past seven years; both news junkies, both avid film buffs and readers of poetry, both ready with a barbed observation but equally disliking cynicism. I had loved him from the moment I met him, through the inevitable disagreements and disappointments of an intimate relationship, through the unfathomable decisions that other people make, salvation from the paucity of emotion in my family or the rapacious nastiness of his.

Yet, here we were, and I could not bring myself to cross the floor to kiss him.

"What is it that you want from Jane?" Harrison asked, as we huddled inside a smaller meeting room on the floor above the

OSC-occupied boardroom. Harrison was taking no chances on accidental contact.

"This is confidential and sensitive family business," Bob said, ignoring Harrison to look straight at me. "It really would be better for us to have privacy, Jane."

"Curly, Larry, and Moe here are lawyers, right?" Harrison said, stabbing his finger in the air in sequence at three men in suits standing in a row behind us. "I'm Jane's lawyer, and I'm staying. David protects Jane, and Middle East knows to keep his mouth shut."

"Jane doesn't need protection from me."

"That's not what it looks like from the cheap seats."

Bob took a step in my direction. "Why do you need a body-guard?"

"You disappear without a trace. I don't know if you're dead or alive, I still don't know if Johnnie is. A strange woman I later come to recognize is Alexandra Hanlon stalks me. The securities regulator threatens to charge me. The list is long, Bob."

"I'm trying to protect you. What you didn't know couldn't be held legally against you."

"Plausible deniability is cold comfort when your world's gone down the shitter."

Bob ran his fingers through his hair, exhaustion written into every cell of his body. "I know exactly what you mean."

The intimacy of the movement threatened to annihilate the tension holding me up. "Please, can we get started?" I said. "I need to get back."

"I'm so sorry, Jane." The timbre of Bob's voice was soft in the way he used when negotiation was required. It was both genuine and contrived. If he'd been able to dictate what he needed done he would have, even if it was only about saving time.

"I've always been there for you in the past. I'd never have missed your big night if it wasn't an emergency," Bob said, voice more formal now.

"Let's sit down," I said, anxious to steer the conversation away from the personal.

"Tell me first why you have a bodyguard. Are you in physical danger?"

"He's also an investigator. I don't want to talk about that right now."

Bob looked at me sharply, while his lawyers arranged themselves at one end of the table. Harrison moved faster than I would have thought possible to sit me between him and David. But was protection from Bob what I needed? All I'd wanted since he'd disappeared was to have him back, yet here I was, seated between two men I hadn't known a week ago, squared off against the person who shared my life.

"What do you know so far?" Bob asked, sitting in a chair directly across from me. "I don't want to waste time on duplication."

"Just start at the beginning," Harrison interrupted.

Bob looked from Harrison, to me, and back again. Evaluating. "Johnnie disappeared a couple months ago," he said. "Didn't come to the office one day, nor the next. Didn't answer his phone or email. Uncle Frank was suspiciously edgy but denied any knowledge about where Johnnie might be. At first, I noticed the oddity, but let it go. You know Johnnie. Anything is possible."

I nodded but kept quiet.

"A little more than a week ago, the OSC sent us a registered letter notifying us that the last filing showed too little working capital. It was only when I went digging, I realized how deep the trouble was."

"The missing forty-five million in liquidity?"

Bob glanced backward at his lawyers.

"I'm a corporate director, Bob," I said. "You need to be transparent with me. If I'd learned what was going on directly from you, the situation would have seemed bad enough. But to keep a poker face while the securities regulator threatened me was difficult."

"They won't charge you with anything," Bob said. "But, yes, I can well understand your outrage. And, yes, there's forty-five million dollars missing in our working capital account."

"It's not like losing the emergency twenty from your wallet," Harrison asked. "Didn't anyone notice?"

"It wasn't until we started investigating that we fully understood the timing issues," Bob said.

"Wasn't there a sudden drop in the regulatory filings?" Harrison said.

"They went from fifty million three months ago to forty million two months ago. We'd bounced around some before, so that didn't trigger concern. But we filed the last report late, just before Johnnie disappeared. It showed only five million left." He paused. "We've been trying to find out the facts and come up with a solution before we sat down with the OSC."

"The genius plan was to avoid them by disappearing?" Harrison asked.

Anger flashed in Bob's eyes at Harrison's flippancy.

"I'm confused," I said. "The OSC told me that the regulatory filings were signed by you, in addition to Johnnie. If you signed them, you must have known the figures."

Bob paused again. "The truth is, our filings were so standard for so long, I pre-signed the blank forms instead of reviewing them every month. It's not uncommon in family firms like ours."

"But it's not legal," Harrison said flatly.

"No," Bob said. "It's not."

"You had no idea Johnnie was taking money?" I said.

"None."

"Did Alexandra Hanlon?"

"No."

"How can you be sure?"

"I am sure, Jane," Bob said, frustration seeping into his voice.

"As chief compliance officer, she should have reviewed the filings, yes? And she signed some of those forms, too."

"What about the Chief Financial Officer?" Harrison asked. "It boggles the imagination that Frank Smythe wouldn't have noticed the missing dollaroos."

One of Bob's lawyers coughed loudly. "At the end of the day, the responsibility is mine," Bob said.

"And Alexandra Hanlon's," I said. "Let's not forget the blond leopard."

"Excuse me?" Bob said.

There'd be time enough for that conversation, I needed to let it go for now. "Johnnie never met a gamble he didn't court, but I have a hard time seeing him as an outright thief. Did he mean to put the money back after his investment panned out?"

Harrison kicked me under the table.

"Investment?" Bob said, looking from Harrison to me and back again.

"We're guessing he didn't steal to buy a new Mercedes," Harrison growled. "Let's keep the forward motion. I don't want to waste any more of Jane's money than necessary on billable hours."

"I'll be paying any legal or security bills," Bob said.

"That's not your responsibility," I said.

"It would be my pleasure if you let me, Jane," Bob said softly, his eyes now dark green pools. "I don't want you to feel abandoned."

"What did your brother do with the money?" Harrison interjected. David was a stone on my other side.

"Johnnie's always been friends with the pump-and-dump mining stock promoters that hang around the edges of legitimate businesses. Freewheeling, heavy drinking. Bombasts. Johnnie thought himself one step above them, but that doesn't mean he didn't still get taken on deals from time to time."

Harrison leaned forward in his chair. "What deal did Johnnie get caught up in?"

"Perhaps you should be telling me."

There was no time for a pissing contest. "We know Johnnie was involved in oil leases in Kazakhstan," I said flatly.

"Jane, stop talking," Harrison said.

"Bob's not going to throw me to the OSC dogs, Harrison," I said. Bob looked offended at the mere suggestion. "And besides, I knew nothing that could have aided the OSC in its investigation, and I did everything I could when confronted by them, including arranging for them to be here today. Is that not true, Bob?"

"Of course," he said, without hesitation. "Jane had no knowledge of any of the business challenges. It's my responsibility not to have told her, and I will testify to that in any court."

A baby elephant snore erupted from Harrison.

"What we don't fully know," I continued, "is what happened to those leases, or why Johnnie disappeared. Do you?"

David glanced at me sideways when I didn't mention Anna Basmanova. I trusted Bob but I'd absorbed his admonishment about keeping one's own counsel, and so I would, until the full view became clear.

"This is what I know," Bob said, picking his strategy carefully. "Apparently, Johnnie got roped into an oil lease deal in Kazakhstan. Billed as the next big development project, massive deposits just waiting to be brought to the surface. They needed a foreign partner with the money to underwrite expensive test drilling to prove the geologist reports. And Johnnie needed a Russian partner to hold title on the leases — a legal requirement there — and to help grease whatever local hands needed to be made pliant."

"David's been investigating since the OSC descended on me," I said. "We understand Johnnie had an original partner, but we don't know who. He eventually sold his stake, presumably for less than he paid for it, in what I've learned is a typical scam. We don't know what happened to the money, or where he is now. Do you?"

"We haven't been able to trace that, either."

"What's being done to deal with the working capital account deficit? I mean, the OSC are here. What have you told them? How much real trouble are we in?"

Bob looked at his lawyers; all were silent. "Johnnie's no dummy," I continued. "If this is a scam any fifth grader could spot, how did he ever fall for it?"

"He's a gambling man. And it wasn't his money."

I shook my head. "Too simple."

Bob got up to pace, taking a full minute before he spoke again. "Eight months ago, I offered to buy out Johnnie's stake in the firm. I'd have needed major financing to swing it, but I couldn't see any other way forward. I was no longer willing to work with him. He refused. I was left with a decision to make. If I fired him, would Uncle Frank and the other shareholders go along? I'd need two-thirds majority on a major decision like this, according to the shareholders agreement. If I couldn't split the vote and they all voted as a bloc to back my brother, then it would have been me out the door, not him."

"Ah," I said, but nothing more came out right away. "You didn't think to tell me?"

"I didn't want to put you in a position of choosing loyalties."

"Haven't I been doing that for seven years?"

Bob frowned. "I was also worried about your responsibility as a director to the best interests of the firm. I didn't want you to have conflict between that and your natural protection of me."

"Because you were going to go what you were going to do, regardless?" I said.

"I wouldn't put it that way," Bob said, sitting back down. "You were right. Johnnie and me working together was always going to be a mistake."

"Did he mean to make a lot of money fast and use it as a leverage tool with Uncle Frank to force you out?" I asked. "It's hard to imagine he did it just to pad his own bottom line."

"I don't know," Bob said. "The explanation disappeared alongside him."

I rooted around in my handbag for some candied ginger to quell the rising nausea. "What we need to focus on now is any legal risk to the firm, and us," I said. "There's no issue with the client accounts, right?"

"Of course not."

"That's what I told the regulators. Johnnie wouldn't steal from people."

"Except me," Bob said.

I nodded. "Except you."

Bob leaned forward to take my hand. "I would have preferred to tell you this privately," he said. "But that doesn't seem possible, so here goes. I've sold forty-nine percent of the firm to make up the forty-five million in missing capital. We need to sign the paperwork in the next twenty-four hours."

I sat back, stunned. Half Bob's birthright, gone. If the money couldn't be traced, or Johnnie had blown it, that was the only solution. But the ramifications of what that meant to Bob, and to the Smythe family, was staggering.

"Jane needs to sign as a board director?" Harrison asked.

"Yes."

"You can't possibly expect her to review paperwork on a deal so monumental for the firm and sign in a day," Harrison said. "We're going to need to add an M&A lawyer to her team."

"This is our only suitor, and the terms are as favorable as we're going to get. The buyer, a London-based private bank I've worked with before, is willing to advance the capital tomorrow, but not until there's a signing of the first round of paperwork."

"This timeline is insane," Harrison said, pounding the table.

"I'll sign."

"As your lawyer, I'm advising you to step out of the room with me right now."

I stood up, prompting everyone else in the room to get to their feet. "I understand, and appreciate very much, that you're trying to protect me, Harrison. But the basics here seem clear. The firm needs to replace the money or be shut down. It's Bob's company to sell, not mine." I looked at Bob. "But the paperwork has to be reviewed by my own lawyer. We'll make sure that happens expeditiously, but I will not sign blind."

"That's reasonable," Bob said. "We'll find a way to make it work."

The day before I was to marry Johnnie, Robert showed up unannounced and dropped a twenty-page prenuptial agreement on my desk. Flustered, I asked for time to find a lawyer to review it, pointing out the clause just before my signature attesting that I'd had adequate access to independent counsel. He reached for my hand, his icy fingers strong around my knuckles, and forced a pen into it. "To be precise, it says you have the option of having your own lawyer review it. And you've waived that. I promised my son there would be no issues here, and there won't be. You and I understand each other, don't we, Jane?"

I shook away the memory cobwebs. "You will also need to give me an affidavit attesting to the expedited time pressures I'm under to review this deal."

Bob nodded. "For sure. But there is also another layer you should consider if you haven't already."

"What's that?"

"The likelihood that Johnnie's will names you as his beneficiary. The last version he filed with our corporate lawyers as addendum to the shareholders' agreement did. I have no way of knowing if he made a subsequent version."

Harrison whistled. "That makes this a very different kettle of fish, indeed."

I was silent for long enough that Harrison put a hand on my shoulder. "Are you okay?"

For more than a decade, Johnnie had been a nettle in my side, reminding me, whichever way I moved, of his presence. Permanently embedded, or so I thought. Once tempted, forever held to account. Could Johnnie really be gone without my sensing it? "Do you actually think he's dead, Bob?"

Bob moved around the table to come stand beside me, taking my hand in his. My peripheral vision narrowed as we looked at each other, grounded in a complicated history that no one else could fully comprehend. "No. But I think we need to consider the possibility."

I ran my thumb across his palm, massaging the base of the third finger, a spot where I knew he carried a lot of tension. "What are the deal terms?"

"Fifty million for a forty-nine percent stake. In a normal situation, the firm would be worth one-fifty, so a forty-nine percent stake should get just south of seventy-five million."

I kept massaging. "A bit of a Boxing Day sale."

"We're not in the best leverage position."

"What about management terms?"

"I need to stay for a minimum of five years to prevent the risk of asset flight. Beyond my five years, I sign a noncompete for another five on top of that. You and I will both retain our positions on the board, in fact we're required to for stability perception. They'll appoint two directors, and we can name the tie-breaking vote, but it can't be Johnnie."

"If he shows up, he'll be banished altogether?"

"I've been transparent with Sandringham & Co, the new partners, about what's happened. No one wants to see Johnnie criminally charged. Beyond personal issues, the firm can't afford the reputational risk with clients. But he can't ever set foot in Smythe again."

I nodded. "What else?"

"Uncle Frank is out. As CFO, he's gotta wear this and besides, the partners want their own guy in here to have a bird's eye view on the financials. If any of the forty-five million disappears or is used for anything other than to replenish the working capital account, their forty-nine percent automatically converts to fifty-one, and they seize control. Ditto if the OSC charges me personally, or if we find ourselves in trouble again with the OSC within a period of two years. Any fine levied by the OSC for this incident must be paid by me personally, not by the firm."

Harrison whistled again. "Pretty steep terms. But not, I guess, unreasonable given the situation."

"And the OSC," I said. "Will they play ball with this arrangement?"

"I don't know." Bob squeezed my hand. "I hope, in acting quickly, they'll understand the problem is contained. Charge us a whopping big fine — their bonus pool is based on revenue generation just like everybody else's — but leave us in business so we can pay it. And for the sake of our clients, which we'll argue, not that they really give a damn about that."

I took a deep breath. "I think you've done the very best possible in an extremely difficult situation. I'm so sorry you're losing half the family firm."

"You know I never really wanted it."

"Regardless."

"There's some comfort in thinking of it as forfeiting Robert's half and keeping Clare's."

The mother who told me once upon a time, so vividly, that she could imagine drowning him. The mother who moved halfway around the world and never came back because losing her son in whole was preferable to losing the fight for his soul, as she saw it.

"I've got to go back now, Bob," I said, picking my words very carefully. "Tell me when the paperwork is complete, and in the meantime, we'll line up a lawyer to review it on an emergency basis."

"I don't want Jane meeting with the OSC," Harrison growled. "I insist on that. If it becomes legally necessary, then we'll comply, but not without representation and not without full briefing in advance."

"Agreed."

"How much of Johnnie's own wealth would be liquid?" David asked, startling us all after having been quiet the entire meeting. "How well could he disappear if he's serious about it?"

"I don't know exactly," Bob said. "I don't know what his personal nut is."

"Nut?"

"Run rate. His expenses. Johnnie's salary and bonus would be somewhere between one and two million a year, depending on performance. But he lived large, so his nut could easily have been half that, or more. There's also his inheritance to factor in, which had some cash and property gifts — although most of the equities were Smythe Financial shares and those are in his account with us, which is frozen. I have no way of knowing how much he's spent, or how badly he's leveraged, or what private deals he did on the side. I'd guess, with very scant real data, that his net worth is somewhere in the neighborhood of twenty-five million on paper. No way of knowing what debts he has against that."

Harrison nodded repeatedly, as if he was running a calculator in his head. "Presumably any money Johnnie realized from selling the oil lease stake he'll have hidden offshore somewhere," he said. "And who knows, maybe the rest of his liquid assets are there, too. But anything based here — at the very least, his properties, investments, and cash bank accounts — would mean coming up for air to access. Which means leaving himself vulnerable to the Russians, your anger, and any potential legal charges."

"About sums it up. Look, we should get back downstairs before the OSC folks come looking for us. They're very diligent," Bob said. "I'd like a private word with Jane first. No business, I promise."

"Please give us a few minutes," I said, remaining silent until everyone left the room.

And then there were two. The silence crystallized in the now-empty room, as if ice shards hung in the spaces warm bodies had occupied only moments ago. Bob reached out to touch my face.

"Nothing but the collapse of the firm, and the potential of criminal charges, would have kept me from your side, on your opening night," he said.

I sighed, placing my palm over his. "This is really not a conversation we can have right now."

"Are you okay?"

"It's just too big a question." I stepped away from his hand, and then forward again to leave a ghost of a kiss on his lips. "Do what you need to do to take care of things. I'll do the same. And if we get through it all, we can sit down and talk."

"If?"

I smiled, squeezed his hand, not trusting words. I grabbed my purse from the chair but paused. "The festival has a new major donor — Darren McGregor. I don't trust him. He says that Smythe handled the sale of his holding company a decade ago. I don't like being in the dark with a man like Darren. Can you please have someone pull the paperwork and send it to me, so I can level the playing field?"

"Consider it done."

I left to find Harrison and David waiting for me near the elevators. I was silent until we were back outside in the sun. "Thank you for that," I said.

"Are you okay?" David asked quietly.

I gave a small, tight nod, as I tried to swallow the sorrow blocking my esophagus.

Harrison enveloped me into a moist bear hug just as a silver BMW pulled up. "That's my Uber," he said, getting into the car. "Keep me in the loop, and for God's sake, Jane, don't do anything precipitous."

"What now?" David asked, as the car pulled away.

"Let's walk for a bit, and then I'll call the driver to pick us up."

"It was more of a global question."

"I know," I said, walking for a few minutes before I spoke again. "The OSC don't seem to know of the RCMP's interest in me. I don't feel confident that eliminating the securities regulator threat eliminates the other ones, do you?"

David shook his head. "Given what we've learned, my gut instinct says that the silent second guy is CSIS or some equivalent the public doesn't know about."

"The spy agency?"

"Intelligence services," David said. "Would make sense if Ms. Basmanova's connections, or activities, extend well beyond the legitimate business world."

I shivered. "What has Johnnie dragged us into?"

"You know where he is? I noticed your hesitation when Harrison asked the other day."

"Maybe. Not for sure," I said. "But call Anna Basmanova and get the paperwork she wants signed. Make no promises, tell her it's a real long shot at best."

"Why do you need to be the person to deal with her?"

"Bob's got enough to handle. And besides," I said slowly, "in some ways, Johnnie is more my responsibility than his. They may share their father's DNA, but I understand Johnnie's survival instinct in a way that Bob never could. It's low and cunning and ugly and desperate. Bob is cut from another cloth."

David looked at me. "So are you."

I looked at him without reply, tears very close to the surface.

"I was in the Israeli army, Jane. I understand doing what needs to be done. And I'm a pretty good read of character. You and Johnnie are worlds apart."

I began to walk as briskly as I could, not trusting myself to speak. David followed. "What do we tell Harrison?" he asked.

"Nothing. He's an officer of the court, I don't want to limit my options," I said. "If you feel uncomfortable with that, I can deal with Anna myself and keep you out of the loop."

"This isn't my first rodeo," David said. "I won't knowingly break the law for you. But that still leaves us lots of rope."

"Comforting visual image."

David laughed. The rarity of it made me jump. "Ms. Basmanova will have eyes in the back of her head, and probably eyes following her. And you will, too."

"Remember, too, Anna and Alexei Panov seem to be connected in some way," I said. "He implied she launders money."

"That would certainly explain the interest of the RCMP."

"Panov's hardly blameless himself. I can't believe Jacob got him sprung, back out there to menace other women. If there's a way to hand him back on a platter to the police, let's add it to the to-do list."

David smiled. "I'll do what I can. And if there's not?"

I thought about the maid whose identity I didn't know. About my mother. Clare. Hazel. The laws that did diddly-squat to protect them, established rules only a jackboot on their necks. "Then I'll find some other way. He's going to be held to account for his sins, so help me God."

CHAPTER TWELVE

Huntley lay curled up in a fetal position on the hospital gurney, head resting on aluminum bars, wrists covered in white gauze, soft brown eyes pleading, "Save me, please save me." Docile, just like my mother.

I told him I'd be right back and walked into the hall to call Devlin's manager. I started in before I was sure whether it was a live person or voicemail. "Devlin's had her fun with the video. If it doesn't stop, I guarantee you that the only parts she'll get offered will require her to boil rabbits or murder small children. No amount of UN work is going to rehabilitate her image when the PR people I hire are through."

I slipped the phone back in my purse and turned to find Samantha had followed me out of the room.

"You understand, right, that they're only surface wounds?" she said. "There was no chance of him doing any harm to himself?"

"You said he was our waif to look after. It's a cry for attention, let's give him some."

I went back into the room and held Huntley's hand. I was too tired to grasp why he triggered my protective instinct, other than I didn't like bullies, and it was now clear in a Devlin vs Huntley match which one had the power. "We've got your back," I said. "Tomorrow, you'll meet a publicist who owes us a very large favor. Franny will scrub your image clean like the little rat-dog warrior she is."

Huntley kissed my hand softly, without opening his eyes.

I turned to Samantha. "I need to get back to the office to meet the intern, and then to the cinema. Burt's been calling. Find someone to take care of Huntley tonight, and I'll meet you there, okay?"

She nodded. I strode out of the hospital, making sure to touch nothing. Months spent with my mother through all her radiation and chemotherapy appointments had instilled in me a profound wariness of the superbugs that clung to the surfaces of hospital wards. My faithful driver waited in a white SUV with a giant RBC bank logo on its doors. I'm sure Victoria would soon add sponsor logo tattoos on staff as part of the donor cultivation strategy. I slipped in the front and laid my head back against the seat.

"Find some opera, will you? *Don Giovanni* or *Così fan tutte*. Full volume. Let's have some sturm und drang to drown out our own."

★ ★ ★

The intern looked impossibly young. Her résumé said she had an MA and a certificate in screenwriting so she had to be twenty-four or twenty-five, only fifteen years younger than me. But parenting my mother and sister had accelerated my aging process, and my cells felt impossibly old and tired sitting across from her.

Valerie was carefully dressed for the meeting, formal in a fitted linen suit, defiant in four-inch pumps and bright-red lipstick.

"Why am I here, Ms. Browning?" she asked, sounding exasperated at my silence. "You know I don't work for the festival, correct?"

"I understand you quit yesterday. I'm curious as to why that was."

"Do you do an exit interview with all the festival interns?"

"Not all of them cuddle with high-profile, married producers."

"I see," she said, yanking at the bottom of her suit jacket and then smoothing out her skirt. "I'm over the age of consent."

"It's not the legalities I'm worried about. It's you."

"I'm not sleeping with Larry."

"But I guarantee you, he wants you to."

"Lots of men and women do. It doesn't mean I acquiesce to them all."

I nodded. "Fair enough," I said. "Have you heard the rumors about Larry's behavior with women? I'm not accusing him of anything specific, as I have no firsthand experience."

"But you're willing to slander his character anyhow?"

I paused to look at her more closely. "I'm not just talking about infidelity here, Valerie. The rumors are much darker than that."

"What exactly?" she said, yanking at the jacket again. "He's very smart, you know. Reads everything. I've never had that insightful a conversation with someone about Toni Morrison."

"I see how that'd be enthralling," I said. "Especially given how powerful he is. But he's also aggressive. Controlling."

"Not with me."

"Yet."

"Are you trying to scare me?"

I sighed. "No, I'm really not. But if he offers you a job at his company, don't take it." Her face fell behind the bravado. So, he had. "If he asks you to meet at his hotel room, do it downstairs in a public space instead. If he expresses interest in a screenplay you wrote, get a lawyer to write as many possible exits into the contract as possible. Do not trust Larry Roth."

"Why? Tell me specifically. Otherwise, it's just one more rumor in an overactive rumor mill that churns out as many lies as it does truth."

"I'm already saying more than I should, and I trust that you'll keep our conversation in confidence." I didn't trust it at all, but this was an impossible situation. I had no concrete details, no proof, only dark suggestions whispered between women in the industry over drinks, quietly, the fear of a libel suit or vendetta ever present. *Larry has a temper. You don't want to be alone with him. How do you think she got that part? It's not like she's the best actress in town.*

"Part of our internship program is to make connections for young programmers and filmmakers with established industry people," I continued. "Would you like the festival staff to do that for you?"

"People who have worked with Larry, you mean?"

"Yes."

"And you plan to stack that deck with people against him?"

"People who can tell you what to expect working with him. I can't prejudge that, since I've never worked with him myself."

"I'm not one of your employees anymore."

"The program's in place, I'd like to see it utilized."

Valerie stood. "I really have to go now, Ms. Browning. I appreciate your concern, and I'll think about it. But, really, I think you're worrying for no reason. I feel positive about the future possibilities. I can take care of myself."

"Please think about what I said and give it some consideration. My door's always open to you."

★ ★ ★

Closing in on one a.m. The cinema for our kiss-and-make-up police screening night was jammed.

Tasked with the challenge of coming up with pro-cop films, our programmers chose a list of older Hollywood movies. *Die Hard, Lethal Weapon, The Untouchables, The French Connection, The Fugitive, The Departed.* We scrambled to clear the screening permissions; the marketing department tweeted teasers from films under #ShowTheBadge, turning up the dial on the distributors to agree.

A private event in a festival full of private events, but I still worried about public perception in a city where opinion on the role and funding of policing was divided. The event went a long way to rebuilding a relationship that was essential to WTFF's operations, but my built-in distrust of state authority made me twitchy.

In a light soft enough to hide the stains on the walls, the cinema's ornate architectural features looked elegant. It cost us a pretty penny to bump the venue's regularly scheduled screenings and to underwrite a three-month free membership extension for their patrons denied entrance, but it enabled us to put "Private Screening. Support Our People in Blue" on the outside marquee.

The audience of police officers took a sharp turn younger after shift change at midnight. The later crowd was looser, edgier, louder — out for a good time, holding on with a death grip to their big Slurpee cups. I figured there was more than Orange Crush in there, but since it was their business to keep the peace, I kept my own.

"I sometimes think life is a reality show, and we're all just one step away from making the loser edit," I said to Samantha, as we watched an officer pushing sixty try to horse around with his younger colleagues in the vestibule. Everything felt amplified — the jabs in the ribs harder, the frenetic movements more pronounced, the laugh more brittle. Something to prove, and no grace left by which to do it.

"Working with folks who pass him by," she said. "That's difficult."

I glanced at Samantha. She'd been at the festival her whole working life, in on the ground floor when the festival was small and mighty and growing with it to end up as executive assistant to the CEO. Now she found herself working for a female, younger boss who had different ideas on how the place should run.

"Divorced, at least once," she mused. "Probably his infidelity, maybe his wife's, too. She was lonely because he worked late shifts or angry because she suspected he was a cheater, or maybe he pushed her against the wall more than once. He worries about growing old alone. Already the adult kids are closer to their mom. She helped them with their homework, he dropped in and out of their lives, either absent when his friends or lovers called or needy of attention when he dropped back in. It's going be state-assisted living for him when he's infirm. That police pension won't cover the services he'll need and the kids won't be lining up to change the Depends."

"That's a cheery narrative," I said, laughing. Had Samantha always had this wry sense of observation?

"All the people who get divorced in midlife. No idea how hard it is growing old with dignity when you're alone. Divorce decrees should come with a warning sticker: opportunity cost higher than you think, hook back up as soon as you can. Don't be the lonely seventy-year-old woman in a hotel room rendezvous with your married lover, aging breasts strapped into a corset and the curtains kept closed to disguise the chicken skin of your underarms."

I peered at her more closely. "I realize I don't know anything about your life," I said, curious but not wanting to be intrusive.

"No, you don't," she said.

David appeared, saving me from having to respond. "There's a commotion outside," he said. "You need to come smooth it over."

"What's going on?"

"The boys in blue outside having a cigarette aren't taking kindly to interlopers trying to get in."

"We said only festival staff and volunteers working this event, and those carrying a badge," Samantha said, looking decidedly animated as she weighed in. "We have to honor that."

"It's your board chair and shiny new donor," David said.

"Yikes." I pushed away from the wall that had been holding me up. "Why on earth are they here at one in the morning?"

"I'd imagine party-hopping, since Darren McGregor looks three sheets to the wind. One of the officers asked him to walk a straight line, which didn't go down well. If he's not careful, he'll get a drunk and disorderly ticket."

"Victoria will have kittens if McGregor ends up in a jail cell," Samantha said. "Jacob should know better than this."

"I'll go, you stay here and keep everything under control," I said, wanting to maintain the slight thawing that had begun between us. "I'm a little worried about how much these police officers have drunk as well, and the potential for conflict inside and out."

"Will do," she said.

As David and I approached the front entrance, the crowd of bodies began to thicken. I knocked on the barn-door back of the man in front of me a few times before he finally turned around.

"No shield, no entry," he said.

"I appreciate that," I said. "Though I'm not actually trying to enter. I want to see if I can help solve what's happening outside."

"No exit, no re-entry."

I admired his ability with simple slogans. "That's slightly less obvious," I said. "Though I am so pleased that you've taken a real sense of ownership over the event."

He squinted down at me, trying to focus through an alcoholic haze. "You're the festival lady."

"Indeed. And I believe my board chair and biggest donor are the ones causing the fuss outside. I want to talk to them and explain the situation."

He opened up a channel with the sweep of one arm, and body-surfed me through. "No shield, no entry," he repeated. "That's what we were told."

Darren McGregor embraced me as soon as I appeared on the sidewalk. I disentangled myself and said, "This is a surprise. Night on the town?"

"Reacquainting myself with my old home," Darren said, his face flushed with booze, sweat beads around the edges of his hair-line and the top of his lip. This was one selfie that wouldn't be making it into his Instagram feed. "This lady's gotten a lot leggier since the last time I lived here."

"Wonderful that you're having yourself a good time."

"And now we're here to party with you!"

I looked at Jacob for help, but he was busy being deliberately mute and blind. "I'm turning into a pumpkin soon — it's an early start tomorrow — so I'm going to leave you to enjoy yourself, two gents out and about, and catch up with you another time."

"No time like the present to seize life!" Darren exclaimed, seizing my arm and moving a few more feet toward the entrance. "I'm with her," he yelled forward to the group of police officers whose semicircle effectively blocked the entrance.

I looked over my shoulder. Jacob had now moved a few feet away, phone to his ear, back purposely turned. The bastard. "I'm sorry, Darren. Tonight is the festival's mea culpa for the crap the police went through two nights ago. We agreed from the beginning that absolutely no one without a badge would get in," I said, speaking quite low so the officers couldn't hear. It had the unfortunate effect of prompting Darren to move even closer to me. "They're adamant about being in control of this screening. I don't want to put you in jeopardy by trying to take you across the line. You might well end up with some kind of ticket, or even detention given the mood they're in."

Darren's hot breath assaulted my cheek as he spoke. "Then let's go to my penthouse suite and have a drink," he murmured, his hand now pulling me in another direction. A gruesome two-step but at least we were moving away from the theater and not toward it.

"That's really not possible," I said.

Darren was taller and stronger but I dug in, back and neck convulsing at the yin of my legs rooted into the pavement and the yang of my upper body being pulled toward him. A guttural yelp of frustration rose out of my chest; it pierced even the willful blindness of Darren. He swung back against me, and in the nano-second where I processed that he was now standing right against me, his hand slid up between our bodies and grabbed my left breast, fingers deliberately and painfully tweaking my nipple. His eyes were half-closed like an Evangelical preacher in a revival tent, face raised toward the hallelujah all the while sizing up the crowd out of the corner of his eye to see what the evening's take would be.

Later I understood that David was the force that pulled me backward; I thought revulsion had propelled me. The endless caffeine on a stomach with little nourishment arose in protest of the sweaty paw print on my white silk shirt and the powerlessness it implied. I leaned forward as my body hurled everything I had.

My ears registered sounds of disgust as heaves in my stomach geared up for a second round of bile only, which hit Darren's back as he turned to leave. A handkerchief was shoved into my hand, and I used it to cover my mouth even as my stomach continued to roil in disgust. David pulled me away and through the crowds. The police line of scrimmage opened to slip us through, and I managed to pantomime that we should go upstairs where it was private.

As soon as the washroom door came into sight, I headed for it.

"I'll make sure no one but Samantha gets in," I heard David say.

Inside, I tried to wash away the mascara running down my face and rinse the vomit residue from my mouth. When Samantha entered, she stopped at the sight of me in the mirror, then took a step forward before stopping again.

"Thank you for being here," I said.

Her eyes kept glancing down at the vomit on my shirt. I took it off and threw it in the garbage.

"There's a theater full of police officers that can take a statement," she said.

"You understand the complications that would ensue."

"This is how men get away with sexual assault."

"I know. And I'm still not going there. Can you please ask David to give me either his T-shirt or his suit jacket if it's got enough buttons not to gap?"

She disappeared back out the door and I stood looking at myself in the mirror. I'd gone for comfort versus fashion with my favorite bra, and my chest looked as pale and tired as the rest of me. All I felt was shame.

CHAPTER
THIRTEEN

DAY 7: *The Dark Knight Rises*

"You need to address Sophia Bennini's Twitter rant," Lina said, as the senior team huddled around the table in my office, newspapers scattered across its surface.

It was Lina's job as vice president of marketing and public relations to brief me before I went into the day's press conference. I was anxious about the media grilling I was sure to get — there were just too many open sores — and about the previous night's encounter with Darren McGregor.

"You haven't done a media stand-up since the *Bin Laden* party, so expect stray questions about the photo of you and Harrison Wex outside the police station, in addition to *State* and the police screening from last night," Lina continued. "It's been uniformly positive coverage of the latter two. Yin Lee's sound bites about Toronto and you are also getting a lot of play. Torontonians do love to have their city validated by others."

Victoria flicked her hand dismissively at a headline that read "WTFF Love-In," accompanied by a photo of large crowds sitting on the ground of Franklin Square watching *State*. "The Chinese delegation is still irate. Yaya Hui calls me all day long looking for us to denounce the film."

"Would it help for me to have a meeting with her?"

Victoria snorted. "A dollar short and a day late."

There was no point giving further oxygen to Victoria's gripe. If it wasn't this one, it'd be another. She was disliked by most of the staff but her success in fundraising for the organization made her invincible with the board. Instead, I pointed to another photo: Larry Roth with his arm around the intern. "Any media questions about this?"

Lina scoffed. "Media question the Vagina Vulture?" Apparently, a nickname I'd uttered once had made the office rounds.

"Unusually high levels of foreign press stayed past opening weekend courtesy of Panov's dick," she continued, turning over a page in the *Sun*. Once he'd made bail, Panov slipped the name of the maid in an interview with a European news outlet, which refused to adhere to the publication ban on her identity. The media swarmed her apartment building and the picture of her fleeing in a tracksuit, hair in disarray and eyes full of panic, would be haunting her forever.

I just shook my head. What words were there? "Look. I'm going to speak bluntly here. The last six months have been enormously difficult. Paul's suspension and the activities that led up to it have caused a great deal of internal friction in our organization —"

"Alleged activities," Samantha said, cutting me off.

Lina bristled. "It wasn't alleged for some of us."

"Either way he's gone, and we need to stop talking about it publicly," Victoria said. "It's the first question I get on every fundraising pitch. We're taking a real hit on our closure rates."

Lina slammed the paper shut. "If TMZ hadn't published those pictures, the board would have kept their collective head up their ass, and he'd still be here harassing women."

"The internal investigation is supposed to get to the full truth," Samantha said, refusing to look at Lina.

"I'm telling you the truth." Lina stood, pushing back her chair in anger. "You can either believe me, or you can call me a liar. There's only two choices."

"Okay, look," I said, standing up, too. Burt and Isaac, senior programmer, the only men in the room, were so still they looked like ice sculptures. "I'm sure the investigative report will have recommendations including how to reconcile the divisions going forward. The tension we all feel has only been exacerbated by the extreme workload of the past few months. Alexei Panov's arrest, the debacle of the *Bin Laden* party, the controversy about *State* — none of that drama has helped."

"Ain't that the truth," Burt said, cautiously putting an oar into the conversation.

"I want to say, on a personal note, that I appreciate all your hard work especially at such a difficult time. Stepping into this role has had its challenges, and I'm grateful for the support you've shown me. We still have another five days left in the festival; let's come together to make sure we deliver for our audiences and our filmmakers. Then we focus on solving our internal problems. Publicity is a double-edged sword, depending on whether you seek exposure or privacy. But one thing is for sure: media companies are a business, and their first priority is their market share. They'll wrap it up in pretty language about public service, but there's nothing pretty about their tactics."

"We're running late at this point, Jane," Samantha said.

"One minute, Samantha," I said, slipping my phone into my pocket but deciding to leave my purse where it was. I waited until everyone else had filed out. "I know you were close friends with Paul DelGrotto, and that this transition hasn't been easy for you."

She paused to look at me closely, I suspect looking for sarcasm. "No," she said finally. "It hasn't."

"You're the closest to me, I'm sure you've gathered I have things in my private life also playing out. They're confidential for others, so I'm not at liberty to share them. I want you to know that I do appreciate your work and your help."

We were both stunned by my little speech. Samantha's unwillingness to believe Lina and the other women involved angered me. If it didn't happen to her, it couldn't have happened. At the same time, she was sincerely dismayed by the situation. And while I'd dismissed her complaint to Jacob earlier as inherited animosity from the Paul DelGrotto situation, I had to admit that I'd been doing everything I could for the last several days to keep her out of the loop, while hiding that fact.

"I also need to feel that you're loyal to me," I said. In for a penny, in for a pound. "We all know that Jacob's not playing straight. I suspect he's been asking you for surreptitious information in order to build a case for dismissal."

Her eyes widened at my bluntness.

"It's my intention to be here for the long run," I said. "At least as long as Paul, if not longer. I hope you and I continue to have a chance to work together. I think, ultimately, we could make a good team."

With that, her eyes narrowed again. The subtext was clear. Gamble against me by helping Jacob and chance being found out. Or stay neutral. If she thought she'd see any loyalty from him, she hadn't taken the opportunity fifty years of living had given her to read human nature.

I paused to give her space to respond, but she stayed quiet. "Okay then, I'm ready to go."

A wall of noise hit me as we entered the hotel conference room. As Lina had so aptly summed it up, Alexei Panov's ascendant body part meant the entertainment press had stuck around past opening weekend, instead of leaving once the biggest films had premiered. Given recent events, the media ranks had swelled to include news journalists, making it a record crowd for a Wednesday news briefing.

"How nice to see you all still here," I said, taking the podium. "To what do we owe the pleasure?"

Laughter rippled through the room. A whack of hands immediately went up, reporters already yelling out questions.

"Let me tell you what I know upfront," I said. "And then you can ask me the same questions over again repeatedly, until we all get bored and leave."

"Did Alexei Panov rape the maid?" a strident Australian accent called from the back of the room.

"We're more than halfway through the festival, and we're so delighted that more than two hundred and fifty thousand people have participated so far, either as ticket buyers or in our free events, up ten percent over last year, itself a record year. We're grateful for their interest in the power of film to build community, and their support of the festival."

A collective groan went up. I continued on, undaunted, even when the same voice called out the same question. Repeat talking points often enough and eventually they find their way into the coverage. And once archived in the great big digital warehouse in the sky, the narrative about my first festival as CEO would become sticky.

"It's a banner year so far for film sales, enabling both emerging and established filmmakers to get their films to market, and of course the two hundred million dollars of economic impact the festival brings to the city is unsurpassed by any other artistic organization."

"You want to send out a press release, put it on the newswire," someone called out.

"While we celebrate the record attendance and highly successful launch of the free forums, we are, of course, watching developments on several fronts very closely."

"Did Alexei Panov rape the maid?'

I paused for a moment. "That's a matter for the courts, not a film festival, to determine."

"The missus is pretty pissed at your failure to defend his character."

"Sophia Bennini requested that the festival interfere in the judicial process to obtain a temporary release for her husband from prison, where he was remanded on criminal charges. The festival's lawyers felt the appropriate route was to have her lawyer either seek expedited bail or the extraordinary ministerial permit she ended up attaining."

"You're saying the festival didn't play a role in Panov's temporary release?"

"I didn't, and none of my staff have reported to me that they were involved."

"Did your board chair?"

"You'd have to take that up with him directly."

"What do you think? About Panov's guilt?"

"I think it's time for the next question. Anyone?"

Fiona Pyper, a *New York Times* journalist in the front row, put up her hand. I nodded at her.

"The festival seems to have a problem with sexual aggressors," she said. "First, the former CEO is caught taking photos of his genitals and sharing the little gems. Then a featured director allegedly attacks a maid. And if that wasn't enough, there's Larry Roth harassing your interns. It's a disturbing pattern, Jane."

My stomach sank. So much for the press not being willing to take on Larry Roth.

"We've discussed the Panov situation. As you know, Paul DelGrotto is on leave from the festival, and the board has hired an independent investigator to do a fulsome review. Any questions you have on that situation are better directed toward the festival's board chair, Jacob Ray. I am in no position to comment." I nodded at a journalist in the third row, who stood up to ask his question.

"Mark Jones, *Bloomberg*. The *Operation Bin Laden* party is rumored to have cost the city more than a million dollars in emergency response. Will the festival be compensating the city for the costs?"

"Before we move on, I have a direct follow-up for Jane," Fiona Pyper interrupted. "As a woman, are you willing to accept anything less than zero tolerance when it comes to sexual harassment and sexual assault?"

But *Bloomberg* was not prepared to cede the floor to the *New York Times*. "We have moved on," he said. "What is the festival's responsibility —"

"Don't talk over me, Mark," Fiona said, now also standing. "The *Sun* is running a picture online of Larry Roth leering at a young woman, arm around her shoulders. The caption says only that she's the festival's intern. Is it part of an intern's responsibility to keep Larry Roth happy?"

"Of course not," I said, chafing at being restricted from what I really wanted to say. "Nor is she currently an intern with us."

"You don't see anything wrong with this picture?"

It was a complete minefield, no matter how I answered it. In the split second where I hesitated, the Australian accent from the back piled on. "Rumor has it that Roth hightailed it on a plane back to New York this morning. Why?"

"I'm afraid I don't know," I said truthfully. "He bought a record number of films in the first half of the festival. Distributors and producers rarely stay past opening weekend. You know that."

"You're obfuscating," Fiona said. "I'd like an answer to my original question. Does the Worldwide Toronto Film Festival give safe harbor to sexual predators?"

By now, the room was increasingly tense, and I was hyper-conscious of the cameras and microphones. I raised my hands in the air. "Calm down, everyone. I'll stay here as long as possible to answer your questions. I haven't spoken with Larry Roth so I don't know when or why he left Toronto. I did speak to the young woman in the photo yesterday. She says Roth is a professional contact. I've encouraged her to take part in our program where we introduce young professionals to a wide range of industry players, in particular women who can act as mentors for her."

"As to the *Operation Bin Laden* party," I quickly continued, trying to change the dial on the questions, "it was an independent party, which we did not sanction or organize. Nevertheless, I've apologized publicly and privately to Toronto Police Services. As you know, we held a special evening last night for police officers to thank them for their service to this city."

A reporter I didn't recognize at the back put up her hand, and I nodded. "Why have you hired Harrison Wex as your lawyer?"

The abrupt change of topic startled me, and I hesitated for a split second. "Did I ever tell you the one about the lawyer, the festival director, and the actor who bumped into each other in a police station waiting room?"

They were smelling blood, though, and I wasn't going to get away lightly. Hands pressed in air, and I answered one question after another with a version of the truth it was expedient to share.

Finally, I signaled that time was up. "I'm sorry, that's all the time we have for this morning."

I headed for the door, as questions continued to rain down on my back. David waited outside in the corridor and hustled me toward the elevator.

A voice from behind me spoke up. "Ms. Browning, I would like a word, please."

There are the grace moments in life when you're able to ride the wave just ahead of the piper, and there are others still when debts must be paid. I turned to find Yaya lying in wait, waving her phone at me.

"You believe in provocation, is that not true?" she said, frowning.

"Not unnecessary provocation, no. Or provocation for its own sake. I don't believe in that, either. I do believe in standing up for one's principles, though."

"Releasing this media announcement on the final day our delegation has to enjoy the festival is standing up for which principle exactly?"

I reached, without success, for the phone. "Our marketing team puts out the releases," I said. "I don't approve them in advance. I'm afraid I don't know which one you're referring to unless I can see it."

Yaya brought the phone closer to read, pushing her glasses up on her forehead to see better. It was oddly endearing. "Roth and Partners are delighted to announce they have acquired the worldwide rights to *State*, a film about massive corruption and criminality within the Chinese government," she read out loud, pausing to frown at me with the last sentence. "'Yin Lee's the next Sofia Coppola,' says Larry Roth. 'The first top-flight director mainland China has produced, the government wants to kill her because her film gives a black eye to the Communist party.' Roth added that the film will open in four thousand screens across North America, with a marketing budget of twenty million dollars and an all-out push during award season."

I whistled, which did not help. Four thousand screens were beyond opening wide; it was taking an Uzi to the distribution chain. Twenty-five to fifty percent of a film's production budget was the rule of thumb for marketing; he essentially matched it dollar for dollar. Larry was taking the fight with the Chinese personally.

"I'm sorry for the timing, Yaya," I said. "Press releases are put out regularly about acquisitions — our market is one of the main attractions of the festival, and so we pump good news about sales. Timing is coordinated with the distributors who have bought films but had I or Victoria known in advance about this, we'd have asked them to wait a day until your delegation left."

"It is better not to be betrayed by a friend."

"Betrayal?" I sighed, without meaning to. "You think this is betrayal?"

"Everyone has an agenda. Even Ms. Lee."

The quiet intensity in Yaya's face moved me. Before I'd seen her as someone doing her job, but I'd missed important tells. The little bumps under the skin between her eyebrows that pulled together. The flecked brown of her eyes that got darker, deeper with emotion. The frustrated abruptness by which she shoved her hair back and pulled her glasses back down on the bridge of her nose. This was not just a duty for her, not an abstraction. She felt personally the dishonor she read in the film.

"Thank you for your partnership on this showcase, Yaya," I said, chastened by my previous failure to read her accurately. "It's been enormously successful. I don't agree with Larry's comments — I think the quality of filmmakers in China is outstanding, and I'm delighted to have had the opportunity to really show that to our city and the world."

She shook my hand politely. "I doubt we will work together again."

"I hope that's not true," I said. "Perhaps there will be a middle ground to be found."

She left, and David stepped toward me. "Can we take a few minutes and go up to the roof deck?" I asked. "I could really use some distance from people. Let's take the stairs. I'm tired of elevators, too."

"Sure," he said. "Do you believe what you said about middle ground?" he asked, as we began to climb up the service staircase toward the roof.

"You're from the Middle East. What do you think?"

"One side always comes out on top. The rest is just window dressing."

"Yeah," I said, as we emerged onto the roof. "Power sharing is a ridiculous term. You've got it, or you're fucked. Any update on Ms. Basmanova?"

David patted his jacket pocket. "Got the paperwork from her this morning."

I shivered. "I guess the game's afoot."

* * *

I'd only been back in my office an hour catching up on emails and telephone calls before Sophia Bennini sauntered through my door, Samantha trailing behind. I stood and moved around my desk to shake her hand. Ms. Bennini didn't bother to look down or outstretch her own.

"You will have heard the news?"

"What news?"

Sophia's snide little laugh made me feel small and insignificant. "The ludicrous charge has been dropped. We're leaving soon for Russia."

I looked at Samantha, who nodded slightly. "Just found out."

"The woman who made the false accusation is being deported," Sophia said.

I blinked. "Pardon?"

"Her visa had expired," Samantha explained. "She filed for an extension while she awaited permanent status, but there'd been a delay in it coming through. She was supposed to leave until it was granted but she didn't. It's an expensive flight to Bosnia and back again. The prosecution won't proceed with charges like these if they can't guarantee the main witness will show up."

"This poor woman is about to get kicked out of the country because she reported a rape?" I said.

"That, in a nutshell, is the problem," Sophia said, her tone both formal and mocking at the same time. "You believed this maid over my husband, without any facts. We will boycott this festival until you are fired. And we'll bring our considerable resources to hurrying that along."

I took several steps closer until I was only inches from her face. It was a pleasure to watch her eyes open slightly — as much as they were able to with all her plastic surgery — in surprise. I reached out to caress the ultra-soft leather of her purse, drawing out the tense silence. A tin whistle played itself rat-tat-tat along my veins. "The problem, in a nutshell, is that you can afford to pay eight thousand Euros for a Birkin bag and the woman has to get on a plane back to a country where that amount would be several years' income. And *you* think *you've* been wronged. Get the fuck out of my office, and my city."

"Jane —" a shocked Samantha said, but I held up my hand to stop her. Sophia Bennini took an involuntary step backward. It was the slightest signal of intimidation, but one had to take one's small victories where they came.

"Let me ask you one question, Ms. Bennini," I said. "Do you intend to stay with your husband in the long run?"

Her expression had not altered with my outburst. "You look down on me because I am not some quivering woman surprised at her husband's infidelity." Her voice dripped with scorn. "You know, yes, that all men can and will commit infidelity if given the means? They'll make up the motive on a dime, and believe their own justification, too, if they're the type inclined to look for absolution. Really, it's just a primal act of fucking to them. My husband bought sex with the chambermaid because she was there and willing, and then she decided to up the ante. He's had affairs, yes, we all know that from the papers. There is always some woman willing to believe the crumbs of attention a man throws her way means something more than it does. Some phone calls here, supportive emails there, maybe he even takes her to the theater, makes time for a luncheon near Christmas, and voilà, she creates fantasies. Really, she is less than casual sex on the side; just one more obligation to manage once the sense of trespass is gone. Who is to be despised more? The man who cannot face limitations or the woman who's the fool?"

I walked back around my desk and sat down. "It's strangely a relief to have my own realism dwarfed by your worldview."

"I am not a quitter and won't be perceived as one. I'll leave my husband in my own good time."

And with that, Ms. Bennini was out the door.

CHAPTER
FOURTEEN

Johnnie stood before me, French cuffs of his shirt stained, the signature Valentino pants rumpled beyond recognition, a caricature of himself. I'd seen Johnnie drunk many times but, still, his air of dissolution stunned me.

"I should have known you'd be the one person who could find me," he said, pulling me into a clumsy embrace, even before I had the chance to step over the threshold. I willed myself to stand still, one of his hands smoothing my hair, the other holding a wine bottle that bounced against my legs.

We stood for as long as I could stand it, Johnnie rocking us from side to side, me trying to keep us from tipping over. Finally, I pulled away.

"Are you going to invite me in?" I asked. "I desperately need a cup of tea."

Johnnie waived the wine bottle unsteadily and pulled me into the penthouse suite. "I can do better than that."

"Tea is all I want. I'm dead on my feet from the day."

"You know how much I hate to drink alone."

"It's past midnight. I need some help staying awake."

"You always were such a sanctimonious cunt about alcohol."

A sharp left into taciturn — Johnnie's specialty when blotto. He pushed me down onto the sofa, and went into the kitchen for another glass, settling down far too close to me upon his return. "How's the new gig?" he asked, filling both glasses to the brim.

"Chaotic," I said. "How are you?"

Johnnie waived his wine glass around the room. "Oh, you know. Surviving."

I took a sip of wine. All the lines I'd practiced on the way over to dig out information without raising his ire dissipated as I wondered what opioid of hope had ever deluded me into thinking that marriage to Johnnie would end any way other than disaster. "I know about the missing money from Smythe," I said flatly. "And about the Kazakhstan oil leases."

Johnnie went still. There was no way of predicting which way he'd go, and I knew better than to rush into his silence. Minutes passed as I looked around the Yorkville condo where we'd lived out our short cohabitation, completely unchanged in the decade since I'd packed feverishly one morning and bundled all my suitcases into a taxi. Three years later, when Robert died, Johnnie moved back into the familial home to keep an eye on Hazel, whose drinking was getting worse — there was no happiness dividend for her in widowhood, the bitterness was too entrenched. Johnnie gloated at the time that he'd sold the condo for double the original price and wasn't it too bad our prenuptial agreement precluded me from profiting.

With Johnnie missing, I'd asked David to check title on the condo. Johnnie continually tested people's loyalties, but not to escape them. More than anyone I'd ever met, Johnnie craved the familiar, clung to it as a way to keep his worst tendencies in check. I thought he might well have held onto our matrimonial home as a bolt hole from Hazel when the need arose.

The ownership came back as a numbered company, and I came knocking on the door.

"The OSC leaned on me," I continued. "I hired a private investigator to find out what was going on."

"Why you?"

"The entire c-suite executive went vamoose. I was left holding the bag."

"Did you tell them where I was?"

"I didn't know for sure."

"You wouldn't have anyhow. Betrayal is best contained within the family, right, my darling? No outsiders need apply."

I stayed silent. Words were hand grenades, and I didn't yet know which one I needed to detonate.

"Bob's gone?" Johnnie asked.

"He's back now. I saw him yesterday morning."

"Where was he?"

"Raising money to replenish the working capital account before we were shut down. Or charged. Or both." I paused, considering how much it was expedient to tell him. "It's best to talk to him directly. I don't know very much about that side of things."

"Sainted Bob. Dastardly Johnnie. And the Prize." Johnnie took a long drink of his wine glass. "Some things never change."

"We're not quite *Casablanca*," I said, giving in and drinking more of the wine myself.

"Aren't I the hunchback of Notre Dame to you?"

"Spare me the hypocrisy of playing the victim, Johnnie," I snapped, slipping far too easily into the rhythm of our ill-suited marriage. "We were both there, we both got the T-shirt."

Johnnie barked a laugh, jumping up to pace. Fighting to regain an upper hand on himself.

He finally sat back down again. "Has my brother raised the money?"

"Yes."

"How?"

"You really need to discuss it with him."

I reached to pick up my wine glass, just as Johnnie's hand darted out to grasp my wrist, sending the contents flying. Even hammered, he had a strength that belied his thin frame.

"Please don't," I said, the humiliation at having to ask almost as overwhelming as the pain. Anger coursed alongside fear in my veins but the muscle memory of forced acquiescence was older, and more entrenched. Johnnie's eyes filled with tears, but still his fingers dug into my skin. He'd spent his life failing to live up to everyone's expectations and I was the only one there to pay the price. "You're hurting me," I said softly.

Slowly, the hold began to lessen. "You know I've never wanted to do that," he said.

"I know."

"You're the only person I've ever loved."

"I know."

"I wasn't a perfect husband, but I gave your mother a better end of life, didn't I?" Johnnie said quietly. "The final tally shouldn't be in the red, darling."

I sucked in air. That wound was still open. "Thanks for that."

We both sat slumped against the couch. At least ten minutes passed in a silence so complete that only a thousand dollars per square foot could buy it. I started to doze off, waking only as I felt Johnnie take the leaning glass from my hand. My eyes opened as I felt his lips on my fingertips.

"You lit up my life the moment you walked into that television studio," he said softly, running my fingers along his cheek. "All day I'd think about you, barely able to wait until I could see you next. At night I'd be on fire, hearing your laugh, imagining your hair across your breasts as you climbed on top of me. Every ounce of me wanted you in a way I'd never known. Or have ever known since." He put my hand back in my lap, patting it. "But you were never really mine. You deliberately moved left when I moved right. I'd move closer and you'd withdraw. I always knew that your ambition was too big to be contained by that town, but you lacked a way out. I was happy to be the ladder, I was happy to take care of your mother, and you. Hell, I thought it was my privilege to do so. To provide the kind of security you'd never had." He paused to wipe away tears. My hand instinctively reached out to his misery. "It wasn't until I finally came to understand it was unlikely a woman in her twenties would have those kind of fertility problems, that I realized just how indifferent you were to me after all."

We sat, holding hands, defeated, until his tears subsided and he pulled away, using his shirt sleeve to dry them. He leaned back, arm slung tiredly over his eyes.

"How did Bob raise the money?"

I didn't want to go there, but it couldn't be avoided. "He sold forty-nine percent of the firm to a British private bank."

Johnnie's body curled in upon itself, like a hedgehog. I put a hand on his back, only to feel him scurry away from the touch. Dawn would break in a couple hours, and I'd be officially declared missing in action. At best, I had one ask of Johnnie and time was running short. Why he took the money and what he did with it was less pressing to me than eliminating the threat Anna Basmanova posed to us all.

"Anna Basmanova is stalking me," I said, trying to use my calmest voice. "I'd like to talk to you about that."

He stiffened.

"I didn't know she was Anna Basmanova at first," I said. "Just an unbelievably attractive woman with an accent I couldn't place appearing out of thin air. Said you had unspecified business interests in common. That she wanted the four of us to get together for a drink. I refused to commit to that, or to give her any information, which provoked her further. I didn't learn the wider truth until David tracked her down."

"David?"

"My investigator and bodyguard."

"Bodyguard?"

"I felt threatened."

Johnnie sprang to his feet and began to pace again. He tucked his shirt in, running his hands through his hair to comb it.

"Though, to be fair, she didn't make an explicit threat to me," I continued, standing up myself to stretch out my back. "She just oozed threat somehow."

Johnnie headed toward the kitchen. "Trust me, Jane, I know exactly what you mean."

I followed, perching on a kitchen stool as he put on the kettle and set about making us a pot of tea. His mercury seemed to be dropping.

"She said you were in a business deal with her and got cold feet, and she's looking for either you or Bob," I ventured, once I had a cup of tea in my hands.

"Bob has nothing to do with this."

"She's hedging her bets on any way to reach you."

"She's a smart cookie," Johnnie said, filling his own teacup. "He'd give me up before you would."

In the starkness of the overhead kitchen lighting, in the middle of a night, some truths were difficult to sidestep. Johnnie was right, and he was wrong. I walked back to the living room and pulled an envelope from my bag, returning to perch once again on the kitchen stool.

"What is it?" Johnnie asked, eyes precisely focused for the first time since I'd arrived.

"I have not, and will not, tell Anna Basmanova, or anyone else, where you are. Ever." I didn't want to spook Johnnie further by mentioning the RCMP.

"But?"

I slid the envelope across the black granite of the countertop. "She wants you to sign the legal paperwork on the oil leases. The 'or else' wasn't articulated, but she doesn't mean to give up."

Johnnie drank his tea, eyes holding my own, over the rim of the cup. His expression was inscrutable. "I'm afraid that's not possible, Jane," he said finally, taking his cup to the sink. "She will need to be incentivized another way."

I nodded. "Do you have any ideas on how?"

"That's up to others to take care of."

"What others?"

"There are authorities, even in Kazakhstan."

"What does that mean?"

Johnnie came around the island to sit on the stool beside me.

"You have no horse in this race," he said. "Keep this David close for the next few days, and by then Anna will understand there's no advantage to intimidating you."

"I don't understand what you're saying," I said, slamming the cup down too hard on the granite counter. The noise vibrated through the narrow space between us, a sine curve measuring the pressure.

"It means," Johnnie said very softly, "I never agreed to sell my stake. She intimated Dimitri, my original partner, into selling his shares to her at a deep discount. But not me. She's powerful and very dangerous, have no doubt about that. But I can't legally sign away the rights to something I no longer own."

His face was so close, the inadvertent spittle from his mouth landed on my own. It was a minute before I pieced it all together. "You flipped your stake in the leases to a third party that's not Dimitri and is not Anna Basmanova?"

Johnnie touched his finger from his nose to my own.

"Who?"

"I'm not telling you that," he said.

"Do you know Alexei Panov by chance?"

"Leave it alone, Jane. Too much information will put you in danger."

"Danger?" I said, despite the voice inside compelling me to back off. "That's a funny thing about all this. Everyone thinks they're protecting Jane by keeping her in the dark, when all they're really doing is putting a fucking noose around her neck."

"It's not a good sign when you start talking about yourself in the third person."

"I know that," I snapped, spinning the other way off the stool and making a beeline for the front door. "Goodbye, Johnnie."

My shoulders were grabbed from behind, and Johnnie turned me to face him. "Don't walk out on me again."

I swallowed, hard. Johnnie could go from deep emotion to intense anger to unspeakable gentleness without warning — or vice versa. A calm before a storm, or a storm before a calm.

He pulled me close into an embrace, mouth to my ear, hand on my hair. "I just need to hold you one last time."

Tears formed in my eyes, both from the futility of our intertwined lives and from the pressure of Johnnie's hand pulling my head back, stretching the neck muscles too far. His breath was hot against my neck. "I will always love you more than life itself," he whispered.

"I know."

"Come away with me."

I watched the dark sky through the window, lit from behind with the streetlights and cityscape. I started to move my knuckles up my body, ready to go for his eyes. "You know I can't do that."

He pulled my hair back so suddenly, and so furiously, that the pain took a moment to catch up to what was happening. Then the tsunami overtook me. Ears roared from the sound of blood vessels popping, or maybe it was me howling, or Johnnie raging. I tried to realign my neck by falling backward but the iron vise of his other arm held me in place, like a grotesque caricature of the old-fashioned dip and kiss. All I could do was look at the tortured regret in Johnny's red, runny eyes as everything faded to black.

When I came to, the sun was higher in the sky than I needed it to be. How many times had I lain in this bed staring at the climbing or setting sun, listening to Johnnie sleep off a foul mood, caused by alcohol or depression or both. He hated waking up alone when an "incident" had occurred, my presence the bulwark against the inevitability of facing whatever damage he'd done in his rage. I learned how to tell time exactly by every shadow the sun and moon made. But this time, I knew the bed beside me was empty.

The pain was too great to stand up. I rolled slowly off the mattress, misjudging the speed so I landed on my knees, not my feet like I had planned. The underwire of my bra dug into my chest cavity, and the elastic band of my underwear was twisted but still on my hips. Invaded in other ways, but not this.

I crawled on all fours toward the door until I reached a chaise longue, which I used to drag myself up, pausing so as to not black out a second time.

I made it to the kitchen, putting on the kettle to boil. Johnnie had carefully laid out all the accoutrements of tea-making for me on the counter, but the air of abandonment was unmistakable. He would not be back. I slowly walked the other rooms, using furniture and walls for support, thinking about the collateral damage people are capable of inflicting on those they claim to love.

Johnnie had tidied up. The suitcases I'd noticed near the door were gone. It was so fastidiously clean that the envelope on the kitchen counter stood as a glaring exclamation mark. I took the time to make my tea before I pulled out Anna Basmanova's legal paperwork and flipped to the last page.

Unsigned.

CHAPTER
FIFTEEN

DAY 8: *Sex, Lies, and Videotape*

I lay facedown under a sheet on a fold-out massage table in my office. Seated on a stool somewhere near my head, Samantha read my emails out loud while Liuzhen's acupuncture needles and massage techniques tried to soothe the strained muscles and torn ligaments. More than once I called out in pain, causing Samantha to pause.

Every time a poker of pain pierced my right eye, the anger I'd been squashing down since childhood threatened to bubble over. Always, a man using me to serve their own needs. Always, a stick to beat me into it. Pastor Glass's thundering sermons a veneer over my father's secrets, cowing my mother and wringing bitter concessions from me in order to protect her. Johnnie's sense of inadequacy instilled by a tyrannical father and indifferent mother, his desperate desire to consume me in compensation for it. Darren McGregor and Jacob Ray, for whom I was a powerless nothing, disposable and insignificant.

A knock at the door. Footsteps shuffled, and then shuffled back.

"You want to be dressed for this visit," Samantha said.

The hands working on me stopped. "Time's up." Liuzhen's eyebrows knitted together in worry as she helped me turn over. "Your body's soaking up the massage like crazy but too much is no good. You'll feel worse later if we continue. I'll come back tomorrow."

"Jane, did you hear me?" Samantha said.

"Jane's ears have stopped working," I croaked.

My throat was still too bruised for easy speech. David's round robin of the staff desks and purses had turned up an alarming range of synthetics including Percocet, Vicodin, and OxyContin. I'd swallowed two Tylenol 3s and resisted asking who owned what. The Tylenols dulled the pain but didn't eliminate it.

That morning, after picking me up in a little parkette near Johnnie's condo, David stripped down and got into the shower with me. I'd closed my eyes against his nakedness, as he washed my tangled hair with tenderness before getting me dressed and bringing me to the office. The fact I'd slipped out of the hotel room to go see Johnnie without alerting him was left unmentioned.

"Well, then Jane won't hear me say she should report whatever bastard did this latest piece of work on her."

I clutched the sheet to my chest, as I attempted to roll over. Using a pejorative word to describe someone was completely unlike Samantha. I interpreted the effort as a sign of solidarity.

"Liuzhen can help me get dressed. Who's waiting?"

"Your lawyer."

"Please tell him I need five. And Samantha — thanks, I really appreciate your concern."

Samantha helped me stand before going out into the hallway. I managed to get my underwear on, but fastening the bra was beyond me. Liuzhen stepped forward. Modesty had no role in our relationship.

Once she'd assembled me, neck collar and all, Luizhen packed up the table, promising to return the following day. As soon as she opened the door, Harrison barreled inside. "Middle East was right to call me. Who the fuck did that to your neck?" he yelled.

"Come in," I said. "I'd rather the office didn't hear our entire conversation."

"You're wearing a big white collar and moving like you're ninety. Trust me, Jane, it's not inspiring confidence." Harrison watched me closely as I eased my way into a chair at the small conference table. "Do you need coffee?"

"That's very thoughtful of you," I said. "Breakfast tea with milk would be great."

Harrison turned to David, who had appeared behind him. "Get one of those minions to bring Jane tea," he said, then unceremoniously shut the door. "You're alone with your lawyer. Tell me who did this to you. David said you refused to tell him, although I have my suspicions."

"It's got nothing to do with the Russian. I'm not in danger of it happening again."

A knock at the door. "Just a minute," Harrison yelled. "It shouldn't have happened the first bloody time. But I need to know who the combatant was, and you need to talk about it. Trust me."

Harrison's puffy, gruff face oozed concern. Despite myself, tears rolled silently down my face. Unanticipated kindness delivered tiny cuts to my defenses. It took me a few minutes before I could speak. "Johnnie."

He took my hand in his. "Not dead, then?"

"No."

"You didn't want David to know because you don't want to have to answer questions about it."

"Yes."

"Do you intend to tell Bob?"

"No."

"Because he'd kill his brother?"

"That, too." I paused to wipe away the tears with a handkerchief that Harrison handed me.

We sat in silence while I tried to force the tangents of memory back into a little metal canister, so I could snap the lid shut. "I think he's left the condo for good," I said. "But I don't want to have to choose whether or not to give up his location. To Bob or the police. To Anna Basmanova or the people following me. Can you understand that?"

Harrison nodded, slouching back in his chair. "People like to make snide comments about my high rates," he said. "And listen, I get it. My largest source of income is keeping the Hells Angels out of jail. But I do a lot of pro bono work, too, primarily for a women's crisis center. Time and again, when these women describe to me what terrible thing's been done to them, they show empathy for the asshole who hurt them. They worry what people will think. They're embarrassed they couldn't stop it. They're so willing to believe they contributed to the situation, because some bullshit self-help book tells them to own their victimhood. These women find a million ways to beat themselves up but if the tables were turned, men wouldn't be blaming themselves, they'd be calling in the militia to seek revenge. So, yeah, I understand where you're coming from in trying to protect Johnnie, at least I think I do. But it sucks."

I didn't know where to look. Slipping his hand from mine, Harrison went to open the door. David entered with a tea tray.

I knew they waited for me to speak first, but I was so weary my eyelids were sandbags and my mind was near to shutdown.

I looked at David. "It was Johnnie who assaulted me last night."

"I figured."

"It was my impression that he intends to disappear for good."

"Anna Basmanova isn't going to like that," Harrison said.

David's glance at me was faster than a magician's sleight of hand, but Harrison's concern had sharpened his intuition.

"Spill," he said sharply. "I can't and won't represent you if you withhold information from me. Unless Middle East here has a law degree tucked into his back pocket, you should think twice about leaving yourself without legal counsel at this present juncture."

Harrison had my back; I couldn't afford to alienate him. He was my advisor, but his experience of combat had been limited to the confines of a legal system where structure and fair play were baked in, even if unevenly applied. David and I had seen dirty combat, one in a war zone, the other from living while female.

"There's a very difficult situation that I'm afraid is going to spiral today, and I'm not thinking clearly," I said. I had to tell him something, and I wasn't yet ready for it to be about Anna Basmanova. "David was there when it happened, and Samantha, too. But I haven't told anyone else."

"What?" Harrison said.

I willed my breath to go up one nostril and down the other as I'd learned to do in yoga class, gasping at first in its refusal to be smoothed out. My arm began to shake. Alarmed, I opened my eyes to see Harrison staring at me, his hand on my left bicep. At least I wasn't having a heart attack on top of everything else.

"Jane? Are you okay?"

"Sorry," I said.

"Just spit out the facts. We can get to context later."

I took a deep breath. "Darren McGregor grabbed my breast during a confrontation on Tuesday night outside the theater where the police screening was taking place. He was drunk and wanted me to go back to his hotel room. I refused. It was a power play, pure and simple."

"It was sexual assault," Harrison said. "Pure and simple."

I reached over for a biscuit from the tea tray. Hunger gnawed at me, but it wasn't physical.

"Jane refused to report the incident to the police present that night," David said.

"Your chances of convincing the police to lay charges diminishes rapidly after twenty-four hours, especially if it happened within feet of their officers," Harrison said. "I'm assuming none of them saw anything?"

I swallowed the remnants of cookie crumbs with a sip of tea. "No, and there is zero chance I'm reporting it. We all know what happens to women who go to the police. I mean, Panov got set free; the maid whose name none of us even knows got deported. Think what the media would do to me. My privacy ripped to shreds, reputation destroyed, the festival blackened by extension. Darren McGregor is our largest individual donor for Christ's sake. Smearing him without solid evidence would just hand Jacob another shiv to stick in."

"Jacob Ray and Darren showed up together," David explained. "One o'clock in the morning, Darren three sheets to the wind, pissing off the police officers by trying to bully his way into the venue. Then Jacob supposedly takes a call which enables him to turn his back on the situation with Darren and Jane. He didn't pay attention again until he heard Jane vomit."

Harrison's eyebrows raised so high they looked like implants on his forehead. "You vomited on the street?"

"I think more of it actually landed on Darren than the pavement," I said. "But yeah."

"How did Darren and Jacob react?" Harrison asked.

"I don't know, I fled."

"It can't be coincidental that Darren's back in Toronto, and in the company of Jacob Ray to boot."

"What do you mean?" I asked.

"Darren may loathe the British for their petty classicism — he's certainly been vocal about that over the years — but there's some part of him, granddaddy the governor no doubt, that loathes the colonies more," Harrison replied. "When he sold his holdings here and left to play Moneybags in London, it was for good. There wasn't a lot of love lost between him and his former partners."

"He made his money in real estate, correct?" David asked.

Harrison nodded. "Also mining, telecommunications, energy, manufacturing. But primarily, real estate. Early on, McGregor developed an uncanny reputation for buying up tracts of lands for ten thousand an acre in places you'd think would take years to develop, and then suddenly, wham, the government announces a big infrastructure project in exactly that location. The public dime responsible for the sewers and roads that, in turn, skyrocket the value of McGregor's holdings to a million an acre. All the big unions and construction companies mysteriously acquiescent so the projects go forward fast without any labor disputes."

"Kickbacks?" David asked.

"You might well ask," Harrison said. "Given how often it happened. Or the familiarity the Italians and my better-paying client base had with him. Darren amassed an early fortune, money that ended up seeding all the subsequent mergers and acquisitions, in partnership with the other billionaire Canadian families, and eventually a web of international players, too."

"Why do you know so much about him?" I asked.

"I've got an articling student digging. McGregor peddles himself now as a clean-living buddha, but he was a businessman without principles, playing the shell game with a complicated and intricate web of holdings and partnerships. People don't change. And I don't believe in coincidence. Why is Darren here now, why is he making such a public donation, and what does he need from a man like Jacob Ray?"

"He says he's here because of his aspiring filmmaker son."

Harrison tapped his head, strange smile on his face. "Maybe not so much. I had drinks last night with someone who shall remain nameless," he said, clearly enjoying himself in the role of raconteur-in-chief. "Rumor is our Darren's the subject of RCMP interest."

"What?" I said. The rabbit hole just got deeper. "That's why they're hassling me? To get at Darren?"

"I don't know," Harrison said. "But I'd bet my left testis it's all connected somehow. He owns an island in the Bahamas — his Instagram overflows with photos of him living his own full potential, or some such shit he peddles. And apparently massive real estate holdings in London still. Not quite as removed from the world of business as he'd like people to believe."

"Wow," I said. "Why bring up the old history with Smythe?"

"That's what got me digging," Harrison said. "Ten years ago. Before Bob's time, but not before Johnnie's. Was he trying to impress you with a personal connection? Rattle you? Warn you?"

I frowned. "It's difficult to believe Smythe was caught up in illicit dealings, even during Robert's reign. He was a cold-hearted bastard, but I don't think a criminal. I asked Bob to send over the McGregor sale files from a decade ago. They arrived yesterday but I haven't had a chance to go over them yet."

"Do you want my junior to read through?"

"You're on retainer to me, not the firm. I think confidentiality considerations mean I need to do it."

"Twenty million donation over four years. Camouflage?" David asked.

Harrison shrugged. "Good publicity in advance of ugly stuff to come?"

"Jacob hired to handle the muck," I said. "Probably to fling it in another direction, that's his specialty. Give the RCMP a new scent to steer them away from McGregor."

I closed my eyes and felt my arm shake again. "You don't have a concussion, do you?" Harrison grumbled.

"I'm just thinking about what's next," I said.

"You keep Middle East here closer by," Harrison said. "No one gets within ten feet of you."

I looked at David. "I want something I can carry for self-defense — not a gun, but something just as effective."

He nodded at me. "You'll have it by end of day."

"With Jacob and the board — there are three days left in the festival. Do I play defense, avoiding outright conflict with him? God knows, there's enough other fire bombs that need my attention. Or do I shift to offense? And if so, what does that look like?"

"Offence is the best defense, or so the saying goes," David said. "How much do you trust Jacob not to take that strategy?"

"I don't."

"Darren's assault was Tuesday night?" Harrison asked.

"Yup. About one a.m. Tuesday night, Wednesday morning."

"It's now thirty-five hours later. Have you heard from either McGregor or Ray since?" Harrison pressed.

"Nothing," I said. "It seemed like a godsend yesterday, but now I wonder what they've been cooking up."

"My advice to you is pick up the phone and dial human resources," Harrison said. "Tell them what happened, and about Jacob being present. They won't be obligated to call the police, but they will be obligated to tell the board and investigate Jacob."

"It will put the donation in jeopardy," I said.

"Not your problem," Harrison said. "It's a big donation, but a small fraction of the festival's budget. You need to lob your own ball, before Jacob's volley comes railing down. Being on the defensive is difficult to overcome."

Harrison clambered to a stand before continuing. "Jacob will try to sway the court of public opinion. He's a master at the dark arts, but he's not the only fake god in town."

* * *

I sat quietly in my office, sending emails to apologize for the three breakfast meetings I'd failed to appear at that morning, blacked out at Johnnie's, and reviewing the legal opinion on the Smythe deal. Harrison had flipped the paperwork to the mergers and acquisition lawyer he'd retained on my behalf. After six pages of disclaimers that she didn't have enough time to adequately review the deal and thus any opinion was so qualified as to be rendered useless, the M&A lawyer finally stated there were no glaring impediments to my signing it.

A knock at the door. I looked up but went back to writing. I'd instructed Jamila and Samantha that I needed an uninterrupted hour to get organized, no matter who might show up at the office. The only open time in my festival schedule should have been after the parties ended, between midnight and my breakfast meetings that started at seven. The past few days had required too much rejuggling by staff having to work around my sudden disappearances. In an environment as intimate and frenzied as this one, it was difficult to stem the tidal wave of gossip.

The door opened, and in walked Jacob. His silver hair looked to be freshly touched up, and his smooth complexion was slightly too orange to be just a tan. His makeup person needed to go a tad lighter on the foundation.

"I've had some troubling news, Jane. Don't get up," he said, as I struggled to get to my feet. "I'm not staying long."

"Please sit," I said, walking over to the conference table. "Or we can stand and speak, whichever you prefer."

Jacob made no move to sit, and so I was forced to tighten my core muscles to support the rest of my battered body in an upright position.

"You're a cowboy, Jane. Time and again, I've asked you to work with me, to keep me, as your board chair, in the loop. But you shoot from the hip, no consideration given for the wider issues at play, not willing to work as a team member. You've refused the volunteer staffing I offered to help you cope with the added work-load and stress which must be impacting your judgment."

I remained silent.

"Human resources called me. Apparently, you've filed a com-plaint against my lack of intervention into the personal situation between you and Darren McGregor."

"I brought them into the loop as to what happened."

"You should have just called me yesterday, and then Darren. We could have cleared up this misunderstanding."

"Are you speaking as the board chair, Jacob?" I asked, pleas-antly smiling, as my foot ground down on the pedal. "Or as his crisis manager?"

"There's clearly been a flirtation going on between you and Darren."

"Calling it a flirtation is a gross misrepresentation."

"He had too much to drink and was unsteady on his feet the other night. Perhaps, when he stumbled, he touched somewhere he shouldn't have, but you can't think it was deliberate. I didn't see what happened because, as you know, I'd taken a call."

"At one in the morning?"

"Of course. My business is on a twenty-four hour cycle."

"The situation was escalating even before you put the phone to your ear. You had the option of not answering it."

"I've tried to ignore your aggression toward me for the sake of the festival," Jacob said. "As you know, I felt the board should remove you; they demurred until the festival was over. But now you're accusing both our largest individual donor and me, your boss, of inappropriate behavior. You've become completely unhinged."

He was in full stride now, scorn dripping from a voice that got quieter with each word.

"And why are you wearing that soft collar? You can't possibly be gearing up to accuse Darren McGregor of grievous bodily harm?"

"I'm not making a complaint to the police."

"How could you? Nothing criminal happened."

Don't rise to the bait, my fingertips tapped out against my leg. I wanted so badly to wipe the smug smile off his face. "I'll call human resources to join us. They said they should be present for any conversation between you and me."

"You understand, yes, that this is an untenable situation," Jacob said. "Darren McGregor is a well-respected philanthropist and business leader. The board is going to have the same difficulty I do in believing he purposely assaulted you."

"The board may view him differently once the truth of his business dealings is revealed."

As soon as the words slipped out of my mouth, I knew I'd made a terrible mistake. *Never, ever, reveal your hand until it's played.*

Jacob turned on his heels and walked out, closing the door precisely behind him.

I made me way back around the desk and into my chair. If I could have physically managed it, I might have curled up under my desk. Instead, I picked up the phone and dialed.

★ ★ ★

I signed away forty-nine percent of Smythe Financial without feeling much of anything. I'd popped more codeine to cope with the pain of doing without the soft collar — questions from Bob about my injuries would derail me, and I needed to be steely enough to get through the six hours left in my workday. The effects of the drug made me feel like a zombie walk-on from *Night of the Living Dead*.

"Might you have time for dinner later?" Bob said, standing close.

"I'm afraid not," I said, self-consciously adjusting the scarf I wore around my neck to make sure the bruises were covered. "I have eight things on the itinerary this evening, and not one has your name on it. Besides, aren't there a million details to settle with the merger?"

"I'm anxious to spend time with you."

I smiled slightly, not sure what to say, and conscious of Harrison standing with Bob's lawyers a few feet away. "Let's talk tomorrow, okay?"

When Harrison and I reached the foyer, we found David waiting in front of a muted television screen.

"Jesus," Harrison growled, when he caught sight of the news footage. "Turn that sound up."

"I don't know where the control is," the receptionist whispered, in full retreat as Harrison came toward her. "We usually only have it on silent to watch the market crawl."

Harrison jabbed his fingers so forcefully around the bottom and back of the screen, looking for the manual controls, that it was in danger of careening off the wall. Voices suddenly filled the cavernous space.

Behind the news anchor, a large split screen displayed the photo of Harrison and me from days earlier coming out of 14 Division, juxtaposed with one of me wearing the neck brace. The scrawl at the bottom of the screen read, "WTFF's Jane Browning: Out of Control?"

I sank into a chair and listened with mounting distaste as the host recounted the numerous challenges with this year's festival, including rape accusations against Alexei Panov that were later dropped and my gender-biased support of the accuser instead of a director in my own festival. They ran video clips of questions from the media briefing, about DelGrotto and Larry Roth, followed by a snide inference about how young I was to be appointed to a job of this stature. The hatchet didn't spare a tour of my "sensational" private life, either. Early marriage to "high-flying hedge fund manager" Johnnie Smythe and a subsequent live-in relationship with his brother and business partner.

My skin sizzled from the sunburn of exposure.

"Karma's a bitch," I mumbled.

"Karma?" David said, turning to look at me with one eyebrow raised. "You think you did something to deserve this?"

"Samantha and I were stuffed full of schadenfreude when Panov was forced to walk the media gauntlet in handcuffs," I said, putting my scarf over my eyes to block out the glare of the pot-lights. A migraine built at the base of my neck. "Like chicken cordon bleu, the middle all fatty ham and oozing cheese. Impossible to keep the glee inside."

"Panov was a perpetrator. You're a victim."

"The TV says I'm an out-of-control polygamist whack job married to two shady businessmen."

A soft touch glanced across my head. I looked up to see David's helping hand. He waited while I ignored it, until finally there seemed to no option other than to give in. "I know, I was there," he said, pulling me gently to my feet.

"This has Jacob's fingerprints all over it. He can't have gotten this together in the three hours since I saw him," I mumbled.

"He'll have been working on it since Tuesday night," Harrison said. "Typical BFA gong show."

David turned to the receptionist. "Please ask security to walk the perimeter looking for bloodsuckers. We're particularly sensitive to the presence of TV trucks."

"He can't leave the downstairs lobby unattended," she sputtered, clearly wondering who this man was to be telling her what to do, but too taken aback to question the innate authority with which he spoke.

"Giving a shit about the safety of your boss's spouse is an effective job-retention strategy," Harrison said, his eyes narrowing at her. "Pick up the phone now, ducky."

She quickly dialed. "Excuse me," she said hesitantly, the phone held out from her ear. "Rahul from security said there's a truck outside with a satellite on top. But nothing in the garage."

"Good job," Harrison said. "Can our driver get access to the garage?"

"Someone would have to stand down there with their electronic access card to open the gate."

"I'm sure you're happy to do that. Middle East, how fast can you get someone here?"

"Probably fifteen."

Harrison sighed. Their lightning-speed dialogue hurt my head.

I put up my hand to interrupt. "I have the extra key fob for Bob's car. Would that help?"

Harrison gave my arm a pat, *job well done.* "Assuming Bob's car is here — yeah."

I fished my keys from my purse and handed them to David. "Can you please drive?"

The three of us walked quickly to the elevator, alighting a minute later in the parking garage. Bob's dark red Jaguar was in its spot. "Thank God a midlife crisis didn't extend to a sports model," Harrison said, as he settled into the front and I got into the back. "Lay that soft collar down on the seat, Jane, and you with it. The only photos those reporters are getting going forward are the ones we control."

CHAPTER
SIXTEEN

Large art pieces hung everywhere, juxtaposed against very white walls. I wandered slowly around David's cavernous warehouse apartment, startled by his choices. Photography, framed tapestry, a large mechanical art piece hanging from the ceiling in a corner, a sculpture of a man at war with himself. The round wrought-iron-and-glass dining table was illuminated by a giant antique gold chandelier. It was both august and intimate.

A long white counter ran most of the length of the kitchen space. Harrison and David perched on stools on one side, facing the giant flat screen that hung like a sleek painting between floor-to-ceiling windows. Harrison channel surfed news sites and peered into his phone while hoovering up Thai food. David sat glued to his laptop.

"The publicist will be here in half an hour," Harrison said, pieces of green chicken curry threatening to escape from his mouth as he spoke. "I told her to keep calling my cell, as we had yours turned off."

"Okay," I said, stopping in front of an abstract painting it took me a minute to recognize was of Marilyn Monroe.

"The libel lawyer should be arriving momentarily," Harrison continued.

"Okay."

"You should eat something, Jane," David said from behind me. "Balance the painkillers."

"Not hungry."

"Snap out of it," Harrison said, his hard edge causing me to finally focus. A Thai eggplant, long and dark purple, hung millimeters from his mouth. "It's a clusterfuck that's not going away. You need to regain some fighting form."

"I know," I said, and then turned back to the art.

Harrison slammed his hand down on the counter. He muted the volume on the television. "Earth to Jane," he said. "The world's coming at you. No choice but to deal. Ditch the fugue state, sit your ass down here, and get to work on strategy. If we can't outmaneuver that fuckwit, we have no business breathing in and out."

I knew fighting back was the only viable option, but whether it was the Percocet, or one attack too many, I couldn't bring myself to put the gloves back on.

David walked over to take my hand in one of his, leading me to a stool where he'd placed an espresso cup and sugar bowl. "Sit."

I took a sip. David pushed a plate of almond cookies in front of me, as well as a spring roll. "Options."

I drank the coffee under his watchful eye, and the combination of caffeine and sugar wormed its way through my bloodstream. Almost against my will, the detachment ceded ground.

"I like being zoned-out better," I said, finishing the spring roll, then helping myself to a cookie.

"Don't we all?" Harrison said, looking at his watch, just as the doorbell rang. "That'll be Jools. Never a minute too early, never a second late. Doesn't wear a watch. Freaked me out ever since law school."

David answered the door and the latest lawyer on my team made her way in. Imposing as Harrison, although they were as different as Abbott and Costello. Tall where he was wide, her gray hair was shellacked into perfect place while tufts of his hair sprouted in all directions. Her blue eyes were intense, and her handshake pulverized the unsuspecting.

"Ms. Browning, nice to make your acquaintance. I'm Julia Ferguson."

"Please call me Jane," I said. "Thank you for coming."

"When Harrison calls, I jump."

Harrison's great guffaw made my aching head pound harder. "Hello, pot."

"Nice to see you, kettle," she said, giving him a hug. "Right in the middle of a high-profile case as usual. Been practicing the media bites in front of the mirror?"

"Before we get into it, is the counter fine, or do we want to move to the table?" David asked. "Can you I get you a coffee or tea, Ms. Ferguson? Or something stronger?"

"The counter's fine with me," she said, pulling up a stool and sitting ramrod straight. "I'll have a double expresso with sugar, since I see you have one of those fancy machines. I had a couple glasses of Barolo at dinner and my faculties are a little less sharp than they could be."

"Jools, before I brief you on what's been happening," Harrison said, "did you happen to see the CBC piece that Jacob Ray planted on Jane tonight?"

"I don't eat dinner in the type of establishment that has a television blaring," she said. "But I did hear the coverage on the radio as I drove over."

I flinched.

"I'm afraid you'll need to get used to it, Jane," she said. "At least for a day or two until another story knocks you out of the limelight. Which it inevitably will, and soon enough, although for you it'll seem like a lifetime."

"We're working on that next," Harrison said.

"I don't want to know," Julia said. "And make sure Jane knows nothing about anything you might do to deflect attention to one or more individuals, especially if it might mean they'd have grounds to sue for slander. She needs to have complete deniability."

"Sue me? I want to sue them," I said, indignation eating up the remainder of my lethargy. "Jacob and the CBC."

Julia took her time to doctor the coffee David delivered before replying. "Jane, tell me. When you come upon a big, steaming turd on the sidewalk, what do you do?" she asked.

"Pardon?"

"It's a straightforward question," she said, voice getting deeper and hands waving in the air. She and Harrison had that much in common, old-time circus masters controlling their audience. "One of your neighbors fails to pick up after Rover's rear end. Say it's a Bouvier, or maybe a Labrador, or some other breed that's bigger than any dog living in a poop-and-scoop urban jurisdiction should be. The size of the excrement is massive. It's July, it's hot, the flies are buzzing all over said excrement. Tell me, Jane," she said, leaning forward. "Do you step your nice strappy sandals into the middle of it, or you do try to avoid the unpleasantness, even if that means stepping onto someone's flower garden?"

"I guess the tulips have to go," I said. "If you put it that way."

Jane sat back, smiling at me benignly. "Good girl," she said, making me feel younger than I could ever remember feeling, even as a child. "Because there's no upside in spending all your time wiping the dogshit off your shoes when you need to spend it saving your job."

"Jacob Ray just gets away with slandering me?"

She shook her head as if disappointed at the need for a remedial lesson. "Do you have conclusive proof that he planted the story with the CBC?"

"No," I said reluctantly.

"Was there anything in the coverage that was demonstrably untrue?"

"No," I said even more reluctantly. "But they strung together a series of disparate things which, together, defamed my character."

"And how has that negatively impacted you?" she asked, her words as slow and persistent as water dripping. I wouldn't want to face those blue bullet eyes in a court of law. "What would justify the court awarding you damages? Have you lost your job?"

"Not yet," I said. "But that's what Jacob's after."

"And if that happens, your first recourse will be a labor lawyer, and we'd also revisit the idea of a defamation suit, especially if you were unable to get subsequent employment. But let's fight the battle we're facing, not a fantasy one."

"I see," I said, still upset at the humiliation of being bullied but also secretly relieved. The idea of launching a lawsuit, where all details would be public, was horrific.

"Having said all that," Julia said, "there's no point in having the best libel dog in the country and barking yourself. I'll send a cease and desist letter to the CBC. Your only response going forward, to any and all media questions, is to refer them to me. 'The matter is in the hands of my lawyer, Julia Ferguson.' Can you practice that with me, Jane?"

I smiled. "The matter is in the hands of my lawyer, Julia Ferguson. I have no further comment at this time."

"Excellent. You're a fast learner. I'll coordinate with your publicist, as necessary, to tell your side of the story, but since you lost first mover advantage in the media, we'll take our time figuring out that strategy, so long as the media's attention is diverted to someone else within the next twenty-four hours. And so long as Jane has no traceable fingerprints on that," she repeated, laying out the broad blueprint the details of which I could later deny knowing. "In the meantime, I'll have a chance encounter with Jacob and casually mention I'm now your lawyer. Let him sweat that one a little. Who's the vice chair of your board?"

"Sheila Waterford."

"Lawyer? Partner at Tory's?"

"Yes."

"I've met her through the women's bar association. I'll have a quiet word there, too."

"Thanks very much, Julia. I really appreciate it."

The doorbell rang, and Julia stood. "That's my cue to leave. Harrison, I'll call you tomorrow. Jane, here's my card, call anytime you need to, cell phone is best. Jacob Ray is a Labrador-sized turd. Hang tough."

I detoured to the washroom while David answered the door. I barely lifted the toilet lid, before I vomited. My neck brace cushioned the impact of the toilet roll holder as I leaned sideways against the wall. With one hand, I tried to extract some toilet paper, but one little square came out at a time. Frustrated, I rubbed the remnants away from my mouth, pieces of white tissue sticking to my face.

"Jane, are you okay?" Franny's knock on the door was remarkably restrained for someone capable of dreaming up a Fuck ISIS signature cocktail.

"Just give me a minute, okay?"

"Take as long as you want. I'll make like a statue and wait."

I gripped the toilet seat to pull myself up. I held my wrists under the running cold water until they were almost numb, and the pain subsided. Slowly, my breathing returned to normal and a modicum of control came back to me. When I'd washed my face with the towel and finger-combed my hair into a top knot, I fished the phone out of my pocket. Twenty missed calls, several from Bob along with a text that read "Saw the TV coverage. Where are you?"

Sheila Waterford, ever the efficient vice board chair, had emailed, texted, and called. Her message was succinct. My presence was required at an emergency meeting, nine a.m. the following morning, her office.

"Okay, we've got thirty minutes for Team Jane talk," Harrison said, when I walked back into the room.

"Shall I go first?" Franny piped up. "I'm having a really rockin' party Saturday night, eight p.m., you all have to come. Red or black clothes only."

"I meant something relevant," Harrison grumbled.

"There's no need to talk to me in that tone," Franny said, not fazed in the least. "This is like super-important to me."

"I'll be there, Franny," I cut in. "I'm sure the others will be if they can. Thank you for helping turn the heat lamp up on Jacob and BFA. I have some ideas to go over with you."

"I think you aren't supposed to know the deets?" she said.

Harrison made the motion of a zipper across his lips. "What Jane means is that she'd like an update on your plans to disincentivize other media outlets from following the CBC's gotcha journalism."

"I've been working the phones since you called. Had a chat with sources at the *Star, Globe, Sun, Post, Huff Post, Vice,* and a few other outlets. Pointed out the problems with the CBC coverage, anyone with eyes in their head could see it was a hatchet job, is that how low your national broadcaster has sunk, shilling fake content as a favor for Jacob Ray. Tried to rile their journalistic pride to prod them to make the story become the story."

"BFA has an unseemly close relationship with media," Harrison said. "They hand Jacob miles of editorial comment and on-air minutes that build his brand for him. Journalists yap all the time about corruption in politics or business or wherever and ignore the incestuous little feedback loop they themselves create."

"I also spoke to a few contacts inside CBC," Franny said.

"Let me guess, no uptake?" Harrison said.

"Not so far."

Harrison snorted. "CBC is a client of BFA, too. Leave them to Julia's legal wrangling and focus on creating competition in the other outlets."

"Jesus," I said. "You'd think in a city this size, there's got to be more than one spin terrorist."

"Jane, are you willing to do an exclusive on-air interview with CTV refuting the allegations from the CBC story?" Franny asked. "They won't allow pre-vetting of the questions; you gotta know they'll ask about everything."

I swallowed the lump in my throat, just as Harrison butted in. "Too risky."

"How about spreading the RCMP investigation rumors?" I asked.

"Oh," Franny cried, "I love those dudes on horses."

I smiled. Franny's uncomplicated enthusiasm was impossible to resist, if you weren't wanting to wring her neck.

"Can't go there," Harrison said. "Potential for collateral damage too great."

"What do we have then?" I said. "I'm running out of time."

"Don't worry, Jane. Command and control ain't what it used to be," Franny said. "There are multiple ways to slice and dice this fucker."

I stood up and began to walk, rolling my shoulders to try to loosen the tension. Thinking. "I'm a big fan of the movie *Citizenfour*," I finally said, my back to the others.

"We're not here to talk about parties or movies," Harrison sputtered behind me. "We need a strategy —"

I put my arm up in the air to cut him off. "The movie poses an interesting question. Is Edward Snowden a hero? Traitor? Communist spy? Jacob despises me, in part, because he suspects I'm the whistleblower who went to TMZ with the DelGrotto photos, or at least I knew about it and didn't intervene."

I stopped to look at them, before continuing to pace. "And he's right. Jacob would argue I wanted Paul's job and I stabbed him in the back to get it. But my purpose was to level the playing field. For Lina. For me. For my female colleagues. Because the board directors made a specific calculation that the CEO was more important to the organization than the VP of marketing. She was expendable and he was not. So why bother investigating, until the photos were published and their backs were against the wall."

"But Jane, that's about job function, not about gender," Franny said. "Of course, the top dog is going to be more important than someone a few levels down."

I stopped in front of her. "Listen, I get that power involves ugly choices and compromised positions. Way more after this week than I did before, I'll be the first to admit. But in the history of the festival, in the history of businesses, and governments, and large organizations, the vast majority of the time the CEO is a man. And the VP of marketing is a woman. And to decide one is more expendable than the other so we'll turn a blind eye — that's all about gender and power."

"Where does Snowden come into your soapbox?" she asked. "He's not the trans whistleblower, is he? So many to keep track of."

"Regardless of what your value judgment is about Snowden, there's no denying he pulled off the most significant data leak in U.S. history," I said, smiling at Franny. "Changed the course of history. Revealed the NSA's nasty little secrets. Set information free . . ."

The lightbulb switched on. "Good morning, Vietnam," she said, hopping off the stool and grabbing her purse. "Gotta get to work. Remember Saturday night."

She was out the door before Harrison or David could offer a word of caution.

* * *

Bob stood in the hallway outside my hotel suite, a vase full of yellow roses in his hand, deep grooves in a forehead etched with concern. His eyes were still as they took in the soft collar. "I hope you don't mind my coming. I wanted to see how you were."

I asked David for some privacy and closed the door behind us. Bob put the vase on a side table and took one step toward me. I let him draw me gently into a hug, sinking into the familiar, before I pulled back slightly.

"Help me off with this cardigan, okay?" I said. "My range of motion is not quite what it should be."

Bob slid the cardigan from my shoulders, and we stood awkwardly looking at each other.

"Sit down," I said, indicating the couch, waiting until he sat first before I joined him, my back next to his leg, and then slowly leaning backward, so that my body was angled into his. I loved to curl up in bed with him wrapped around me, feel his nibble on my neck, his lips on my ears. "Jane," he'd whisper softly, as he caressed me. "Do you like this? How about this?"

Now we sat as best we could, the soft collar an impediment, his arms around me, slowly rocking back and forth.

"I'm not up for a lot of conversation tonight," I said. "My PR people have a strategy in place about the media coverage, but I really don't want to go into details now. Can we just sit like this for a while? And then I'm going to go lie down."

"We'll do whatever you like."

I closed my eyes and listened to the rhythm of his breathing in and out, quick at first, as our bodies made contact for the first time in more than a week, and then slowing, as his arms tightened and our bodies found their jigsaw groove again.

"My injuries happened last night," I said. "When I went to see Johnnie."

"I'm so sorry, Jane."

"It's okay, it's just any pressure at all is painful."

"I'm so sorry I left you alone. I'm sorry you felt like you needed to go see my brother. I'm sorry he would do this to you —" By now, Bob was crying.

I patted the back of the hands that lay crossed against my abdomen. There was nothing left in my reservoir that would give me the energy to manage the complexities of his emotions. "Johnnie's actions are his own responsibility. We both know that," I said. "I just need you to know the truth. Johnnie disappeared once I'd passed out —" I paused, feeling Bob's body recoil, and the sound of a wounded animal escape. It pierced the fog, and I picked up his hand to kiss it. "I'm barely holding it together, Bob. I need you to do the same."

"I'm sorry." He hiccupped in his attempt to deal with the tears, not wanting to move his hands away from mine.

"It's okay," I said, leaning away from him slightly so he could move. "Why don't you go get some Kleenex, and I'll just wait here."

I didn't turn around but heard him pad through the other room, all the way to the bathroom and then blow his noise in a big honking sound. It was only a minute before he returned, folding me back into the crease of his embrace.

"I don't mean to upset you about Johnnie, I just need you to give you the bare bones, and then we can talk another time."

"Okay."

"He lost control and pulled back my head out of frustration that I wouldn't leave the country with him. But he didn't lose full control, if you understand what I mean by that."

"I think I do."

"I really don't know where he's going, or what his plans are. Except I'm pretty sure he's not coming back. There were packed suitcases by the door when I arrived; they were gone when I woke up. He told me nothing that would give you any insight into where the money is, or whether he ever intended to give it back." I held my tongue against telling Bob anything more.

"Not surprising."

I closed my eyes and leaned in more. The intimacy of the room surrounded me, and our breathing soon fell into sync. I didn't realize I'd dozed off until I heard little snores escape through my nostrils. It was only when Bob's snores saw mine and raised me one that I moved around enough to wake us both up.

"I have to lie down," I said. "I really need to make it up to my staff by actually meeting some of my obligations tomorrow. They've been on a scramble to cover my commitments."

"Might I stay?" Bob asked. "I'll sleep on the couch to make sure you're not crowded in the bed. But I would feel better keeping you in my sights tonight. I imagine your bodyguard is probably lingering somewhere in the hallway —"

"I bet the staircase."

"It's for my own sake," he said. "I'd appreciate it."

I smiled for the first time in what seemed a very long time. "If you help me into my nightgown, you can sleep in the bed," I said. "But you can't fling those long arms around over your head like you do sometimes. It's only a queen-sized bed."

"Non-retractable arms on humans are a real design flaw," Bob said, helping me to my feet.

I laughed, then paused for a minute. It seems so ungracious to utter what I was thinking, and I looked at him, searching for a soft landing. "It's my honor to be your concierge into sleep tonight," Bob said, reading my mind. "And there my duties shall end."

CHAPTER SEVENTEEN

DAY 9: *Kill Bill*

My childhood fear of Johann, Pastor Glass's oldest son, remained even as I grew taller and smarter, and his stagnation became clearer. Angry acne blisters had crawled out from the pit of his teenage angst to cover his neck and face and the disfiguration just made him meaner. He took out his frustrations on me whenever he could, with taunts about my mother's inadequacy or by beating me up on my way to, or from, the school we both attended.

This ended a year after I'd made the deal — video camera for God-mongering. As big and clunky as the camera was, I perfected ways of being surreptitious in my filming. When I dared, I poked my lens through Pastor Glass's windows, working to decode the enigma that had turned our lives upside down.

Johann performed his daily salutations to the patron saint of clear skin in the basement washroom: a mass of creams and astringents and clumsy fingers that attempted to pop the engorged whiteheads. One morning I bribed Johann's younger brother, Peter, to leave the washroom window ajar, so I could film the ritual. The following week, as I cued up the video in art class, I felt a healthy twinge of remorse but I played it anyhow, not hitting pause until Johann had fled the kind of cruel, relentless mocking that only children and psychopaths are capable of, overturning his desk on the way out.

Were my actions survival, pure and simple? Force Johann from school to save myself further beatings? Was it justifiable revenge, an eye for an eye as the Old Testament provided? Or was it a betrayal of the strange intimacy of our entangled lives?

Betrayals are never as black and white as we would like to them to be. My father showed up that night to confront me, Pastor Glass in tow for an unprecedented visit inside the house. Johann would be transferring schools. My father would help pay for his new private school to atone for my sins. Did I have anything to say for myself? Did I want to unburden myself through confession?

For once, I did not pause to weigh the odds. "You should have enough money saved from shortchanging Mom all these years," I said. "We eat Kraft dinner and meatloaf, so you can play large down the street."

Tracy started crying in the background. My father put his hand on my shoulder and shook his head slowly from side to side. "One day you'll understand what it is to strive and fail," he said quietly. "To seek forgiveness."

Pastor Glass was not going so meekly into that good night. The door slammed behind him so loud Mrs. O'Flynn was sure to hear it next door over the sound of the Hoover, and my father followed his lover out. My mother turned up the television and

Tracy fled into the kitchen for food to dull the pain. I didn't speak to my father again until my mother's death, and then only that once. Perhaps he'd found salvation with Pastor Glass and his children. I didn't know. He hadn't bothered to look for it with us. You can't grant something that isn't sought.

"We have a very serious situation on our hands," Sheila said, as the WTFF board directors sat grouped around one side of table, Jacob a silent, looming presence sandwiched between Sheila and Carole. "We met an hour ago with the human resources department to discuss the incident you reported. And, of course, we've all seen, or heard, or read, the news coverage."

"There wasn't any news in that hatchet job," I said quietly, sitting across from them. I'd ditched both the soft collar and the codeine. I needed to appear sharp and professional, but the effort was taking its toll already. "Just a combination of disparate things edited together with the deliberate attempt to slander me."

"Are you accusing the CBC of libel?" Henry, the lawyer, asked.

"That issue is in the hands of my lawyer, Julia Ferguson," I said. "She's advised me not to comment on it further at this time."

"Yes, I know," Sheila said wryly. "She showed up at my gym at this morning. Remarkable coincidence. Never seen her there before."

I kept a neutral expression on my face. "When Jacob showed up at my office yesterday to threaten me, I told him I didn't intend to go to the police about what happened with Darren McGregor," I said. "I don't want to risk further exposure for the festival —"

"Nothing criminal happened," Jacob inserted, his voice rising to drown out mine. "That's why you're not going to the police, not some altruistic impulse. And I didn't threaten you. I sought to deescalate a misunderstanding that you've now built into a hysterical witch hunt."

Sheila put up her hand to interrupt Jacob. "We reviewed with HR how we'd communicate with Jane," she said. "I suggest we stick to that." Tension filled the room, with the rest of the directors looking anywhere but at each other.

"Obviously the festival can't simply ignore this situation," I said flatly.

Jacob stood and walked slowly toward me. The height advantage was clearly a psychological warfare tool; annoyance flashed across Sheila's face.

"He apologizes unreservedly for his drunken behavior, but says he did not, to the best of his memory, touch you in any way," Jacob said.

"I repeat what I asked you yesterday," I said, Jacob now paused behind my chair. I refused to pivot my head to look at him. Beyond his desire to intimidate me, my neck was too sore, and this wasn't *The Exorcist*. "Is McGregor a client of yours? And are you speaking to me as the chair of this organization who, as my employer, has obligations under the Employment Standards Act regarding a toxic work environment? Or as his crisis manager?"

"He has no crisis except the one you're trying to fabricate," Jacob said, reentering my peripheral vision on the other side. "He says you accepted flowers from him last week, and also a card with his private contact details. He feels he made his interest in you completely transparent and that you were welcoming of it."

"Untrue," I said. "I was friendly on behalf the festival and his transformational gift, as I think you called it. But I repeatedly made it clear that our connection was professional, not private. I declined to spend time alone with him."

Carole piped up. "Even if what Darren is saying is true, that doesn't mean he had any right to touch Jane unless she expressly gave him permission to do so."

"Thank you, Carole. But let's be very clear: he *is* lying."

"Careful," Jacob said, in a mocking tone. "Calling someone a liar is grounds for libel."

I sat back, fists clenched at my side. "I'm not responsible for his refusal to take no for an answer."

"For the record, I believe you, Jane," Carole said. "But I also think that's beside the point. What we need to decide as a board is what, if any, association we want with Darren McGregor."

"Part and parcel of the same issue," Jacob said. "Either Jane is credible, or Darren is, and we've seen her bad judgment in dealing with *State* and with Alexei Panov. His grudge against Jane keeps intensifying."

"That's ridiculous," I said. "I followed our legal department's advice with Panov. And the charges were dropped because they deported the woman, not because they were proven to be untrue."

"We're getting off track," Sheila protested.

"Let's cut to the chase," Jacob said, still standing. "We can accept Darren's gift or reject it. He tells me he's still keen to support the festival."

"Yesterday, I made a comment to Jacob that I believe caused him to go nuclear on me," I said slowly, looking around the table.

"You should think carefully of the legal consequences before you speak further," Jacob said softly, staring at me.

Pausing now would gain me nothing; the only potential win was with bayonet pointed straight at Jacob. I took a deep breath. "I understand from one of my lawyers that Darren McGregor and his business practices may be the subject of RCMP investigation. I told Jacob. Hours later the CBC did a hatchet job on me. Any reasonable person might assume those two things are connected."

A stunned silence, except for Jacob. "But isn't you, Jane, whom the RCMP is interested in? Perhaps to do with Smythe Financial?"

"You're a master at misdirection, Jacob, I have to give you that," I said, willing my voice to remain cool and under control. "You showed up in the middle of the night to an official event with an inebriated donor and then turned your back to give him carte blanche to assault me. Your actions are not just negligent but willful and deliberate."

"The festival has more than ample cause to terminate you, Jane. Throwing knives at me won't camouflage the liability you represent to this organization."

"Shup up, Jacob," Henry snapped. "You're giving Jane even further ammunition for a civil suit against you and the festival."

"Let's take a five-minute breather," Sheila said, standing up. "When we come back, we'll focus on what needs to be done in terms of immediate steps to handle the media and donor relations. The larger questions can be dealt with next week, post-festival."

Jacob picked up his briefcase. "I told you upfront I had a hard stop this morning," he said, heading for the door. "I'll be in touch with the board this afternoon."

Jacob closed the door behind him. The rest of them stared at me like the grenade carrier I was. "We need to prepare for the media attention to get worse," I said finally, when it looked like no one was leaving the room for a recess after all. "I was the target of the original CBC story, but it's inevitable that will widen today, especially with a story so thin you can see through it. They'll need more red meat to feed their editor and circling back to Paul DelGrotto will be a route of least resistance. The festival's PR department is excellent, but they're also staff of this organization, so there's inherent conflict in covering stories that involve the board. You might want to bring in a third-person PR firm to help shape the messaging on this."

"Thanks, Jane, we appreciate your proactive stance," Sheila said.

I cleared my throat. "It probably goes without saying, but bringing in Jacob's firm would be a massive mistake. Beyond the obvious conflict, the tide is turning against those kinds of super-aggressive, NDA-pushing firms. The tactics are the message, and the message is under greater scrutiny."

Sheila nodded, standing up. "Understood. I think the discussion about Darren McGregor's gift is best left to the board to decide. Thank you for your time today."

The dismissal was clear. I walked around the table shaking each of their hands, hoping it wouldn't be the last time I did so. Like with Johann, I'd moved to stem the bullying but it did not make me proud. Only determined. I did not want to be a beautiful loser. It was time to hedge the odds.

★ ★ ★

"If you seek legal advice from me in order to facilitate the commission of a crime or a fraud, then some quarters say I'm not bound to consider that confidential information protected by solicitor-client privilege."

Harrison was not best pleased.

"I'm not asking you to commit a fraud."

"Feeding Jacob to the RCMP for breakfast without proof he committed a crime could be perceived as fraud."

"I only suggested you have a talk with your friend who's nameless but plugged in enough to know about the Darren McGregor investigation. Jacob sent the RCMP on a wild goose chase by trying to implicate me and Smythe; all you're doing is correcting the record."

"You don't have proof it was Jacob and you don't know it's unsubstantiated where it comes to Smythe."

"Early this morning, before my board meeting, Bob and I dug through records of the transactions that Smythe handled for Darren, and the communications between the two firms. All on the up and up; the business evaluation and sale was the extent of the involvement. Doesn't clear McGregor — it would have been a surprise if any illegal activity was put through the books of his main company, and besides it's been a decade, he's had plenty of time to grow his wingspan. But it does clear Smythe and, by extension, make the RCMP's interest in me illegitimate."

Harrison downed the single malt in front of him in the hotel restaurant where we were having lunch and signaled for another round.

"Don't do anything that makes you uncomfortable," I continued. "I can just meet with Inspector Wallace directly."

"Don't try to jam me up, Jane. Emotional blackmail doesn't sit well with me."

I put my fingers over my heart. "Scout's honor. It's not my intent."

"You're not going to meet with them directly. That would be suicidal, and you're way too good at chess to make that kind of mistake."

I indicated the soft collar with my hand.

"Point taken," Harrison said. "I'll clear the record about Smythe. Also point out that you're not a police officer. It's not your job to investigate for them or to be dangled like a target, a witness to be neutralized. But I won't mention Jacob Ray's name, since we have no hard evidence of wrongdoing."

"Thank you," I said, taking a sip of my gin and tonic when it arrived, camouflaged in a water glass in case media lurked. It was stupid to have a drink at lunchtime; I needed my wits about me for everything still to come. But the decadence of a quiet half hour in the early afternoon, huddled with Harrison in a booth, as the warmth of the alcohol dulled the body pains and psyche aches, was a balm I wasn't giving up before I had to.

"One more thing," I said.

Harrison guffawed so loudly the waiter started over. "Jane, with you, there's never only one more thing."

"Alexei Panov. Maybe I've seeing conspiracy everywhere, but . . ."

"But?"

"Last Saturday he and Anna Basmanova had a confrontation. It was clear they were well acquainted and antagonistic. He was overly curious how she and I know each other, Jacob too. Jacob claims pulling the political favor to get Panov out of jail was done to protect the festival, but Jacob does nothing that doesn't benefit himself or his firm. Later that night, David saw Alexei and another man hovering near me at the *Bin Laden* after-party when they had no reason to be there. The next day my hotel was searched. I asked Johnnie if he knew Panov, given his dust-up with the Russian oil sector but he just warned me off. None of it means anything in isolation, but I have a hard time believing in random coincidence. Could Panov be the person Johnnie flipped his stake to?"

Harrison took a long pull of his drink. "If you get fired, maybe you can write screenplays."

I punched him lightly in the arm. "I think Panov is worth a look."

"Any other debts you'd like the RCMP to collect?"

"I wouldn't put it that way," I said.

"If Panov tossed your hotel room, or followed you at the after-party, it's more likely intimidation than anything else. He's made his hatred of you so well-known, he may as well hire an airplane to write it in the sky."

"That doesn't explain his connection to Anna or to Jacob. Or how Johnnie knows him, for that matter."

"We need to double down on the immediate issues at hand, Jane, and not split our focus. Let's assume legal officialdom is placated, at least for now. All bets are off beyond the immediate term, if criminal activity or money laundering is taking place and they think shaking you down will help information float to the surface. I notice you don't jump as readily to Johnnie's defense as you do to Bob's. Seems to me he's perfectly capable of dealing from the bottom of the deck."

I raised my eyebrows at him. "It's more nuanced than that. But, for sure, he's not picky about the character of those he associates with."

"What we do know is Jacob's still your board chair, and he's still gunning for you. We need to turn the tables on him and the negative media coverage. And unless she's gone vamoose, the specter of Anna Basmanova haunts us still."

I took a drink, keeping silent about Ms. Basmanova and the oil leases.

"Drink up. Middle East is in the building," Harrison said, nodding to front doors of the restaurant where David scanned the room for us.

"I can't tell you how much I appreciate everything you've done for me, Harrison. Regardless of how things turn out."

Harrison clinked his glass against mine. "It's how we roll."

* * *

David and I sat side by each on a park bench. "Do you have the paperwork?" he asked.

"I do."

"Did Johnnie sign it?"

I paused momentarily. "It's signed. I'd like to meet Anna Basmanova alone, although I'd like you to have eyes on me."

David gave a slight chuckle at my adoption of his terminology. "Of course, re the latter. But are you sure re the former?"

"I am. Look at it as girl talk."

"Uh-huh."

"Better you don't know the details."

"Got the concept, Jane."

"I'd rather do it today than wait. Maybe six? There's only two days left of the festival, but still there are some things I need to attend tonight. If I wait to see Ms. Basmanova, it'll be late and I'll be pretty zoned out."

"Agreed." David pulled out his phone and dialed. "This is David Levy. Jane will meet you at six, if that works?" Brief pause. "I'll call with the location later this afternoon. It will need to depend on Jane's schedule, and that shifts throughout the day." Another pause. "Yes, and yes." David hung up.

"Why don't we want to tell her location now?"

"Not that I think she'll bring surprise visitors, but best to limit the option. Plus, I'm assuming you don't want the conversation bugged."

"Didn't think of that."

David gave me a brotherly punch on the arm. "That's because you're not a spook."

"Not yet, anyhow. I get fired and you never know. Think the Mossad is recruiting?"

"Always. Too much competition these days from the high-tech sector and private security. Need to fill their ranks somewhere. They have a nice website where the goyim can apply."

"All right, wise ass," I said. "Make like a bodyguard and help me up. Fresh air break over. We can talk strategy for Ms. Basmanova on the way back to the office."

CHAPTER
EIGHTEEN

Alex looked pale at finding me on her doorstep. I smiled, a little,
at the leopard-spotted blouse she wore over black leggings. How
often do we become our own cliché without even knowing it?

The sound of children behind her in the house was a surprise.
Why hadn't I considered that possibility? She came out on the step
and closed the door behind her. "What the hell are you doing here?"

"You said it was urgent we talk about Bob," I said. "Let's talk."

"Are you crazy? This is my home. My kids are here."

"Grab your purse and we'll go for tea. Or we can sit out of
hearing range in the backyard."

"You can't just show up here."

"You drop unannounced into my life, but I can't into yours?"

The red door opened behind her and a much older, harried-looking man put his head out. "Your mother's on the phone again," he said. "Hello, I'm Jeff, Alex's husband."

I put out my hand to shake his. "Jane Browning."

"Nice to meet you. You're Bob Smythe's wife, right?"

"They're not married." Alex pursed her lips as soon as she spoke.

"I just wanted to have a quick chat with Alex, but it appears I've disturbed your family time."

"No bother at all," Jeff said. "Come on in. If you don't mind hip-hop blaring up from the basement, or *Guardians of the Galaxy* on at full blast. I've just put on a pot of decaf, although happy to switch back to wine if you'd like a glass."

Whether confronting Alex would make me feel better was unclear to me on the way over, but I knew I couldn't let her earlier aggression toward me go unanswered. Now, though, Jeff's warm and easy manner made me want to go inside and hang out. Sit at the marble kitchen counter, shabby chic roman blinds drawn against the darkening sky and drink a glass of pinot noir, maybe share a little harmless laughter when Alex went downstairs to yell at the kids to turn the music down. No stakes. No stress. Just normal family life.

"You're very kind, Jeff. I won't keep you."

"I'm really sorry for all that's happened with the firm," Jeff said.

"He doesn't know anything confidential." Alex's voice was sharper than a single-bladed razor.

"I'm sorry —" Jeff started to say, but I waved him off.

"Not to worry. I'm sure you can be trusted. Right, Alex?"

Alex had seemed destined to bring danger into my life on opening night. With her carefully orchestrated entrance, hair back-combed within an inch of its unnaturally blond life. The kind of woman some men want to climb inside, and other women find ridiculous. But after everything that had happened in the past nine days, what was lost and what was retrenched, it was time to pull focus on the future. Alex was ultimately irrelevant, and now she'd be gone.

"I don't imagine I'll be seeing either of you again," I said. "Now the sale is in the hands of a very specialized team, Smythe needs to revamp its c-suite execs with the new partners in mind. I'm sure you and the kids will be happy to have Alex home more than she's been in the past year. And it goes without saying that Bob and I will make sure her departure is taken care of properly."

I spoke directly to Jeff but could feel Alex staring at me, mouth agape.

"What are you talking about?" she hissed. "I'm needed on the transition team."

"No," I said, "you aren't. As chief compliance officer, it was your job to make sure the regulatory filings were accurate, and they weren't."

She took a step forward. "You can't blame me for that," she said. "Johnnie's at fault."

"Yes, he is. But you should have caught it earlier," I said. "Nothing to be done about that now, but our focus must be on the future, on a fresh start, and building the team that will give the new investors the comfort they require."

"You better believe I'll be talking to Bob about this the minute you leave."

"Go ahead," I said. "I'm certain he agrees. And anyhow, I now control two votes out of three on the board." I put out my hand to shake Jeff's. "Again, my apologies for the intrusion."

I walked down the path and into the SUV the faithful WTFF driver had waiting.

★ ★ ★

"Thank you for meeting me," I said, sitting down across from Anna Basmanova. It was discombobulating to see a woman so precisely beautiful as Anna seated at a Formica table in front of the McCafé in the food court of an office tower.

"Is there a reason why we're in a location such as this?" she said. "Beyond your amusement, that is."

"It would have been difficult for you to set up recording equipment here in advance, should you desire a digital copy of our conversation. Although, my bodyguard did take the precaution of planting a cell phone jammer nearby. He — David — has us within eyesight, just in case you didn't come alone."

"Charmingly honest," she said, continuing to sit so tall she almost levitated above the insult of plastic molded chairs. "Is there a reason you think I wish you harm?"

I raised my eyebrows at her. "Are you kidding me?"

"I made no threat against you. I simply needed to have legal paperwork signed, and you were the best conduit to get that done. Speaking of such —" She let the sentence hang.

"I have it with me," I said. "There's a cost to handing it over."

"Which is?"

"You and I must come to an understanding, and then I never want to see you again."

"Now, who is threatening whom?"

"Not a threat, just an understanding of the necessary quid pro quo."

"I bought those leases."

"Did you actually pay Johnnie for his?" I said. "Or did you force the sale of his partner's, and now you're attempting to jam him for the remaining portion?"

Anna's blue eyes looked at me for so long that I could count the black flecks in the irises. "What did Johnnie say?"

"He kept his cards close to his chest."

"Except he did sign the paperwork, so presumably he sees the legitimacy of my claim."

"I've found, in my experience, never to presume anything with Johnnie."

"He is your legal husband, I understand."

I nodded. "Although that functionally ended many years ago."

"Are you his legal heir?"

"Why does that matter to you? Were you thinking of having him killed?"

"What an active imagination you have," she said smoothly. "Besides, what need? You have the signed leases. Is your question to me about money? Is that what you seek from me?"

"Definitely not." I paused. "What I seek is for you to leave us alone."

"I don't even know where Johnnie is. Do you?"

"Not anymore. But I was referring to Bob and me."

"I see," she said.

"For your own clarification, you should know that the provenance of the money Johnnie used to buy those leases is unclear. Should we wish to legally challenge it, we could. My lawyer has a team researching the anti-money laundering laws and bodies in Russia and, of course, is well connected with FATF," I said smoothly, referring to the Financial Action Task Force, a global body Harrison said was the eight-hundred-pound gorilla on cleaning money for illegal activities.

Anna took a quick intake of breath. "You'd make life very difficult for yourself."

"Nothing worth having is easy," I said. "I just note this as a precursor to our understanding."

"That if you hand over the leases, I will leave and never contact you or Bob again."

"Yes."

Anna was silent for a moment. "I have heard rumors, yes, that there may be another party already involved. That perhaps Johnnie has not kept his word to sell me his leases."

"Did he give you his word?"

"You said earlier that Johnnie gave you no concrete information. Why would you doubt me?"

"I didn't say I did." I grew up in a cul-de-sac; I could do circular. "This whole thing has been quite out of character for Johnnie."

Anna relaxed her body and fell back in the chair, laughing. "Please, Jane. Do not insult my intelligence by saying that Johnnie Smythe has ever played by the straight and narrow."

I smiled back. It was, on some level, impossible not to be seduced by her charm. "If there was ever a bending arrow, it's Johnnie. But not crooked, if you get the distinction."

As soon as the words slipped out, I clenched my jaw in the futile attempt to get them back. It was not a motion that went undetected; Anna Basmanova's eyes searched my face and then did a quick scan of my body language. Johnnie had implied that the unidentified third party who now owned his stake would soon be a thorn in Anna's side. Best if she thought Johnnie double-crossed her than to suspect me. He'd thought it necessary to disappear from the menace. Bob didn't even know the threat existed. If I could buy us enough time, hopefully Ms. Basmanova would soon be consumed with fighting whoever had bought Johnnie's stake. I prayed it was someone at least as powerful as she.

"Do you have any other demands?" Anna asked. "I've been in your city far longer than I had planned. As charming as it is, I am rather anxious to get home and on with things."

"No," I said, opening my purse and removing the envelope. I slid it halfway across the table, keeping one hand on it.

"Do I have your word?" I asked.

"If you are dealing straight with me. If the documents have

Johnnie's signature. And if Johnnie does not show up suddenly and try to renege. Then, yes, we have a deal."

I released my hand and sat back. "A couple more things," I said, slipping my hand into a pocket to pull out a USB key. "We've done a deep dive into your past, your business holdings, and the company you keep. That stick contains the results of what we've found. Obviously, this is not the only copy."

"Really, Jane, you are the most distrusting person."

I smiled. "I've never been to Russia or Kazakhstan, so I don't know how things are done. But I'm from Windsor, Ontario, and there we know a little insurance policy is never a bad thing."

"Indeed," she said, taking the stick. "What else?"

"If Alexi Panov were to run into difficulty, the world cinema would not lose a giant."

"You are looking to bargain here?"

I shook my head. "I'll do what I say, regardless. And I won't consider myself in your debt if you do it. Just a little karmic suggestion from the women of the world."

"You wish to stab the pig in the belly?" she said, this time with a smile that reached from one end of those incredible cheekbones to the other.

I assumed that was a proverb a little lost in translation, rather than a literal intent, but I did a general nod. "He uses his power to hurt women. Maybe if he has less power, there'd be less hurt."

"It is not an easy world for our gender. Yes?"

I gave her a calculating look. "You seem to have a faster adaptation cycle than some."

"You make presumptions," she said. "But survive, yes I have. What choice is there?"

"I once told my mother that there were always choices, it's just that many of them are unpalatable."

"Did she believe you?"

I shook my head. "I was about as convincing as my Sunday school lessons peddling the cleansing power of forgiveness."

"Perhaps in Russia we see things in more black-and-white terms," Anna said. "You live. Or you die. The question is how well you are going to do either. For some people, they find no way to influence the outcome. I refuse to accept that. There is collateral damage in everything. Better it be someone else's than mine."

"I have a bit of a delicate question to ask you," I said. "Did you by chance break into my hotel room a few days ago?"

Anna paused, then shook her head.

"I didn't think so, since I hadn't gotten the paperwork from you yet. Alexei Panov was intensely curious how you and I knew each other last Sunday at his screening. Later that night, he stalked me at a party. The following day my hotel room was searched. Maybe it was just intimidation on his part. Or maybe someone else broke into my room. Or just maybe Alexei, too, is after information about Johnnie."

Anna's eyes drilled into mine. "Thank you for sharing that with me," she said, standing and slipping the envelope inside her jacket. "I trade you honesty for honesty. Your house I did search. Found nothing, heard you vomit, left."

"I see," I said, slowly coming to a stand in front of her. "One final thing. Do you know Darren McGregor?"

She gave me a calculated look, before pulling me forward into an embrace. She alternated kissing my cheeks three times. "Goodbye, Jane," she said, before turning sharply on her heeled boots and walking away, looking nowhere but straight ahead.

David appeared a few minutes later. "How did that go?" he asked, his usually placid expression slightly wrinkled.

"I think we have an understanding."

"One you can trust?"

"Can't imagine that. But it is what it is, for now. One strange thing. I asked her if she knew Darren McGregor; she declined to answer."

"Could mean anything," David said. "What next?"

"Two film intros and a handful of receptions. And hopefully bed before it turns into tomorrow."

"And the masterplan?"

"Relentless incrementalism of the turning of the screw."

★ ★ ★

It was after eleven when I finally slipped back into my hotel room. A dozen red roses had appeared to keep company with the yellow. Perhaps orange would appear the next day. A note lay beside them.

Dear Jane,

Just a quick update. The deal with Sandringham & Co has been signed, the money transferred to the working account, and the OSC notified. Thank you for signing the paperwork. Smoke signals from the OSC so far are positive.

Might I take you to dinner on Sunday night?

Love, Bob

CHAPTER
NINETEEN

DAY 10: *Citizenfour*

"Data Dump!" screamed the headlines of every print paper in the city. A gleeful column from one of the more independent writers at the paper previously known as BFA's lapdog made it past his editor with the lead:

Crisis management firm BFA finds itself in crisis itself today as hackers steal and dump thousands of confidential emails onto a public website that reveal how Jacob Ray and his employees really feel about their clients, and the dark arts they employ to advance any endgame deemed necessary. Libel lawyers will lick their chops as they sort through endless emails about the city's biggest movers and shakers, from politics to business to the arts and beyond, revealing personal and embarrassing details. There's no bar too low, so don't eat before you read, and keep the kiddies out of sight of the computer screen.

I dialed. "Tell me officially you had nothing to do with this hack."

"I had nothing to do with this hack. You can't call a publicist at seven a.m. unless you're paying emergency rates." Franny sneezed, then blew her nose. "Which, I guess, technically you are. But unless planet earth is on fire, I gotta go. I've got a million details to deal with for tonight. You're coming, right? Eight?"

"I'll be there. Why is this so important to you? What's going on?"

"Gotta go. Love you." Click.

Love me? I'd known the girl tangentially at best for a couple years through her work with film clients. I dialed Harrison. "Sorry I woke you. Have you seen the news?"

"Woke me?" Harrison said. "I've been up for two hours combing through the website. Tell me you have no direct knowledge of the illegal activity of hacking."

"I have no direct knowledge of the illegal activity of hacking."

"Man, BFA is fucked," Harrison cackled.

"Anything about me or the festival?"

"It's an endless scroll, and I've gotten more than a little distracted by all the politicians doing shitty things, but yeah, of course, I've found some. The tip of the iceberg, I'd imagine. If I were a betting man — and I do love a hot blackjack table — he's gone as your board chair by noon."

I sat back, trying to take it all in.

"Do yourself a favor and don't read this stuff," Harrison went on. "I gotta go for my workout soon, but I'll put a junior on reading everything. You don't want to get caught up in this shit. Smell the daisies and move forward with the plan."

I laughed, but he'd already hung up. Smelling the daisies was not something I'd ever been accused of, but perhaps there was a first time for everything.

★ ★ ★

The senior team sat drinking coffee and indulging in a mountain of chocolate croissants around the conference table in my office. For the first time since the festival started, I'd been ravenous in my earlier breakfast meeting, consuming scrambled eggs, smashed avocado on toast with hazelnuts, and frites. But I was eyeing the croissants nonetheless. "How do we minimize the impact on our funders?" I asked.

"The board has to distance itself immediately from Jacob," Victoria said. "The longer they delay, the worse the mop-up is going to be. By tomorrow, I'll be asking the Cosa Nostra for a cleaner recommendation."

"Did you read some of the things he said about you?" Isaac asked me. "Where he does get off?"

"A wise woman told me to walk around the dogshit, and I'd suggest you do, too. Don't waste your time reading it. Except for Victoria, of course. This is going to impact our relationships with funders."

"I've been going through seedy email by seedy email." She sighed. "He takes some pretty vicious swipes at other festival board directors, mostly the women. He then repeats those comments to our funders, some of whom turn out also to be BFA clients. Talk about conflict of interest. And you're right, Jane, it looks like he did advise Alexei Panov on the legal stuff. I should warn you there are bitchy emails in there from me complaining about the *State* screening."

"Anything you didn't say to my face?"

"Not really, plus or minus fifteen percent."

"The flood of media requests after the CBC piece on you moved into tsunami territory this morning," Lina interrupted. "I told you before I wasn't comfortable with the 'no comment' approach. Better to preempt a situation than leave a vacuum into which everyone else can spill their bullshit. But we're well beyond that situation now; we need to revisit the strategy."

"Okay. Yesterday, I suggested to the board that they bring in an independent PR firm to help. Your team is immensely capable, Lina, but it's a tricky situation given Jacob is still our board chair."

"HR spoke to me about it," she replied. "I agree it's a good idea, whether Jacob stays or goes. Although if there's any justice in this world, the fucker gets nailed to the wall. The board really screwed up with DelGrotto; they have some serious image problems. I don't think it's our responsibility to rehabilitate them."

"Agreed." I looked at Burt and Samantha. "You're both pretty quiet. Anything to add?"

"It's all just shite," he said.

I nodded. "Indeed."

"I'm sorry Jacob turned out to be such an ass wipe," Burt continued. "I'm sorry I didn't get a chance to say that to you before now."

"Thanks, Burt. That means a lot."

"You're not wearing the collar today. Those Chinese needles doing some good?"

I nodded. "Liuzhen's hands are like magic. I'll spring for a day of acupuncture next week, if anyone wants to give it a try."

"The board needs to publicly turn a page on the controversy," Victoria said, as she reached for half a croissant. "But they can't keep turning them, if you know what I mean. If they're dumping you — no offense — they should make that announcement at the same time as DelGrotto and Jacob. Bundle it with some big new strategic plan, and the team who's going to implement it."

"No kickboxing classes today?" Burt said. "Feeling the need to bring it inside?"

"Jane's a big girl," Victoria said, licking her fingers. "She doesn't need me to feed her pablum."

"They're bloody incompetent if they fire Jane," Burt said. "She's smarter than Paul, and one more turnover is the last thing we need."

My phone dinged with a text. "I'm your new board chair. Can we meet Monday?" From Sheila Waterford.

"Ding dong, the Brawler's gone," I said, reaching over to grab the other half of Victoria's croissant as an intense wave of emotion hit me. It was a few seconds before I could speak again. I looked at Lina. "Jacob out, Sheila in. Presumably a female chair means the board will be more receptive to changing the culture around here. Who's got a bottle of bubbly?"

★ ★ ★

"Jane, can I have a word," Samantha said, as the rest of the staff filed out, a little drunk from the two bottles of champagne that appeared courtesy of Victoria's team. "I know you've got to leave in fifteen for the Shangri-La, but I'd like to talk first."

"Of course," I said. "Sit down."

She sat stiffly in her seat. "In our conversation on Wednesday, you bluntly said that you didn't trust my loyalty."

"What I remember saying is that you should think about where your loyalty best lay." I looked at her a long moment before speaking. "A lot has happened since then."

"I don't want to lose my job," she said. "I've devoted my working life to this festival, and this is the most senior administrative position."

"I understand that," I said. "I've worked my butt off to get into what for me is the dream job, and I don't want to lose it, either."

"I don't think the board will dare replace you at this point. The optics would be brutal."

"I'd like to think there are other reasons to keep me in my job," I said.

"What do you think will happen to Paul?"

"It depends on what the independent investigator finds." I paused, trying to figure out the most generous way to word what I was going to say. "It's difficult, when people are important to us, to open our eyes to their faults."

"You think they'll fire him," she said flatly.

"I don't think they're going to have any other choice."

"Do you plan to fire or reassign me to someone else?"

"If I got rid of someone every time I didn't trust them, I'd be pretty solitary." I paused. "More seriously, Samantha, I want a productive working relationship with my EA. The six months since Paul was suspended have been a complete vortex. It will be equally busy going forward, but it's got to be more productive. I'm never going to be the person who confides all my secrets or inner thoughts to anyone. We're never going to be best friends."

"I'm not asking for your secrets. Just not to be always on the outside."

"Fair enough," I said. "Paul and I have very different ways of working. I'm unlikely to change. Reassignment to someone else is also a possibility, if you prefer."

"I don't."

"Then I need your loyalty. I don't want to know if you fed information to Jacob all along. There's just too much to do, to waste time and energy on a forensic examination that will only keep us stuck in the past. But if that were to happen again, I'd fire you. HR will make notes in all our files about the past ten days, including yours. And mine. I know you initiated a complaint against me, and you have every right to continue to pursue that. Although I'm sure you're aware that if they find a conflict, they'll definitely move you to another position in the organization. I'll leave that to you, and to them."

Samantha stood up. "Okay, thanks, Jane. Good to know where I stand. I'll meet with HR and tell them I'd really like to stay in my current position, pending your approval."

She put out her hand to shake mine, and I held it for a second longer than necessary. "On a personal note, Samantha, I appreciate your support and protective instincts at a difficult time for me. I won't forget that."

She nodded and walked toward the door. "We need to leave in fifteen for the volunteer lunch. I bought the thank-you stickers. I signed your name, since I didn't think they'd recognize your writing one way or the other," she said. "We can walk around and stick them on each volunteer."

"That's great, thank you."

"And I also got a nice bottle of craft whiskey for the volunteer driver," she said. "He's become very fond of you. I think he might get your name as his next tattoo."

"Oy," I said. "That's the last thing this festival needs."

★ ★ ★

Unknown caller. I looked at the screen, debating whether to pick up or not. Had Anna Basmanova not gone quietly into that good night? Had Johnnie?

"Jane speaking."

"It's never wise to make an enemy of someone with a long memory and extensive networks," Jacob said, voice all the more insidious for its quiet calm.

"I had nothing do with your data leak."

"It's impossible that you or your cronies were not involved."

"I don't know anything about it."

"I've resigned from the board, but we're a long way from finished. You have no real idea of what you've done."

"What's that supposed to mean?"

"The circle of those with real power is actually quite small, and many of them are not nice people. Revolutions fail all the time. À la prochaine, Jane."

Click.

Shivering, I sat thinking for several minutes before rooting through my desk drawer. I pulled out the card that Darren McGregor had slipped into my pocket a week earlier.

* * *

I slid into the cool, smooth luxury of the Porsche's tan leather seats, right hand circled around the specialized self-defense key chain that David had given me. Its ultra-rigid metal balls fit between my knuckle joints and would take out an eye if necessary. I didn't anticipate Darren would attack within view of his driver — but I was through taking any more chances with my well-being.

"I must apologize for the other night," Darren said, as the car pulled away from the curb in front of my office. He turned to look at me, sincerity written into his expression. "I have no recollection of the events that you allege, and I think of myself as a perfect gentleman. But I've been known to drink too much, a problem I struggle with, sometimes more successfully than others."

"I'm not here to talk about that," I said, unconvinced but cognizant of needing to endure the half-hour drive to the airport where Darren's private plane was scheduled to return him to the U.K. "I'd like to focus on the festival."

Darren sat back in his seat. "I've decided to withdraw my donation," he said smoothly. "I don't want to cause you any further consternation."

I'd rehearsed with David various scenarios on how the conversation could unfold, including this one. "I've come to think that's not a good idea."

"Jacob told me of the board's conversation," Darren said. "A man knows when he's not wanted."

"I'm sure you saw the papers this morning," I said. "One could argue that his advice is no longer worth the money you paid for it — if it ever was."

Darren was silent, but I could tell from his body language he was paying wary attention.

"I know the RCMP is investigating you," I said pleasantly. "I think brand-building here in Canada in advance is still the good idea it always was." No denial, which I took to be a sign to continue. "You should make your gift as planned to the festival, although I think moving it up to an immediate gift rather than over four years will buy you the ink you're looking for. Journalists are a strange mix of the cynical and the idealistic — they like to cast themselves in the starring role of savior. Make the gift big enough, name it for your son, dedicate it to emerging talent, and the media will eat it up."

"Interesting take," Darren said.

"Personally, I'll look at the fund as the reminder to keep one's hands where they belong but that'll be a private thought, not a public one."

"Is this a threat, Jane?"

"No. I already told the board I would not be going to the police or public with this. But I want us to be clear with each other."

"I see," Darren said. "Are you going into the crisis management business yourself?"

"I hope I've done nothing bad enough in a previous life to justify being reincarnated in that profession," I said.

"I'll give it serious consideration," Darren said, and we both lapsed into silence as the car sped along the highway, and eventually onto the grounds of the airport, pulling to a stop beside a Gulfstream.

I got out, slipping the killer key chain from my palm into my purse as I did. Darren came around my side of the car. I had my hand out waiting to divert any attempt at a hug. "Until the next time," he said, eerily invoking Jacob's phrase. "My driver will take you back to the city."

I looked behind me to where the festival's white SUV was pulling in, David riding shotgun. "Thanks," I said. "But I have a ride."

CHAPTER
TWENTY

Of course, the boat Franny chartered dwarfed the imagination as soon it came into sight. Red lanterns hung from every pillar of the multiple decks, glowing warm and soft as the sun disappeared below the horizon. A quartet played on the top deck, jazz spilling from the boat onto the boardwalk, where people stood waiting to board in a slow-moving queue, drinking flutes of champagne courtesy of the waitstaff.

"Get the hustle on, Jane. A gentleman of my stature needs more than this whistle of booze," Harrison said, coming up behind me as I stood in line.

I turned to find David there as well. I held up my glass to click theirs. "I am so grateful to have had you both in my corner."

"You're not going to cry like a little baby, are you?" Harrison said, downing his glass.

"Maybe."

"Then drink up, and at least you'll have an excuse for being all sloppy," he said, pushing his way through to the gangway, elbows out, David and I hustling to keep up.

"It's been a real pleasure to get to know you, Jane," David said. "You've got a fighting spirit. I'll be surprised if this is my only tour of duty with you."

A young singer with waist-length black hair and tall red boots joined the quartet set up on the third deck just as we reached it, and Harrison finagled us another round of drinks. Festival staff stood grouped around several tables. Franny hadn't spared either the invites or the expenses; there were probably three hundred people on the boat.

The singer opened her mouth and out poured out a throaty, knowing voice that felt as old as a lifetime.

"Let's dance," David said, downing his glass of champagne.

"I thought you'd never ask," Harrison replied.

The makeshift dance floor was soon a writhing mass of bodies. I was still too tender for accidental contact, so we created our own little dance area. Victoria made her way over, shimmying her taut frame all around David. The stars glimmered in the darkening sky. I wished I could relax and savor the victory over Jacob, even if it proved to be momentary. But there was one more difficult conversation to come.

The band wound up the set and we trouped over to where Burt stood at a cruiser table, drinking his beer. The sweat from the exertion gave me goosebumps as it cooled. I hadn't noticed that the boat had set sail, and we were now cruising the inner harbor. David pointed to the level at the very top deck. "I think they're gearing up for speeches."

Sure enough, a sound technician fiddled with two mics and a mix board. Slowly, the noise on the boat hushed to a murmur. Franny and Huntley moved to stand in front of the microphones, Franny in a long black gown and Huntley in a white tuxedo, wrist bandages blending in nicely. Trailing them was a priest, in full red sartorial glory. The three gave a half-wave to the crowd, as if from a royal balcony.

"You can't be serious." I said, downing the glass of champagne I'd just been handed. "They've known each other all of what, seventy-two hours?"

"More like ninety-six, I think. And anyhow, Franny said they'd met previously once or twice."

"Probably not even a Hollywood record," David pointed out.

"I guess it's possible that marrying someone you barely know is the key to a happy marriage."

"They live in L.A., Jane," Victoria pointed out. "Their marriage is fucked no matter what."

Franny tapped the microphone until there was quiet. "It's mine and Huntley's wish to make a life commitment to each other tonight before all of you," she said, voice unusually restrained and dignified.

"I hope any donors present don't think a monetary wedding present would substitute for a donation to the festival," Victoria said, so only our immediate circle could hear. "Not that I don't wish them well, of course."

"Shush," Harrison admonished. The priest was just beginning the wedding vows. My heart ached at Huntley and Franny's hopeful excitement.

★ ★ ★

I tried to resist the Uber driver's attempts to talk; he was a chatterer, this one. His career as a musician, his parents back home in Brazil who refused to acknowledge the fact he was gay, the clubs where he danced until the wee hours.

Mr. Brazil and I finally pulled up outside Bob's house. I gave him the hug he requested — apparently my advice about a truthful conversation with his conservative parents was a genuine bonding moment, the irony of my being considered an expert on the topic not lost on me. I stared up at the house. After several minutes, during which Mr. Brazil chivalrously refused to abandon me to the night, I walked back up the front path.

Bob sat on the couch in the kitchen, his iPad and a stack of books all around him.

"Jane," he said, starting to move things to get up.

"It's okay," I said, waving a hand. "I'll just come join you."

He made room on the couch beside him, but I chose the armchair across instead. He looked beyond me to the front door.

"Where are your suitcases?" he asked hesitatingly.

I shook my head several times, before I could bring myself to speak. "I've left them in the hotel," I said. "I'm going to stay on there for a while until I figure out what's next."

Bob got up, books and iPad falling onto the floor as he crossed to where I sat. "Please don't say you're leaving me," he said, taking my hand in his.

I stood up and let him envelop me in a hug. I could barely breathe. I wasn't sure if it was how tight he was holding me, or how badly I wanted things to be different than they were.

"I don't know, Bob. I don't know what the future is. But I know I can't walk back into this house — into our lives — as if nothing happened."

"You said you wanted a fresh start. I want a fresh start, too."

"I said that to Alexandra Hanlon," I said, disentangling myself from his embrace. "Not to put too fine a point on it."

He looked at me with such pain in his eyes that my stomach contracted.

"Let's sit down," I said. "And have a gentle conversation." I curled up on one side of the couch, legs pulled up under me. Bob sat inches away.

"I'm so sorry about everything, Jane," Bob said. "I've let you down, and I've let myself down."

"I don't think a lengthy accounting of who's done what is going to get us anywhere meaningful," I said, taking his hand in mine. "No gnashing of teeth, no wearing of hair shirts. For you, or for me."

"That's very generous of you to say. But it doesn't negate how I feel."

"Look, it's close to midnight, so I don't think tonight is prime time for discussing the future of our relationship. But you left me that note, and I knew you were assuming I'd come home when the festival wrapped. I wanted to be honest with you. And I didn't want to do it over the phone."

Bob kissed the hand that held his. "Of course, I want you to come home."

I sat quietly for a minute. "At any point after you found out about Johnnie's embezzlement, did it not occur to trust me with the truth?"

"I didn't see it that way," he said carefully. "I saw it as my problem. He's my brother, and despite your advice, I left him in the firm after my father died. It was my mess to clean up. I didn't want to ruin your big moment."

"But you did," I said, as gently as I could. "Worrying about you, being completely in the dark, having strange women stalk me. How was I supposed to be at my best in my job?"

"Alex should never have gone to speak to you," he said. "I don't know what she was thinking."

"That's the problem with trying to be in control of everything, Bob," I said, giving his hand a squeeze. "You think you can keep things separate, but people have a way of climbing out of their compartments."

"I wanted to limit the blowback on you," Bob said, tears forming. "Deal with all the crap that had been circling for weeks, for years, so you could shine and not have to worry about it."

I shifted myself, so I could lean my head on his shoulder. I worked to parse the thoughts that had tumbled themselves into some kind of coherence over the previous week. "Your family, my childhood, Johnnie. It's remarkable we were able to build a relationship that made us happy for seven years."

"I think it can still," Bob said, voice breaking. "I love you. I've never loved anyone but you."

The echo of Johnnie's words was a painful thorn. "I love you, too," I said. "I always will. But this relationship takes up a lot of space and I need it for myself right now."

"You said it had made you happy."

"It did. More than I ever thought possible," I said, pausing. "Life hasn't given either of us much reason to trust people — our parents to look out for us, our siblings to share the burden, the world to treat us gently. But I thought we'd come to a place where we could trust each other."

"Alex was a momentary indiscretion caused in the stress of the moment," Bob said, hand gripping mine tightly, sentences rushed together. "I am not my brother, Jane. I'm not. I'm not my father. It will never happen again."

"Shush," I said. I stroked his hand until his breathing slowed and mine did as well. I thought of my conversation with Yaya about betrayal, of all that's really contained in that word. "I know you're nothing like Robert or Johnnie. And I actually don't care about Alex, in the grander scheme of all that's happened. That's not what I'm talking about."

"Could you explain a little more?" Bob asked carefully.

"It's not like you or I have ever had any role models in successful relationships, but I think when someone's your partner, they're meant to be a full partner. You share the good times and the bad. You give them a heads up about where the speed bumps lie. You consult about major actions or decisions you're about to take. That kind of thing."

"Isn't that something we can work on?"

"Maybe," I said. "But not right now. The last ten days have been too hard. The tortured patterns of your family still play themselves out with us. I know Johnnie isn't dead, but I do believe he means to play it that way. I should warn you — I will follow the legal rules to have him declared dead. I wanted to be his ex-wife, and I betrayed myself because I was afraid to push for it. I'll settle for being his widow."

Bob was silent for a moment. "I'll help however I can. You'll inherit his estate. It will make us business partners in Smythe."

"Speaking of that. You said I need to stay as a corporate director, and anyhow I want to protect my interests. I intend to be a fully active corporate director going forward. Never again will I be caught unawares by the regulators or the business dealings of the firm."

"This was an extraordinary situation, Jane," Bob said.

"I know. But lightning does strike twice, and you and I are magnetized for drama. If it's going to happen to anyone, it'll happen to us."

Bob laughed and used the arm I wasn't leaning against to dry his eyes. "It'll give me more excuses to see you," he said. "I'll respect whatever boundaries you establish, but to be transparent,

I want you back and I'll work as hard as I can to make that happen. Might we go to therapy?"

I shook my head instinctively, and then paused. I had my own family patterns to navigate and resistance to the outside gaze huddled near the top of the crowded list. "At least not yet. I need to spend the coming year focused on my career, rebuilding the relationship with the board and senior staff, putting in place an outstanding festival next year. It's do-or-die time for my career, for my dream. I need to focus my energy there."

"Understood," Bob said. "I hope we can continue to talk like this."

I thought again of the malevolent silence of my childhood home. "Not my strong suit. But I'd like to try."

We stood, but suddenly scared at the sense of finality, I clutched Bob in an anguished embrace.

"I think we'll be okay in the end," Bob said, drying first my tears with his hand and then his own.

I kissed him on the lips. The desire to pull him upstairs and crawl under the warm duvet in our king-sized bed and make love was so all-consuming that it took me a couple more minutes before I could speak. Finally, I picked up my purse. "Drive me back to the hotel?" I asked.

EPILOGUE

When I was five or six, for one glorious summer, my mother packed up a picnic dinner almost every weekend, and we would rattle off to the drive-in movies in our old station wagon. Just the two of us. I'd be dressed in an outfit that she'd worked hard on, scouring my closet and then hers, scissors in hand, gamely seeking what could be stitched into something new. If stumped, we'd trip through the second-hand stores, scouting for clothing or fabric to add to our costume department.

Our happy escapes lasted only that one summer, as my father increasingly refused to be left alone with my sister, Tracy, a child who cried much of the night, and my mother grew weary, pulled as she was in every direction, including dead-end work that stole the hours and sapped the will.

I thought of my mother now, the spontaneous one I'd had just to myself, she of nimble fingers and generous spirit, still optimistic for what life might bring, as the staff and I gathered on the rooftop of our office building, waiting for it to get dark enough to start the movie. Samantha had organized monthly outdoor film screenings to take place during good weather as a team-building exercise.

Instead of the chopped egg on Wonder bread and a thermos of milk my mother had prepared, the picnic baskets were filled with smoked chicken and avocado baguettes, bottles of wine and beer, and real cinema popcorn that Burt had acquired from downstairs. But the same childhood excitement and anticipation bubbled through my veins.

I looked again at the dog-eared photo of my mother and her sunflower T-shirt that I carried in my wallet. She was younger than I was now, although we would be instantly recognizable as mother and daughter. The red hair, the shape of the eyes, the smattering of freckles across the bridge of the nose. This woman who produced me, but who seemed incomprehensible for much of my life. I ran my finger across the photo, wishing more than anything that I could hug her. Had I shown enough affection while she was alive? The lifelong narcissism of being someone's child; my hurt, your bad. Reduced from personhood to parenthood, held forever to account.

I slid the photo back into its place and turned to look at my colleagues, all of whom wore custom-made t-shirts with a decal of that beautiful giant sunflower, then up to the gorgeous tall sky. "Take flight, Momma," I whispered. "I love you."

ACKNOWLEDGMENTS

I'd like to thank everyone at ECW Press for being such an author-friendly house, and in particular my terrific editor Susan Renouf, copyeditor Crissy Calhoun, and the team of Shannon Parr, Susannah Ames, Elham Ali, Caroline Suzuki, Jennifer Gallinger, Jessica Albert, Aymen Saidane, and David Caron. I'm grateful also for Sarah Miniaci's expert help with publicity (not to mention her delicious pasta recipes).

I spent many years in the arts as a publisher, editor, and producer before finally creating the space for my first love — writing. I will be forever grateful to the late and greatly missed Priscila Uppal, for her generosity and steadfast encouragement in mentoring me through the first two drafts of this novel. Author David Layton picked up the baton from Priscila and cheerfully guided me through more drafts than I care to remember as I worked to carve out the real story I was telling. To them both, I will always be enormously grateful.

I also thank very much Rabindranath Maharaj, Anna Porter, and Barbara Berson for reading various drafts of this book and providing editorial feedback.

If Priscila was the impetus I needed to carve out the time to write, the inspiration came from the hundreds of writers it has been my good fortune to work with over the years at Diaspora Dialogues. Their talent, good humor, and determination have been so motivating to witness. I thank them for the sense of community we've created together.

Many thanks also to the Tyrone Guthrie Centre at Annagh-makerrig in Ireland for sheltering me through two residencies where I wrote chunks of this novel, and to Clare and Mark Meredith for housing me every August in their centuries-old big stone house in South Queensferry, Scotland, where I joyfully attend the Edinburgh festivals and write.

Finally, to my mother, Jessica, herself a writer and a ferocious advocate always in my corner. And my partner, Michael, for his unwavering support and that calm voice that assured me during periods of self-doubt that, yes, this book would be published and maybe I could just give people a few hours or a day to answer my email.

This book is also available as a Global Certified Accessible™ (GCA) ebook. ECW Press's ebooks are screen reader friendly and are built to meet the needs of those who are unable to read standard print due to blindness, low vision, dyslexia, or a physical disability.

Purchase the print edition and receive the eBook free!
Just send an email to ebook@ecwpress.com and include:

- the book title
- the name of the store where you purchased it
- your receipt number
- your preference of file type: PDF or ePub

A real person will respond to your email with your eBook attached. And thanks for supporting an independently owned Canadian publisher with your purchase!